W9-CAZ-396

Praise for *Poison Flower:*

"Fans of Jane Whitefield know what to expect from this fearless Indian guide in Thomas Perry's quick-witted capers: cunning strategies, clever disguises, ingenious escape tactics, and breathtaking cross-country chases. Perry delivers to order in *Poison Flower*."

—Marilyn Stasio, *The New York Times Book Review*

"At a time when franchise characters are publishing gold (Jane Whitefield) is the sort of protagonist most crime novelists would kill for."

—*The Wall Street Journal*

"Jane's confidence and her warrior mentality are irresistible, and it's just plain fun to see her out-think those who underestimate her. If you have not read Thomas Perry before, run out and grab as many of his books as you can find." —*Charlotte Observer*

"Spellbinding . . . Jane shares some traits with another outstanding protagonist, Lee Child's Jack Reacher. Both are resourceful, fearless and whip-smart." —*The Seattle Times*

"Perry's heroine, Jane Whitefield, continues to be one of the most original and intriguing characters in contemporary crime fiction. . . . Perry plunges us into his patented nerve-wracking, extended chase scenes before the novel's harrowing climax." —*Booklist* (starred review)

"I love the nuances of finding ways to make people disappear, to give them new identities and to wipe away any traces of where they have gone. It is an intriguing concept, made more so by Jane's Native American background and her strong determination to help those who can't help themselves. I heartily recommend this book and all the others in the series."

—Terry Brooks, #1 *New York Times*
best-selling author of *The Sword of Shannara*

"A tour de force . . . an hours-long jolt of pure, adrenaline-fueled plot."

—*Kirkus Reviews*

"Exciting . . . Perry ensures the characters shine." —*Publishers Weekly*

"Anyone who has read Perry knows the anticipatory pleasure that comes just from holding a new book with his name on the cover. Fans of Jane will enjoy this elegantly written tale of pursuit and revenge."

—*Library Journal*

"Perry has created a credibly strong and extremely dangerous hero who does not cloak herself in politically correct trappings to achieve her goals . . . a chilling book . . . it is the story, and the fiery hoops that Whitefield must jump through, that keep the reader in the seat and coming back for more . . . readable, intriguing, and compelling from first page to last."

—Bookreporter.com

"The author once again has crafted a terrifically entertaining, meticulously plotted and suspenseful novel, one I couldn't put down until the final page. It is, obviously, highly recommended."

—*Spinetingler Magazine*

"Perry's credibly strong hero comes back once again with another breathtaking adventure . . . the originality of the main character and the tension in which the author puts in his plots keep the reader in the seat and coming back for more."

—*Mystery Tribune*

THE
MYSTERIOUS
PRESS

POISON FLOWER

Also by Thomas Perry

The Butcher's Boy

Metzger's Dog

Big Fish

Island

Sleeping Dogs

Vanishing Act

Dance for the Dead

Shadow Woman

The Face-Changers

Blood Money

Death Benefits

Pursuit

Dead Aim

Nightlife

Silence

Fidelity

Runner

Strip

The Informant

The Boyfriend

POISON FLOWER

A Jane Whitefield Novel

Thomas Perry

The Mysterious Press
an imprint of Grove/Atlantic, Inc.
New York

Copyright © 2012 by Thomas Perry

All rights reserved. No part of this book may be reproduced in any form or by any electronic or mechanical means, including information storage and retrieval systems, without permission in writing from the publisher, except by a reviewer, who may quote brief passages in a review. Scanning, uploading, and electronic distribution of this book or the facilitation of such without the permission of the publisher is prohibited. Please purchase only authorized electronic editions, and do not participate in or encourage electronic piracy of copyrighted materials. Your support of the author's rights is appreciated. Any member of educational institutions wishing to photocopy part or all of the work for classroom use, or anthology, should send inquiries to Grove/Atlantic, Inc., 841 Broadway, New York, NY 10003 or permissions@groveatlantic.com.

Published simultaneously in Canada
Printed in the United States of America

FIRST EDITION

ISBN-13: 978-0-8021-5511-5

The Mysterious Press
an imprint of Grove/Atlantic, Inc.
841 Broadway
New York, NY 10003

Distributed by Publishers Group West

www.groveatlantic.com

13 14 10 9 8 7 6 5 4 3 2 1

To my family

POISON FLOWER

1

James Shelby sat in the white prison van looking out the tinted window. The tint was so dark it was hard to see out, and the grate on the inside that kept inmates from touching the glass made it worse. He was shackled to a ring welded to the side of the van, so he couldn't move around much.

Five prisoners were going to court this morning. Everyone in the California Institution for Men at Chino had already been tried and convicted, so they all knew the routines—how they should stand, how their facial muscles should be set, where their eyes should be aimed. Three of the five men were going to be tried for crimes they had committed before they'd gone to jail—one man whose DNA had been taken at his prison intake physical and later matched to the sample swabbed from a rape victim, another man who had turned up on three bank security tapes committing robberies, and a liquor store bandit whose gun had been matched to a killing.

The fourth man was shackled a few feet from the others on the opposite side of the van with Shelby. His name was

McCorkin and he was the former cellmate of an embezzler. McCorkin was going to testify that the embezzler had been bragging about using the money to buy drugs for resale. This was McCorkin's fourth trip to court to testify against cellmates, all of whom seemed to tell him things they hadn't told anyone else.

He and Shelby were shackled away from the others because they were both considered informers. Shelby had not concealed the name of the man who had stabbed him in the back two months ago. Being seated with McCorkin had its advantages. None of the others wanted to say anything in his presence that he could use to get more privileges or a shorter sentence. They didn't want him to be aware of them, because his mere notice brought with it a risk of future prosecutions.

Shelby looked out at the road, and not at his companions. From the start he hadn't let his eyes rest on any of them, because they were volatile. And today they were more dangerous to him than ever, because all any of them had to do was notice that something was odd about him and say so. If they even joked with him about being different today, the guards would hear it. He knew the malice and perversity that had tangled the prisoners' minds. If they knew he was planning to escape, they'd be resentful that he wasn't freeing them, too. They would be envious that he had a plan, because they didn't. And the ones who considered him an informer would find it simple justice to snitch on him.

On the way into Los Angeles there were mountains, then dry-looking pastureland and a succession of telephone poles, and then a big highway with cars driven by bored civilians who saw the marshal's logo on the side of the van and the reinforcement of the side and back windows, and tried to see through the tinted glass. They wanted to see a sideshow, a few ferocious beasts whose ugly faces would give them chills, and maybe even more, the poor, sad bastards who didn't look mean or crazy. Shelby was one of those. If they could have seen him through the glass, they would have said he looked just like their brother or nephew or cousin—a man in his late twenties with light hair and a reasonably handsome face. There was some unholy fake sympathy in people that made them think, "There, but for the grace of God . . ." and not mean it. The idea that they were the favored ones seemed to titillate them. They were not the ones inside the bars with the monsters and the freaks, and never would be.

The ride took another hour, and then the van pulled off the freeway at Grand Avenue, and went south to First Street and then up Broadway toward the Clara Shortridge Foltz Criminal Courts Building. It was still early morning. Through the tinted glass Shelby could make out lots of people on the sidewalks of the court district. The lawyers all wore suits, mostly in shades between light gray and charcoal, with white shirts and neckties. The female city bureaucrats all wore pantsuits, and the males had dress pants and light-colored shirts and ties, and all of them wore plastic badges dangling on lanyards from their necks like jewelry. The jurors dressed more casually. Each of them had a red-and-white paper badge for jury duty stuck in a plastic holder with an alligator clip to hold it.

In the period of his life long before his troubles started, Shelby had lived for a year in Los Angeles. He'd served on a jury here, so he knew. They always started the day by herding a couple of hundred men and women into that small assembly room on the fifth floor. Then they waited, and at irregular intervals one of the clerks would come out of their office and read some juror numbers.

Benches lined the hallways of the court building, and they were always occupied by lawyers, their clients, witnesses, and the defendants' families. The first time he had seen the hallways, they had reminded him of the marketplaces in the Middle East, with people haggling and gossiping and scheming, their private conversations all out in the open, but unheard because there were too many people talking at once. Everyone had something pressing of his own to worry about at that moment—legal papers to look at and stories to repeat and get straight before going into the courtroom, or plea deals to evaluate before they were withdrawn.

The building was modern, with floors marked by rows of identical windows a person couldn't see into. The main entrance consisted of steps descending into a sunken patio. At the edge of the patio were glass doors leading into the building. The court building seemed worn. Everything had been walked on, rubbed, touched by human hands so many times that it was old while it was still new. Inside the tall glass doors was a security area that could have been transported from an airport. Long lines of people waited to put their belongings on conveyer belts that took them through X-ray machines, and then waited to walk through the arch of one of the three metal detectors.

Big, hard-eyed male cops and a few women cops operated the machines and funneled the mass of people into single-file lines and off into the rows of elevators on both sides of the lobby, first the ones for floors twelve through nineteen, and then the ones for floors two through eleven. During the past weeks Shelby had spent hours remembering every detail he could bring back.

Shelby prepared himself while the van pulled up behind the building and then into an underground garage. The van stopped. The guard yelled, "Listen up," and paused to hear the silence. "When you're unlocked, get out on the right side through the open door. Follow the man in front of you and line up in that order with your toes on the yellow line. Do not walk, do not move, until I tell you."

Shelby and the others got out and remained in line. They were all experts by now at hearing the order and following it without allowing it to linger in their minds to chafe. Following orders had become the only way forward in their lives.

The second guard got out with them and stood a few feet back, so they couldn't rush him without getting shot. The driver pulled the van ahead and around to an extra-long parking space reserved for the vehicles from the lockups. He came back and stood near his companion. "All right. We're going in through that door over there. When we're inside, you'll be given instructions and taken to a holding room. Walk."

The group of shackled prisoners walked ahead in single file to the door and then continued inside. The second guard handed a police officer a piece of paper, and he read it and handed it to another police officer at a desk, who used a pen to check something off against a list and wrote something down. All of the cops' faces were set in a wary distrust, making sure they were seeing the same things they'd seen ten thousand times before, and not something new.

The men were shackled to a railing that was attached to the wall in a holding room, in the same two groups. Shelby wondered where the black-haired woman was right now. He had listened closely to what she had told him during her visits to the California Institution for Men at Chino. She had told him where things were going to be and how he should reach them, but she'd never said where she was going to be or what she would do. Now he couldn't help wondering whether she hadn't told him because what she intended to do was insane, and she had been afraid he would lose his nerve. Maybe she had already set everything up before dawn, and had taken off, to be as far away as possible before things began to happen. She'd said only that she would give him a chance to free himself, and he had to be ready.

There was a television set on a metal stand high up in a corner, but it wasn't turned on. On the center of the wall was an electric clock. He and the others sat in silence for a long time watching it and waiting for something to happen, but nothing did. He began to worry again that he was not exuding the same air of bored emptiness that he had on other days, in prison. If he seemed nervous or unusually alert, one of the other inmates would know that he was hiding something. He half-closed his eyes and pretended to be dozing, but he tried to figure out where the guards were. About once an hour one of the sheriff's deputies in tan khaki shirts and green pants would come through the room as though he were taking a shortcut to somewhere else. Twice Shelby heard prisoners' names called over an intercom, but they must have been in other holding rooms.

At eleven thirty Shelby began to get nervous and agitated. The time was coming. Either it would happen soon, or it would not happen. There were a hundred reasons why it couldn't happen, and only one reason why it might—the woman's sheer mad certainty—but as long as that one reason wasn't dead, the tension in his chest kept growing. In a half hour he would be free or he'd be dead. Less than a half hour, now.

His eyes began to lose their ability to stay focused on one spot, because they weren't able to rest anywhere long enough. A cop came to the door and called out, "Shelby!"

"Yes, sir," Shelby said.

"There's an attorney waiting to speak with you. Stand up."

He stood and the cop unlocked his shackles from the rail on the wall and guided him out the door. Shelby took deep, even breaths. This was the start, and he was going to need to be sharp. The cop led him along the back hallway to the first open door, a room with a small window that started head-high with steel mesh over it. The cop ushered him in and closed the door behind them.

Seated at the table was the woman with black hair. Today she was dressed in a black suit, and she had draped a black raincoat over the table. The cop led Shelby to a chair across the table from her and began to shackle Shelby to the ring welded to the table.

The black-haired woman dropped something that sounded like a pen, and crouched to pick it up. For a moment Shelby and the guard lost sight of her under the table. The guard suddenly released Shelby's chain and stepped back. "Hey! What are you doing?" He reached for something on his belt and took a first step to go around the table toward her. Before he could make the turn, his legs bent at the knees and he pitched forward. He fell to the floor, and rolled over to get his radio off his belt, but she batted it out of his grasp with her hand, and it clattered across the floor.

She held up her other hand to show him a hypodermic needle she had used on his leg. "It's a low dose of anesthetic. It won't hurt you, and the effect will be gone in a little while. I'm sorry."

The cop stared at her with wide eyes, but he didn't seem to be able to move. In a few seconds his eyes closed. She said, "He'll be out for a half hour." She knelt; unbuckled the cop's utility belt with his gun, mace, and handcuffs and set it across the room in a corner; reached into his breast pocket to get his cell phone; and took the battery and put it with his other equipment.

Shelby saw that the cop hadn't managed to close the hasp to lock his chain to the ring, so he pulled it through and freed himself.

She took the key from the cop's limp hand and removed the chains from around Shelby's waist and between his ankles. "Take off the jumpsuit."

Shelby unzipped it and stepped out of it, then stood in his underwear feeling cold and vulnerable. The woman looked out the screened window and took off her suit pants, which had been rolled at the waist to conceal their length, and cinched with a belt at her hips. She took off her black stretch turtleneck and handed it to him. This left her in a pair of tight black pants and a fitted vest over her white blouse. The suit coat she had left inside her raincoat when she'd taken it off, she now extricated and handed to Shelby. He put it on, and it fit reasonably well. She put on her raincoat.

She turned to him again, and he felt the blue eyes sweeping down from his face to his feet.

"How do I look?" he asked.

"Not like a prisoner." She knelt again beside the cop, took off his black shoes, and handed them to Shelby so he could put them on. He kicked off his plastic sandals, stepped into the oversize shoes, and tied them as tightly as possible. The last thing she handed him was her briefcase. "Ready?"

He nodded. She unlocked the door with one of the keys from the cop's belt, and went out to the narrow, empty corridor. There were doors all along the left side that led to rooms like the one they'd just left, and one windowless steel door at the end with a clipboard hanging on it. The sheet on the clipboard listed Kristen Alvarez, but she took out a pen and added the name Gregory Campbell to the list with the same entry time as Kristen Alvarez. She looked at her watch and signed them both out. They stepped out into the main hallway of the building. As they walked, she and Shelby looked straight ahead and never met the eyes of passersby. Shelby noticed that any eyes passed over him and lingered on her. She was beautiful, tall and erect, and took long, purposeful strides. They made a turn and stepped through the exit door into the staircase.

They hurried down four floors without meeting anyone on the stairs, and then she stopped at a small glass door with a fire extinguisher inside. She opened the door, reached behind the extinguisher, and produced a red-and-white juror badge in a plastic holder and clipped it to Shelby's breast pocket. She looked at her watch. "We're on the fifth floor.

Just go out into the hall near the jury room and sit on one of the benches. In three minutes it will be noon."

"How can I ever thank you?"

"You're not even out yet. Make sure you get one of the first elevators."

He nodded and went out into the fifth-floor hallway. In two and a half minutes the staff in the jury assembly room would let the two hundred or so bored prospective jurors go to lunch, and they'd all stream out to jam the hallway and the elevators and stairs. He walked toward the jury assembly room, but stopped outside the door and sat down on the bench by the wall closest to the elevator to wait.

JANE WHITEFIELD RAN DOWN THE stairwell the rest of the way toward the first floor, but just as she was reaching for the door handle to go out to the lobby, she heard a door a few floors up flung open, and she could hear the measured sound of leather-soled shoes on the metal stairs, and the murmur of voices—jurors. She almost smiled, but instead kept her face blank and serene as she stepped out into a narrow corridor to the back of the lobby near the elevators.

Then Jane saw the three men. Shelby's sister had given her photographs of them when she had come to Jane in Deganawida, New York, to ask for her help. "I took these during Jim's trial," she said. "These are the three who helped frame him. They bribed some witnesses to say that Jim had done violent things when he got mad at people, some to say they saw him sitting in the parking lot waiting for Susan to come home that night, and scared at least two other witnesses away so they couldn't be found in time for the trial."

The pictures had been taken from different angles: one photo of them taken as they were coming out of some public building together, one taken when they were getting into a car, and one taken through the open side window as they pulled away. The men were all about thirty to forty, with short, well-barbered hair, all wearing suits. They looked like lawyers or business clients arriving for a case.

Jane watched them. They had already passed through the metal detectors to get in, so they couldn't be carrying guns. But they were moving against the crowd of jurors and lawyers departing for lunch, standing in front of the bank of elevators, and as each door opened to let jurors out, the three men moved a little closer to get in. There were six elevators on each side of the lobby. There was still a good chance that when James Shelby's elevator arrived they would be entering another one, or at least not looking in his direction.

Jane moved closer to them. This was developing into a situation where she might have to pay a high price for James Shelby. She had prepared herself for this possibility a long time ago, something that was implicit in the promise she made to her clients. If she was going to save innocent people from the enemies who wanted them dead, there would be times when she must fight.

She was close to the three men now, almost to their backs. The door of the elevator to their left opened and she saw James Shelby. He was in the middle of the crowded elevator, and as the door opened he spilled out with a dozen jurors, all pushing forward, weaving to get past the surge of people wanting to get in. A hand shot out as one of the men in front of her grabbed Shelby's arm, and Jane pushed off with her back foot to throw her body into the arm, wrenching the hand off Shelby. The man grunted in pain and surprise and half-turned to get a look at her over his shoulder, but she pivoted, her back to him and his companions as she moved toward the main exit. Ahead of her she saw Shelby heading across the lobby with the torrent of people.

"That's him!" the man yelled.

"What are you talking about?" That seemed to be one of his companions.

"It's Shelby! He's leaving!"

The voices were behind her as she caught up with Shelby and pushed him out with the crowd into the narrower space at the glass doors.

"Stop him!" the man said. "It's him!"

Jane got Shelby out onto the sunken patio outside the entrance where the steps went up onto Broadway. "Go!" she said to him. "Just as we planned."

He looked at her in panic, but his legs took him up onto Broadway, and he kept going.

Jane planted herself at the foot of the steps. She reached into a pocket of her purse, took out a black elastic band, gathered her hair in a ponytail and slid the elastic over it, then tucked it under so the hair was tight to her head. She stood straight and held on to her purse.

The man who had grabbed Shelby had wasted fifteen seconds keeping his companions out of the elevator and another fifteen getting them to plow through the crowd and across the lobby. The people in the crowd were unwilling to let anyone push them aside to get out of the building ahead of them, so getting out took time and the three men weren't much faster than anyone else.

Jane felt the seconds passing. Shelby should spot the parked car soon. Within another minute or two he should get in, find the keys, start the engine. Next he would head for the freeway entrance. Maybe the crowd would delay the men long enough.

But the three men burst out the double doors. They had been craning their necks to see what went on through the glass while they fought their way to the exit, so they all dashed toward the steps where Shelby had escaped to the street. Jane knew Shelby was still not completely recovered from the stabbing two months ago, so he would be slow. Not enough time had passed since she'd freed him from the man's grasp. They could still run him down if she didn't stop them.

Jane took two steps and turned on the bottom step to face them. She could see that they still hadn't grasped what she was. To them she was a lady lawyer, and they planned to push past her and endure her look of irritated disdain.

The first one was easy, probably because he was bigger and faster than the other two. He didn't seem to be aware that she could possibly be a lethal opponent. He charged ahead, barely seeing her as he dashed to the steps. All Jane had to do was sidestep, trip him, place one hand on his spine and the other on the back of his head to direct his face downward into the steps. Her push increased his momentum enough so he hit hard and lay still.

The second man was the one who had grasped Shelby's arm in front of the elevator, so he was ready. He didn't try to get around her, but went straight for her with both his hands up, preparing to throw a punch. Jane knew she couldn't fight toe-to-toe against a male opponent who outweighed her by a hundred pounds, so she never did. She retreated up two more steps to place herself beyond the man's fallen companion. He took a wild swing at her with his right fist, and when he missed, he had to put one foot on his unconscious comrade to keep from falling over him.

Jane swung her purse into his face. He grabbed it, and she wrapped the strap around his wrist, tugged him toward her over his unconscious companion, and delivered a quick jab to the bridge of his nose. When both of his hands went to his face, she stomp-kicked his kneecap from the side. He went down, landed on his friend, and rolled down the last step clutching his knee while his nose bled down the front of his clothes.

Spectators were beginning to gather, jamming the crowd that was still trying to leave the building. In the corner of her eye Jane caught the third man moving up the steps toward her back, but he threw his arms around her from behind in a bear hug before she could evade him. In a single motion she threw her head back into his nose and upper teeth, heel-stomped his right instep, made a fist with her right hand, and swung it behind her into his groin. She felt a puff of his hot breath on the back of her neck as he released her and rocked back.

His momentary distress seemed to give bystanders courage. A dozen men swarmed in at once, getting between Jane and the three attackers, holding them back and pinioning their arms. It was surprisingly quiet, just a bit of grunting and "You don't want to hit a woman, pal." "Calm down." "Just don't struggle." "Fight's over."

Suddenly there was a loud, authoritative voice. "Stand aside. Police officers." Five big cops in black LAPD uniforms moved in, parting the crowd as they made their way toward the three men.

Jane turned instantly and walked off, away from the center of the crowd, adjusting her steps to put as many people as possible between her and the policemen. She hurried along the sidewalk in front of the building and into the other, separate crowd of curious people who had retreated half a block before stopping to watch. As she burrowed deeper into the group, she took off the black raincoat, pulled the elastic band off her hair, and shook her long hair out. She set her face in a slightly amused expression, an implication that whatever had been going on down there had nothing to do with her and was, in any event, incomprehensible.

She got past the spectators and moved on with the stream of people going to lunch. She walked downhill on Broadway to First Street, and turned right to head for the Metro station at Hill and First. She walked quickly, taking long strides that carried her past most of the other pedestrians. The sidewalks were full of people wearing juror badges clipped to them or security ID on lanyards for the city and county offices in the civic center. There were male lawyers with thick briefcases and female lawyers pulling cases on wheels with long handles like suitcases. She spotted the tall red sign with an "M" on it, glanced behind her to look for anyone running, and kept going.

She reached the sign and turned into the walkway toward the escalators. A plain, dark blue Ford Crown Victoria sped up Hill Street toward her, veered to the curb, and stopped. Two men in suits got out quickly. One of them yelled, "Stop right there, miss. Police." He opened his coat and she could see a gold badge clipped to his belt. His companion stayed by the driver's door, but he had pulled out his gun and was steadying it on the roof of his car, not quite aiming at her, but showing it.

Jane's mind raced ahead. If she managed to get down the escalator without being shot by one police officer or wrestled to the pavement by the other, she might reach the platform and have to wait ten minutes for the next train. She couldn't outrun their car on these streets. She stood still and held her hands out from her sides. "What's the matter, officer?"

"Just stay where you are, with your hands in sight." He ran up to her, grasped her right wrist and brought it behind her, snapped a handcuff on it, then took the left behind her and closed the other handcuff on that wrist. He clutched her arm and tugged her toward the car. "Now come with me. We're going to get into the back seat of the car. Keep your head down."

He opened the door and put his hand on her head to keep it from bumping as she slid onto the seat. He moved in after her, and the lock buttons clicked down. The driver put away his gun, put the car into gear, and drove.

The car went up Hill to Temple, turned left away from the court building, past the cathedral and the concert halls, and swung onto the Hollywood Freeway moving north. Obviously, they were taking her, not back to the courthouse, but to their precinct station. She decided to introduce doubt.

"You've got the wrong person," she said. "I haven't done anything wrong."

"I didn't ask you," said the cop beside her. "There will be plenty of time to talk later." He had small, close-set eyes and the sort of thick, dark hair that went down too far on his forehead so it looked like a cap.

"I was just getting on the subway and you came along and arrested me, so you must think I did something." She had begun the urgent business of keeping them from holding her long enough to connect her with Shelby's escape.

"I didn't say that."

"But whoever you're looking for is back there somewhere laughing at us. She's getting away." She didn't have much hope of persuading them it was a case of mistaken identity, but she had to keep probing to see if she could derail the inexorable process of getting her into a jail cell, where she'd be when the escape was discovered.

The cop beside her sighed wearily. "You had a little scuffle on the courthouse steps, didn't you? You hurt some people. Does that ring a bell?"

She knew cops lost their sympathy when somebody lied to them, so she'd have to try something that didn't contradict what they'd seen. "I was in front of the building when these three men rushed out of the building and attacked me. There are at least a hundred witnesses who saw what happened."

"These men just attacked you for no reason."

"If they had a reason they didn't tell me what it was."

The cop shrugged. "Could it be because you had just helped James Shelby to escape?"

"Escape? All I was there for was to get excused from jury duty."

"Consider yourself excused," the driver said.

"Those three men were trying to hurt me."

The cop beside her said, "I'm not arguing with you. I believe that's what happened."

"So why are you arresting me?"

The cop beside her said, "When you see three men who mean you harm, how do you know that there aren't more?"

The driver laughed. "There could be a couple more waiting in a car nearby."

Jane turned to face the man on the seat beside her. "What are you?" Her hands were cuffed behind her, but she used them to grasp the door handle.

"We're the guys who caught you pulling a jailbreak."

She kept her eyes focused on his, but she was watching the speed of the fixed objects passing the window behind him—trees, buildings. The freeway was crowded, but the car was still moving about forty miles an hour. Even if she managed to survive a fall to the pavement at that speed, she would be hit by at least the car behind, and probably the next two after it. She had to wait and hope there was a bottleneck somewhere ahead that would slow the traffic to the stop-and-go crawl that was typical of Los Angeles freeways.

She said, "Since you're not cops, this is kidnapping, false imprisonment, and about eight other things. If you drop me off at any police station and say you saw me get James Shelby out, they'll arrest me and you'll be heroes."

"Sorry. We've got orders, and that isn't what they are."

"Whoever told you this was a good idea isn't doing you any favors. Will he be with you while you're serving a life sentence in a federal prison?"

"Nobody's going to prison," said the driver. "Just sit back and relax for a little while, and everything will be fine."

"There's nothing fine about this," she said.

She watched for her chance impatiently, but the car never slowed below forty. It was still only a few minutes after noon, so the traffic was moving smoothly. She watched for police or highway patrol or sheriff's cars, but the only one she saw was an LAPD car about a quarter mile ahead, taking an exit onto a surface street.

They drove outside the city and into the dry, brown hills to the northwest. Beyond them there were the same rugged gray mountains that loomed like a wall on the east all the way up the coast from the Mexican border to Oregon. The traffic sped up instead of jamming.

Jane waited and watched. If she had suspected that the men weren't police officers, she would have made her stand before she got into the car. The badges, the guns, and the make and model of the car had fooled her. If she hadn't been in the middle of the criminal court complex, expecting the police to be chasing her, the thought of impostors might have entered her mind, but it hadn't. She had allowed herself to be kidnapped in daylight on a city street without ever suspecting it was happening. She kept remembering what the experts said about kidnapping. Never get in the car. Once you're in the car, you're dead. If you're going to fight, you have to do it before then.

The car wasn't going to be stalled in traffic on the freeway, so she began to work out an alternative plan. Sometime they would have to pull off the freeway onto an exit ramp, and an exit ramp usually came to a stop at an intersection. If there was no traffic signal right away, there would be one soon afterward. As soon as the traffic stopped, she would unlatch the door with her handcuffed hands, lean out, and roll when she hit the pavement.

If she was lucky, the two men would panic and drive off. If, instead, the two tried to drag her back into the car, she would kick and scream that she was being abducted. She might be able to delay them long enough to attract help, or at least get someone standing nearby or in a passing car to call the police.

A few minutes later, at five after one, the car began to coast, then moved to the exit lane, and she saw the sign for

Route 23 North toward Moorpark. She prepared herself. Their course seemed to be taking them from crowded places to empty ones, so this might be her only chance.

She felt the car losing momentum, heard the tires bump over the crack that separated the freeway from the ramp, felt the brakes slowing the car. As the car rolled to a near-stop, she pushed the door handle down, and the door swung open. As the car started to move forward again, she pushed off with both feet and propelled herself out. She hit the pavement hard, rolled with the momentum, went backward over her shoulder, and landed on her knees at the top of the ramp.

"Help! Help me!" she shouted. "They're kidnapping me!" A car with a frightened woman at the wheel nearly hit her as the woman swung past. "Call the police!" Jane yelled at her. "Help!"

The two men didn't drive on. They both flung open their doors and ran toward her. The man who had handcuffed her took out his gun. As Jane dived toward the bed of ice plants beside the exit ramp she heard the shot and felt the brutal impact of the bullet, and then the explosion of pain.

JANE'S RIGHT LEG FELT AS though it were crushed and on fire, throbbing with each heartbeat. She must have lost consciousness for a moment, because she didn't remember being dragged back into the car. She was strapped tight by the seat belt with her hands still cuffed behind her. The pain was like fire that seemed to grow hotter and hotter. The leg was weak, and if the bumping of the car moved it, the pain shot inward from her thigh to her spine. Jane could manage only shallow, quivery breaths that rasped in and out. She tried to keep the breaths quiet, to hide her weakness from her enemies, but she couldn't control them. She knew she had been shot only a few minutes ago, but she couldn't imagine living much longer with this pain. She fought the impulse to close her eyes again. She had to remain aware of what was around her.

Since she had come to, the man beside her in the back seat had been talking to her in a hiss of hatred, his face close to her right ear. What was he saying? "You bitch. You stupid bitch. You did this to yourself. We would have found out what we wanted and then let you go—dumped you someplace so it would take you time to get to a phone. But you couldn't live with that. Now you're going to be crippled, or lose your leg."

To give herself strength, Jane gathered her pain and anger, like two hands scraping crumbs together and compressing them. "I doubt it."

"Oh? You're a doctor, too?"

"No, but I can see I'm bleeding out."

He looked down at her right thigh, and his eyes followed the dark wetness that was soaking her black pants, and where the blood dripped to the floor he could see a pool forming. He said to the driver, "She's bleeding a lot."

The driver said, "Then do something. We've got to keep her alive."

"Do something? What?"

"Stop the bleeding," the driver said. "Use a tourniquet."

The man unbuckled his belt and pulled it off, then wrapped it around Jane's thigh just above the wound and tightened it.

"Ahh!" Jane shouted.

He cinched the belt tighter and held it there. Jane could tell he was happy that he was inflicting even more pain.

Jane leaned back in the car seat but kept her eyes open, searching for signs—a street, a city, a direction. There was a shopping mall, but she couldn't see its name. They were passing the delivery entrance, and the sign was facing the other way on another street.

She wasn't sure she should have mentioned the blood. She might soon wish she had bled to death before these two started doing things to make her give up James Shelby.

Her husband Carey's image appeared in her mind, but she blinked and glared at the sights flashing by—chain-link fences around parking lots, low gray or beige buildings with trucks parked at loading docks. She couldn't let her own feelings distract her. She had to be alert to the next chance to save herself, and not think about losing the world full of things she loved.

She was held upright by the seat belt, and she kept her eyes open, scanning the lines of cars in each direction, looking for a police car. That would be all it would take—a police car. She could attract the cop's attention, and this would be over. She watched for what seemed to be twenty minutes, but she knew it couldn't have been that long.

The police car never seemed to appear, and the pain of the gunshot wound was worse and worse. She felt sweat at her temples, the back of her neck, her sides. She kept fighting waves of dizzy nausea, then faintness. She couldn't lose consciousness now, or she might miss her chance to stop the two men before they got her out of sight somewhere.

The car slowed a bit, sped up, slowed, and she realized the driver was looking for an address. As he did, other cars began to pass him on the right—a chance. The seat belt, the handcuffs, and the man's hand holding the tourniquet tight would prevent her from moving anything but her head now. She shrieked as loudly as she could, her voice tearing the air, and threw her head against the side window of the car. She shouted, "Help! Call the police!"

A man driving the car beside her looked shocked. He slowed, then stared at her. Her captor put his arm around her shoulder and pulled her inward. He held up his badge and gave an authoritative wave to tell the gawker to move on. The man pulled over and turned right. She screamed, "No! They're not cops!"

The man holding the tourniquet tugged on it and the pain shot up her leg. "You really are stupid," he said. "There's no need to kill yourself. Leave something to us, for Christ's sake."

The driver was staring intently in his mirrors. "That guy's gone, right?"

The other man looked out the rear window. "Yeah. It's safe to go in."

The car turned left and went between two one-story gray buildings that looked like small factories or warehouses into a parking lot. There were three more low buildings ranged around the lot. The car stopped beside the door of the second one. "Let's get her inside."

Jane's world was becoming a place with dark patches that would join at the periphery of her vision and then spread like a stain. The man swung open the car door, but she mostly heard it, because almost instantly the pain in her leg was sharp and deep, like a blade thrust into the muscle. She felt as though the knife's serrations were scraping the bone, and then the men had her arms over their shoulders, half carrying, half dragging her to a door, and then inside.

The inner space was huge, like a small high-tech factory with brushed concrete floors and acoustic tile ceilings. "Let's put her on the couch." The voice had a slight echo as though the place were entirely empty, but it wasn't. There were rooms of some sort built along the side—offices, maybe.

The two men, now just shadows, dragged her to a couch and then lowered her onto it. The pain always grew, never diminished. Every movement seemed to set off a spasm, bending her body over like a hook. The two shadows stayed there, two blots in the middle of her burning red pain. One of the shadows said, "If you want to scream now, go ahead. That's why we brought you here. But while you're doing it, start thinking about something. You're going to talk. Everybody does."

2

Jane woke up and saw that a new man was beside her, wearing a surgical mask, headgear, and gloves, using a pair of curved bandage scissors to cut along the outer seam of her pants. A doctor. He pulled back the flap of fabric and examined her wound for a few seconds, then began to talk to the man standing above her behind the couch. His mask muffled his voice.

"You had to shoot her?" He was angry. "This is going to make everything harder for you than you can even imagine. She could die." He had a foreign accent, but with the mask she couldn't place it. His skin was light brown, and his eyes were dark.

"Then make sure she doesn't die."

"Easy to say after the bullet has been fired."

"There was no choice."

"She'll need daily care to control the bleeding, prevent infection, and get the wound to heal properly. She must have antibiotics, painkillers and sedatives, IV feeding."

"You'll be well paid for everything you do, and for once you won't have to testify in court that your patient got hurt in a car accident."

"Very funny. I'll need to bring my nurse to assist me."

"Is she worth all this trouble?" The second man was standing somewhere beyond Jane's head, where she couldn't see him.

"What do you mean?"

"Is she even going to live?"

The doctor's voice became contemptuous. "The bullet passed through her leg and exited the other side, which is why there are two holes. She didn't die of shock, or of blood loss, and the femur wasn't broken, all of which I attribute to luck. The care she gets will determine whether she lives or not. You could take her to a hospital and her chances would be very good."

"I don't think so. I want to hold on to her."

"Then we'll have to do our best here. I'll clean and dress the wound now, and then set up the rest tomorrow morning. Let me give her a painkiller so we can move her to the table." He took a very small bottle of clear liquid from his bag, unwrapped a hypodermic needle, filled it, and swabbed Jane's leg with a cotton ball. She smelled the strong, almost nauseating odor of alcohol, and then felt the needle.

EVERY TIME JANE AWOKE SHE tried to sit up, but there was something tied across her under her arms that prevented her. She was aware, as in a dream, that if she could simply overcome her confusion and gather her thoughts, she would be capable of escaping the restraints. But each time, she exhausted herself and fell back to sleep.

In her dream it was a winter night somewhere in the north. She could feel the clear, freezing air and see the light dusting of snow on the ground, indented with many footprints. She was in a big enclosure of straight tree trunks with the bark still on them, sharpened at the top, and in the middle there was a single fire that gave no warmth but illuminated the space with a flickering light. There were other people—women and children mostly, with just a few men here and there. She knew they were all captives. They wore dark, dirty, torn clothes she couldn't even tie to one period or style, and they stayed in the shadows. Some of them limped or crouched or tried to bind up their wounds.

Jane walked, wandering among the people, listening to the things they said to each other. She tried to be unobtrusive, slouching and lowering her eyes to look at the ground as she passed. "Do you think they'll just keep us here until we die?" There was no attempt to answer. "Who are they?" "Strangers. Enemies."

She looked up, and she could see his eyes looking at her long before she could make her way through the crowd to reach him. He stood alone, even though there were people on all sides of him. He wore the same gray polyester sport coat with a faint greenish tinge. He had worn it when she had met him, and even though the elbows were faded on that day, probably from countless hours of leaning on poker tables, he wore the coat later when she was taking him into hiding. He must have had it on when he died. As always, he had on brown dress pants that were shiny in the seat and knees, and scuffed shoes.

Harry Kemple was her only mistake, a gambler who had heard murderers burst into his poker game while he was in the bathroom and kill all of the men at the table. He had opened the door a crack and seen them leaving. They had hunted him, so she had saved his life, taken him away, and given him a new name. Years later she had been fooled into leading one of the hunters to the forger who had made the documents for Harry's new identity, and in two days he was dead. Since then Harry sometimes visited her in dreams.

"I was coming to find you," he said.

She came closer. "Where are we?"

"Just one of those places between life and death. It's a convenient place for people from both sides to meet."

"Sleep?"

"You're not asleep. You're closer to death than sleep."

She looked down at her wounded leg, and at her feet there was blood in the snow.

"Your blood is leaking out of you. Those stitches the doctor put in your leg and the bandages are only slowing it down." He lifted his face to look upward and pointed at his throat, where the medical examiner had put some crude stitches to close the gaping wound where the knife blade had passed. "Nobody knows more about bleeding out than I do."

"I'm so sorry, Harry," she said. "I thought he was a runner who needed my help. It never occurred to me that he was using me to find his way to you."

Harry raised an eyebrow and stared at her for a couple of seconds. Then he said, "Every time we meet I have to listen to the same apology. Forget it. If he hadn't collected on the contract on me, there would have been a car crash or a microbe or a blood clot. When you're dead, the way death got you is just one thing that happened among thousands. You don't care more about that day than any of the others, just because it was the last day. You'll see."

"Are you telling me I'm dying?"

He frowned. "At the moment you are. You're losing blood, and you're in the hands of enemies."

"Is there any way I can save myself?"

Harry held up his hands and shrugged. "How do I know what you can do or can't do? You're the only one who has any way to guess. These things aren't determined ahead of time. The grandsons of Sky Woman fight. That's all we know. The left-handed twin Hanegoategeh raises his arm to strike, but the right-handed twin Hawenneyu reaches up with his right, like the image in a mirror, to block it. Creator and Destroyer, life giver and killer, they struggle, and their constant fighting is what makes the world we pass through into a battlefield. Sooner or later, everyone is a casualty. Everybody sheds his blood, like me. And like you."

She followed his eyes downward, and looked at her leg. The big white bandage that was wrapped around the wound was bright scarlet, and the blood in the snow was pooling. She raised her eyes again. "I've lost blood before," she said. "I want to do better than to lie on that couch waiting to die so the pain will end. What can I do?"

Harry sighed. "You know I love you, but you made your choice a long time ago—day over night, life over death. You think you're on the side of the good twin, the Creator twin. If he made you, then he must have made you what you are for his own purposes. We can't know the scheme, because he's trying to fool his brother, and the left-handed twin might read our minds."

"But that doesn't tell me what to do."

"If you're Hawenneyu's creature, be exactly what he made you, because you have a part to play in the fight. If he made you a fox, he must need a fox, so be the fox he made. Don't think you're smart enough to improve his strategy."

"And if I die?"

"You will die. You know that."

"I meant—"

"I know. Gather your strength now. Your biggest trials are coming soon. Remember the Grandfathers, the ones who chose to stand and fight to block the trail while their friends escaped."

Jane awoke. She was in the big, dimly lit room on the couch, covered with a sheet. She was sweating, and she was very conscious of the tight bandage wrapped around her leg. Her white blouse and vest had been replaced by a man's shirt. She was terribly hot. She wondered if she had a fever and if it meant that the wound was infected.

Her eyes moved, following the weak, dim light to the source, a reading lamp on a small desk far off on the other end of the room. It seemed to flicker, and she realized there was also a laptop computer on the desk. A movie was playing on its screen. Jane hoped it was an online version, and not just a DVD playing. In less than a minute she could use a computer to e-mail her husband Carey or the local police. There were a pair of earphones on the desk, but nobody was visible.

Jane welcomed the extra light because it illuminated her surroundings, and gave her a chance to explore without moving. There were six windows in a row about fifteen feet from the floor, but they looked like immovable glass installed to let daylight into the building but not to open. They had been covered with blackout fabric taped to the glass so no light could pass in or out—had they simply been painted black? They had no latches. The right side of the big room had a wall with four doors, but the wall seemed to extend only to the acoustic tile ceiling.

She heard a door open, and when it did, she heard water, like a toilet tank refilling. The door closed again and a woman in hospital scrubs and a pair of white sneakers walked to the computer. The woman had very dark, curly hair gathered into a bushy ponytail behind her head, and she wore glasses with rectangular lenses and black frames.

Jane tried to evaluate her features. Did she look cruel or dishonest? Jane saw no sign of either. She might be foreign and might not speak English well enough to know that Jane had been kidnapped. But then, what could she imagine had happened? If she was a nurse, she knew Jane's wound was from a gunshot, and she certainly knew this industrial space wasn't a hospital.

Jane decided the woman in scrubs couldn't be much help. Then it occurred to her that the nurse and the doctor might help her unintentionally. At some point, the men who had brought her here were going to try to force her to tell them where Jim Shelby had been heading when he'd left the courthouse. Maybe having the medical people here would restrain them a little.

And the doctor and nurse had medicines and drugs. The doctor had injected Jane with a couple of things—an antibiotic and a very strong painkiller that had put her to sleep. She wondered if it was the same kind she had stolen from Carey's office and used on the guard in the courthouse. She had filled the syringe she'd gotten from a diabetes kit, then broken the bottle and left the pieces inside the cardboard box, as though it had been dropped in shipping. A mixture of Midazolam and Fentanyl, it was an anesthetic used for minor surgeries, or as a pre-op sedation before a general anesthetic. She had read on the Internet that it was safer than most of the drugs used for that purpose, and a full dose wore off in about two hours.

Jane kept looking out into the room, taking in the small bits of information that her eyes brought her, and then turning them around in her head to examine them from different perspectives. But she was careful not to move. The sooner the woman she thought of as a nurse knew she was conscious, the sooner she would notify the men who had kidnapped her and the really horrible stuff would begin. Every minute Jane could lie on the couch pretending to be asleep, Jim Shelby got farther from Los Angeles, and farther from the people who were looking for him.

And perhaps every moment, the police were coming closer to finding her. She had been taken in a busy place. Many of those big public buildings had multiple security cameras going all the time. There were also the subway entrance and the major intersections around the court buildings and government offices. One of these cameras must have caught her fake arrest on tape.

Jane lay there counting each minute as a point for her side. Whenever she partially opened her eyes, she would see that the woman still had the earphones on and was still staring at the computer screen. After a long time, Jane dozed off again.

When the doctor came in, he switched on bright overhead lights and talked loudly. "You can assemble the bed over here, in the center of this room."

As the pieces were brought in from the truck and assembled, the bed took form. It was the size of a twin bed with a steel frame. After less than thirty seconds they were going back out for the mattress. They set it on the steel-mesh spring.

The nurse took off her earphones and said something to the doctor in a language that didn't sound familiar to Jane, and he answered her in the same language. The nurse went to the truck; came back with a set of sheets, a pillow, and a wool blanket; and made the bed quickly. As soon as she was finished, the doctor said to his employers, "You two are going to have to help us move her onto the bed."

"How do we—"

"I'm about to tell you," he snapped. "It's important that you do exactly as I say. We're going to put the blanket under her partway." He and the nurse unfurled the blanket and tucked it under her, then slid her onto it. "Now lift the blanket." Then the four lifted her again onto the new bed, and the nurse arranged her pillows.

The doctor said to his nurse, "I need to have another look at the wound. Bring the dressing kit."

The nurse laid out various implements and dressings, and prepared a hypodermic needle. Jane said, "What's in the needle?"

"It's a painkiller."

"I don't need a painkiller," she said.

"Yes you do. I haven't begun yet." He injected the painkiller into her arm, and in a short time, she felt limp and sleepy, and then there was darkness.

When she awoke the doctor was gone, her mouth was dry, and her leg hurt a bit more than she remembered it hurting, as though the doctor had disturbed it somehow.

"So where is Jimmy Shelby?" The voice sounded friendly. It seemed to her the voice was a little bit like the voice of a country singer. She opened her eyes and looked at the man who had spoken. He was ten feet away. He had the reddish skin that some pale-complexioned people had when they'd spent too many years in the sun. The sunburn never seemed to go away. He was tall and lanky, wearing a pair of boots, with the legs of his blue jeans down over them, and a black sport coat. His short blond hair was spiked on top, and it struck Jane as grotesque, because his face looked a generation too old for the style.

"I don't know," she said.

He looked at her with an expression of mild surprise, which seemed to blossom into sincere curiosity. "Now why would you say that?"

"Because I don't."

"You broke him out of the courthouse, left a car for him to drive, and then used delaying tactics to keep anyone from getting to him while there was still time. Are you denying that?"

"No."

"So you have to be a pro, somebody who has done this kind of thing before, and who knows the way things work. You knew there was a big risk, and you might be caught. You must know where he went."

"I didn't want to. It wouldn't make either of us any safer. If I don't know, I can't tell."

"I sure hope you're not telling the truth about that," he said. "If you don't know, you have nothing to trade. All you'll be is a woman who freed a man we put in jail, and hurt three friends of mine doing it."

"That's all I am," Jane said.

"Are you *trying* to get me to kill you?"

"I'm just answering your questions truthfully right now at the start, to avoid a lot of fruitless conversation later. You'll make your own decisions."

He looked at her closely, his brows knitted. Then he called out to his men, "I think she needs to focus her mind. Ask her again." He turned and walked across the big room and out the door. When it opened she saw that night had come. She heard the sound of a car engine, and then silence.

The man who had shot her and the driver came in from one of the doors along the side of the room. Each was carrying a bamboo stick about three feet long, and about the thickness of a cane. Without any preliminary threatening, the man who had shot her simply raised his cane and brought it down across her shin. She squinted, and the other began to beat her too, hitting her across the stomach. She was strapped to the bed with only a man's shirt and a sheet over her, so the blows fell on her head, stomach, arms, feet, knees, and shins without padding to soften them. The men avoided hitting her right thigh, where the bullet wound was, but otherwise, they seemed bent on hurting her everywhere. She lost count of the sharp, stinging blows, but she could tell the two men had not. She suspected they must have orders to hit her a certain number of times. She turned her head to avert her face, but that was all she could do in her weakness. As though at a silent signal, the blows stopped.

"Where is he?" It was the man who had shot her.

"I don't know."

"You have to know his first stop," the driver said.

"Why do I have to?"

"He's hurt, has no money, no clothes, no shelter. You must have help waiting for him somewhere. Tell us where."

"I offered to get him out of jail. He said yes, so I did. Since then he's been on his own."

The driver hit her again, a sharp, sudden blow that was aimed at her knee, but which hit an inch higher. "Which direction did he go? East?"

"I don't know."

The other man's bamboo stick slashed across her ribs, and she glared at him, but refused to cry out.

The questions came, and after each one, a blow. After a while, they stopped waiting for her to say, "I don't know," and just hit her after each question.

As the blows fell, Jane withdrew her mind from the room where the men were beating her and concentrated on the past, on the wars of the forests her ancestors had fought. Often, when members of a war party were returning from a raid in a distant territory, they would be running to escape, and a much larger force would be pursuing them. Sometimes, if it became clear that they were going to be overtaken, a lone warrior would stop at a narrow, strategic spot on the trail and turn back to delay the pursuers. Most of the time he would fight until he died. But the enemies always wanted to take him alive. They would surround him and try to wound and exhaust him if they could. When all of his arrows were gone and he had swung his war club many times, they would rush him from all sides at once, drag him down, and subdue him.

The Seneca warrior would be brought back to the enemy village bound and wounded. He would be the only representative of the war party that had struck and probably killed a few of the enemy, and he had probably killed more in his fight to buy time for his friends to get away. He would know that the only thing in his future was pain.

But a captured warrior was still a warrior. It was his job now to be indifferent to physical torment. Before he died, he wanted to demonstrate his superiority so convincingly that his captors would be terrified of the next Seneca they saw.

She imagined that the first stages of his torment would be like what she was suffering now. As he was dragged in, the villagers would beat him with sticks, poke and pound him, teasing him with the taste of the pain that was to come.

He would give them no satisfaction. He would pretend that their blows were not frightening to him, and that his death meant nothing. The last, best thing he could do for all the Senecas who came after him was to plant in their enemies a secret, lingering fear that would make them timid and hesitant, so they could be struck down.

Jane felt the blows, and she knew the other torments that would be coming, probably better than these men knew. They were simply doing what they guessed might force her to talk, but she had already thought through all of the tortures that were likely to occur to them as they tried again and again to break her. Each attempt would be worse. Every form of cruelty seemed ready-made, tried long ago, but also reinvented in every human brain because when a person was afraid it took effort not to think of all the things he didn't want done to him.

What the men were doing was just like the entry into the enemy village—a prisoner with a debilitating wound, a beating to announce to her that they were willing to cause her more injury and pain. Probably only a day or two would pass before the novice torturers began to introduce refinements that would make a person shudder and feel ashamed of the species. Then Jane would have to be brave the way the old warriors were, always alert for a way to kill one of them or force them to kill her.

The beating ended. She lay on the bed on her back and silently allowed each of the places where she'd been struck to report the damage. There would be welts on much of her body, and big bruises where they had hit particularly hard. There seemed to be no broken bones in her forearms or wrists, no broken fingers or toes yet. She looked down at her thigh. Blood had soaked through the bandage and the sheet, but it wasn't the sort of bleeding that would kill her.

3

Jane awoke again because she heard a woman's voice. She knew from the way her wounds felt—dry and angry—that a few hours had passed, but there was no day or night, no light or dark. The woman had come back again and was standing a few feet from her, talking on a cell phone. "You should see her. I'm telling you, this is crazy. It looks like they hit her with clubs or something. All nearly identical contusions. Arms, legs, abdomen, chest. . . . Not the head, that I can see. And not the wound on the right thigh. If this is going to be a murder, I'm out. All right, I'll see you later."

Jane had heard, in that short conversation, more than the woman would ever have told her. The woman came closer and looked down at Jane. Today she was wearing burgundy scrubs and a different pair of bright white sneakers. "You're awake. If I help you, do you think you can get to the bathroom?"

"Yes." Jane looked at her calmly, watching her undo the restraints and support her back as she sat up. "You're a real nurse." Jane slowly swung her legs off the bed; tried twice to stand in spite of the pain; then used the headpiece of the bed to support herself, stood, and walked with the nurse. The nurse protected the IV needle stuck in Jane's wrist, kept the tube from tangling, and moved the aluminum stand with the IV fluid bag hanging on it.

"Yes," she said. "I work for the doctor who saw you the other day."

It was the first confirmation that at least two days had passed since Jane had been here. The doctor must have seen her the first day, right after she had been shot; cleaned and closed the wound; and given her antibiotics and painkillers. "Were you here when they beat me?"

"No. The doctor said I shouldn't come in until tonight, after my shift. He didn't know what they were going to do, and neither did I. I swear."

"He's your boyfriend, isn't he?"

"I don't know if I'd say that. There's nothing official." She was smiling, almost blushing, as though she were in high school, talking to a friend.

Jane thought, *A doctor would never get you involved in something like this if he didn't think he could control you for a long time. If you ever reported him for what's already happened, he'd lose his license and go to federal prison.* "Is he smart?"

"Of course. He's a doctor."

Jane couldn't help thinking about her husband, Carey. He was brilliant. "I know some doctors who are very smart, and some who don't have that advantage. All they can do is follow the rules they've learned and the methods they've practiced, and hope they do everything right. That's the way most people are, and I think it's not so bad."

"Well, this doctor is smart."

"Good," Jane said. "That's good news for you and me." She had planted a tiny germ of worry in the woman's brain. She wasn't hopeless. She might be in love with the arrogant little doctor, but she was clearheaded enough to have seen the welts and bruises on Jane—maybe, because of what she'd seen, she had checked for other signs of abuse while Jane was asleep—and called her doctor boyfriend to complain. She wasn't hopeless. She helped Jane get to the toilet, and waited in the doorway.

The nurse said, "He probably saved your life."

"I might be able to save his," Jane said. "And yours."

"You can't use my cell phone."

"I'll make it clear that you helped me, and that you had no idea what was happening until you saw they were hurting me."

"I still don't know what this is about." She looked frightened, anxious. She helped Jane up, flushed the toilet, and helped her walk to the bed. Then she hurried to the sink, brought a cold, wet cloth, and pressed it against Jane's bruises. "We need ice to make the swelling go down."

"Those men are criminals," Jane said. "Somebody—probably one of them—killed a woman about three years ago, and they framed her husband, a man named Jim Shelby, for it. He went to prison. I got him out, and they want to make me tell where he is."

"Won't he just go back to prison if you tell?"

"No. They don't have any way of getting him back to prison without the authorities asking questions they can't answer—what they were doing in Los Angeles, why they would look for Shelby, and how they found him when the police couldn't. And of course, they can't let me go. Kidnapping and torture would mean life sentences for them."

"Oh, my God." The girl walked a few paces and sat down on the chair at the desk. "All this is such heavy stuff, out of nowhere. They just told the doctor there was a private patient who had an injury and wanted to pay for special care."

"That's the way trouble always comes—out of nowhere, with no warning. When it does you have to decide quickly."

She waited, watching the girl sitting at the desk, staring at the wall. "Will you please let me use your cell phone?"

"You just said it was a kidnapping and torture thing. Everybody would go to prison."

"Not you. You'll be the hero."

She looked sideways at Jane. "How do I know you'll twist it that way, and not the other way?"

"Someone who helps me will be my friend. They're just getting started on me." She waited, but the girl didn't seem to be able to make up her mind. She looked paralyzed. "Are you worried about your boyfriend?"

"I told you, he's not officially my boyfriend." She was irritated. She started to walk away, and it seemed to make her remember why she was there. She hurried back to the bathroom and returned with cold, damp hand towels she put on Jane's bruises.

Jane watched her. *It doesn't matter if he hasn't declared himself to be your boyfriend. You've had a big fat crush on him for a long time, and one slow day in the office, he came on to you in an examining room. Or he came to the office one day with flowers and asked you to dinner. Whatever it was, you're committed to him, and you have an intimate relationship now. I can hear it in your voice.*

The nurse went to the medical supplies and returned with Neosporin, which she gently applied to the scrapes left by the bamboo sticks.

Jane said, "I'm perfectly happy to include the doctor in the hero category too. I'll say that the next time he comes in is the first time I was conscious when he visited, and as soon as he knew what was up, he helped you save me. I know he has nothing to do with these men or framing Jim Shelby. But you've got to help me. The longer this goes on, the harder it will be to make up a story that keeps him innocent."

"I've got to have time to think. I should talk to him, too." She looked at Jane again. "Are you married?"

Jane wasn't wearing the ring, but there was still a pale line on her ring finger, and the young nurse must have seen it. "Yes." After a second she added, "I wouldn't ordinarily tell anyone that."

"I knew already, because there's an indentation on your ring finger. I'm glad you didn't lie."

"Sometimes a person in my position has to lie. I've got to lie to those men. I don't want to lie to you, though. Will you please help me?"

"I need time to think."

"We don't have much time. The next stage of this is going to come pretty quickly."

"The next stage? What's the next stage?"

"They'll think of things to do to me that hurt, that will make me so afraid I'll talk. The next stage will be heat—hot irons, or fire. You may be used to seeing things others haven't, but you don't want to see this."

"Why can't you just tell them, and we can all go home?"

"These men are implicated in a murder. No matter what I tell them, nobody's going home but them. They can't let any of us go."

"You're scaring me."

"We have to save ourselves. Either let me use your phone right now, or you use it as soon as you're a mile or two from here and positive you haven't been followed."

The woman took a deep breath, and let it out. "All right. Here."

She came to Jane's bed and held her cell phone out to Jane. They both heard the door at the end of the building swing open. Jane shook her head and the girl pulled back her cell phone and retreated to the desk and the computer. She pretended to be composing an e-mail.

Jane looked up at the men coming in the door. First came the tall man with the western accent who seemed to be in charge, and the others trooped in after him. He eyed the nurse as he passed her, then stopped at Jane's bed. "I see you're awake again. That's convenient."

"Why?"

"I didn't want to wake you up." He turned to the nurse and said, "Okay, honey. Why don't you go take a break? We'll call you if we need you."

"Yes, sir," the girl said. She stood up, walked to the door, and went outside. Jane saw that the parking lot was dark.

Jane watched the tall man. He took his time apprais-ing the progress of her decline. He stared at her bruised and swollen arms and hands above the sheet. "Do you have anything to tell me yet?"

She moved her head from side to side slowly, not taking her eyes from him.

"The thing is, we're in a bit of a bind here. You've taken something of mine. Not to mention hurting several friends of mine in a public place, where they couldn't really give you an idea of the consequences."

"You're persuading yourself that whatever you do to me, I deserve it, and that you'll just be paying me back. That's not true. Nothing you or your friends have done was legal or justified."

His eyes narrowed. "I don't think you're going to help your cause any by pissing me off. Fair warning."

"I don't have a cause."

He looked angry. "Not much of one. So, before things get a hell of a lot worse, I'd advise you to listen to me for a min-ute. The doctor tells me you're too weak to run away, even if you could get out of your bed by yourself. What you've man-aged to do by getting shot is to delay things by three days. Your boy Jim Shelby has had seventy-two hours. He could be anywhere in the country by now. Isn't that true?"

"If he drove most of the time and didn't stop long, sure."

"What that means isn't what you seem to think. His arriving where he was going doesn't take the responsibility to talk off you. It makes you even more important. You're going to have to tell us where he is."

"I still don't know."

"Tonight, I expect to find out if that's true. Each time you don't answer is going to cost you. Maybe it will be a finger. Maybe the next thing will be an ear, a toe, or an eye. I can tell you that it's best to give in early."

"I don't have anything I can tell you," she said, "so it will be a very unpleasant waste of time."

"Well, in a little while the others will get here with the tools, and we can get started. So sit tight." He walked off.

Jane tightened the muscles in her uninjured left leg. That was still strong, and so were her hands and arms. But her right leg would barely hold her, and she was too weak to put up much resistance.

The air where the tall man had stood still held his smell. A smoker. He had probably just gone out for a cigarette. He certainly would before he began to torture her. That was the way the habit seemed to work—a cigarette before anything and one after.

She wondered where her purse was now. She had sacrificed it when she had fought on the courthouse steps to buy time for Jim Shelby to get away. Inside it was a bottle of a particularly strong batch of water hemlock she had harvested and processed last summer.

Some people in upstate New York called the plant cowbane, because now and then a cow would eat a bit and die. The Latin name for the plant was *Cicuta maculata,* and it was related to the carrot, but the water hemlock was the most deadly plant on the continent. The traditional Seneca method of suicide was to take two bites of the root. About once a year Jane went to swampy places to look for the tall plant with tiny white flowers arranged in a flat circular group. She cut the roots from the stems and mashed them to get the clear yellowish liquid that held the strongest cicutoxin. Then she repeatedly strained the liquid until the particles were gone, and distilled it to remove most of the water. One swallow from the cut-glass perfume bottle she carried in her purse would have killed her in minutes.

Without the water hemlock, Jane would have to wait and see what tools her captors planned to use on her. If they were the right kinds, maybe she could use one to accomplish her death. If her hands were free she could tear out the stitches in her leg and get the blood flowing again. Maybe the men were novices who would accidentally cut an artery and she'd bleed to death quickly.

The nurse returned to the desk and sat in front of her computer. As the man walked by her, he said, "Take the rest of the night off, honey. We'll take care of her. And if the doc ever brings you back, don't bring the computer or a cell phone with you. Leave them at home. Understand?"

"Yes, sir." She looked terrified. "I understand." She hurried to pack up her things. She started the shutdown process on her laptop.

"I hope so," he said. "Because I'm not going to tell you again."

"I'll be sure to remember." She moved quickly. She had seen the marks on Jane and was eager to get away from the people who had made them. She closed the laptop even though it had not fully shut down, slid it into her bag, and hurried out the door.

Jane stared after her. She could not quite guess what the girl would do next. Jane had carefully nudged the girl's mind, inch by inch, until she was cornered, unable to think of a reason not to let Jane call the police. She had been ready to give in. But this had been a terrible, frightening experience for her, and Jane had seen people react to danger in many different ways—some had a first impulse to be heroic that carried them only through the initial moments and got them killed. Some people ran not only from the danger but even from the memory of the danger.

It was possible that the girl would get out of here, think about getting her boyfriend and herself into legal trouble or about bringing on them the hatred of an unknown number of violent criminals—six and counting—and pretend that she had never seen Jane. She would tell herself that Jane would talk and be released, or if Jane didn't talk, the consequences would be her own fault. And the girl would stop thinking about her. In a month Jane would seem like a dream. In a year the experience would be so far back in her memory that she would never revisit it.

Jane lay on the bed and studied the man. She hadn't had as much time to observe him as the others, but had no desire to be around him a second longer than she was forced to be. Clearly he was in charge. He was taller than the others, and spoke louder. When he was gone, the others all waited for him to come back and tell them what to do. When he was here, they all watched him and unconsciously mirrored his movements and expressions. But there was something else, and listening to him talk to the nurse helped her identify it: people were instinctively wary of him. There was a volatile, vindictive quality to him that was so strong that people timidly observed his moods for signs of change, and humored him.

He came closer and sat beside her on the bed. Jane was acutely conscious of the restraints on her arms. "Now we're alone for a few minutes, and we can talk." His voice and expression were friendly, almost conspiratorial. "If you'll give me some help and say where Shelby is likely to be now, we can avoid bringing everybody in here to spend the night thinking of new ways to make you tell us. We can avoid wear and tear and loss of limb." Jane decided to play him for time. If the girl did call the police, it would do no good if they didn't have time to get here. She had to keep him talking.

"So what you're saying is that if I give you Shelby, then you will let me go. Is that right?"

He nodded, his face earnest, but then began to modify his expression. "After a reasonable interval. I'd have to send someone after Shelby to be sure you told me the truth, of course. And we would have to be able to get some distance away before you were loose. Probably we'd get on an airplane and fly somewhere, and then make a call from there to let a person of your choice know exactly where to find you. Sound fair?"

"It sounds like a plan that would give you unlimited chances to change your mind and kill me, or just leave me here to die."

"Of course you have to remember that you're my prisoner. I'm not your prisoner."

"That's hard to forget."

"But aside from my leaving myself some wiggle room, do we have a deal?"

"No," she said. "I don't know where Shelby is."

"I'm sure you do."

"I got him a car and a change of clothes and some cash. If he doesn't make any mistakes and drives somewhere that's reasonably free of cops and people who hunt fugitives for a living, he can be invisible for months. He didn't tell me what his destination was, and I didn't suggest any."

"Did you get him credit cards?"

Jane saw the trap. "No."

"How about false ID? A driver's license?"

"No."

"Why not?"

"I didn't want to know what his new name would be," she said. "If people had his new name, they could eventually get his new address."

He looked at her closely. His blue eyes had probably looked innocent to many people over the years, and that was why he was trying to use them again on her. But to Jane his eyes looked cold and opaque, like flat metal disks. He manufactured a half smile. "I don't think I understand you yet. Is this about the money? Is somebody paying you a bonus for each day Shelby stays hidden?"

"No. Nobody's paying me anything."

Suddenly, she understood what he was doing. After the captured warrior had been brought into camp, he would sometimes be bathed and his wounds would be bandaged, and he would be allowed to rest. That evening he would be brought to an important man's dwelling, fed, and treated as an honored guest. Some enemy peoples would even formally adopt him, so he would become a relative. In doing these things the captors were trying to make his body stronger and his will weaker, to force him to live through the cruelest treatment, all the time feeling the terrible contrast between the feast and the torture. Almost the minute after the feast was over, the captured man would face the first of the major torments that would end only in his death.

The tall man looked at her with a friendly, concerned expression, as though he genuinely cared about her. "If you're not getting paid, then why would you put up with the kind of treatment you've been getting, and what's about to happen to you?"

"As you've said, you've got me. I don't have you." His hand shot out suddenly and slapped her face. She had watched for it and decided in advance to take the blow. If she did anything to deflect it or counter it, she would reveal how strong she really was, and this was a secret that might be important to her later. Her face felt hot and sore, and she knew it was probably turning red.

His smile returned. "You just reminded me that I can do whatever I want."

Jane heard cars pulling up outside the building, and her heart began to beat harder. The young nurse must have gathered enough nerve to call the police and say she had been hired to care for a kidnapped woman. Jane lay there, her eyes on the tall man. She knew that when the police came through the door he would either try to use her as a shield, or kill her. She would have to roll off the bed and stay low. Maybe she could deliver a kick to distract him for the police. She bent her strong left leg so she would be ready to push herself off the edge of the bed.

She heard the door swing open, and after a second he called out, "It's about time you guys got here."

The man who had driven the car when she was caught walked in carrying three bags against his chest. He said, "It took us a while to find all this stuff."

The man who had shot her said, "You wanted to talk to her alone. Should we wait?"

"She's buying time and bullshitting. We might as well get ready."

The men brought in a folding table, opened it, placed it about six feet from Jane's bed, and then began to take things out of the bags and lay them out on the surface. Jane considered not looking, because the fear would only weaken her, but she reminded herself that she needed to see what implements were going to be lying where she might be able to reach them later.

There were assorted knives, some of them serrated and some smooth, a package of steel skewers for barbecuing meat, a small handheld blowtorch. So this stage of her ordeal was going to be what she had expected—cutting and fire. There was a car battery, and a set of insulated wires with alligator clips. Just another kind of fire.

The tall man disconnected the IV needle from the back of her left hand and wrapped the tube around the steel stand.

"Here. Roll her over on her stomach and use the restraints to secure her wrists to the bed."

The two men turned her over roughly, and tightened the Velcro restraints on the bed frame around her wrists. She heard a cigarette lighter, and then a hiss. She turned her head toward the sound and watched the tall man holding the lighted torch, adjusting the feed valve until the flame was a small blue point.

The tall man used the torch to heat up a set of four steel skewers while the driver held them with a pair of long-handled pliers. Jane pictured the warrior, tied to a stake by now, watching the embers being heated, the torturers' eyes glowing like cats' eyes in the reflected firelight. The proper response was complete indifference. The warrior would pretend to be unafraid, would show calm when the pain came, would pretend that he felt no despair.

Jane could see that the skewers were red and glowing. The driver pulled the oversize man's shirt she was wearing up to her shoulders, and the tall man simply laid the skewers, one by one, across her back. Her muscles tensed, and her vision narrowed, with a red halo at the edges. Her eyes were wet, the tears spontaneously running as the hot steel seared her back. She believed she smelled her own flesh cooking, but she pictured the warrior's eyes staring into hers, silently urging her to endure the pain and the horror, and remained still.

The tall man picked the skewers up with the pliers. "Hot enough, you think?" She couldn't tell who he was talking to, and it no longer mattered. "You know, that was a shame. You really did have a beautiful back. I hated to ruin it with those burn lines. Well, guys? What should we try next?"

Another voice said, "We should have just killed her when we got her here."

"You shot her. You could have fired again or just aimed higher and said it was an accident." He was enjoying her ordeal, but it seemed to be making his friends uncomfortable. "She has a lot of determination, doesn't she?"

The driver said, "Maybe she told us the truth. Maybe she doesn't know where he went."

"Then she's really stupid. You should always have something—one precious thing—that you can use to keep this kind of shit from happening to you." He was heating the skewers again, and this time, he dropped all of them on her back at once. Jane's vision clouded red again, with only a small point of light in the center. The muscles in her arms and legs tightened in a spasm, but she held back the scream, kept the air moving in and out through her nostrils so it wouldn't pass her vocal cords and make a sound.

The burns on her back were now throbbing from the first attack, the air sweeping across them and making the pain flare again. She felt the bruises from the beating under her, and the burned flesh on her back, and together they seemed to overwhelm her nervous system until she was barely aware of the men and their movements.

"You know how to make this stop. All you have to do is give us back what's ours."

It was getting harder to keep silent. The bullet wound in her leg hurt again. Her body was a raw, throbbing, aching set of nerve endings, all sending hot, screaming alarms to her brain at once, and she couldn't soothe herself, couldn't turn away, couldn't even move. Inside her closed eyes she had a vision of her husband, Carey—not wishing he could save her, not wishing him into this horror at all, just feeling the loss of him.

What the tall man did next came with no warning, no sound that reached her ears, but brought an explosion of pain, and then the red cloud in front of her vision closed the point of light in the middle, and went black.

At first the darkness was like being in a pocket, but then she sensed that it was big, like a starless, infinite space. She wondered for a moment if she was dead. Moving was impossible, and she couldn't feel her body touching anything. And then, without warning, she felt all of it. The skin of her back was on fire. Her eyes opened like a camera shutter, and closed again at the glare of the lights.

She tried to look at the men again, and saw that they had gone. She couldn't see them or their shadows or hear their voices. She was cold, and she suddenly realized she was wet. She looked around at the table, and saw that someone had attached the two insulated wires to the car battery. That was it. They must have given her a shock, and she had passed out. She wondered how long she had been unconscious. She tried to run an inventory of pains, but she didn't detect any she hadn't felt before. They had let her alone after she passed out. They wanted her to feel every single sensation. There was no point in hurting a person who couldn't feel.

She had lost track of time. She had heard from people who had been broken in interrogations that losing track of time had weakened them. A person had to feel that there was a whole world outside his prison where time proceeded in an orderly, uniform way, where the sun rose and set as it always had. She realized that this was part of the distress she had felt when she had first been dragged in. The high windows that had been blacked out had scared her a little, and the single dim desk lamp had been worse. It was always gray twilight in the big room.

Jane took a deep breath, asked herself how long she could hold out against the pain, and realized that she was still willing to die. As long as she didn't reveal where Jim Shelby was, she could buy him time, and keep these men occupied with her instead of searching for him. Shelby and every one of her earlier runners would have another day of safety, another day for their identities to mature and be more solid, another day to make a friend who might help them. And another day would give Jane's captors a chance to get impatient and careless.

She thought about her runners. Over the years she had taken dozens and dozens of them away. Shelby was only the most recent. They had almost all come to her in the last days of wasted, ruined lives, sometimes just hours before their troubles would have changed from dangerous to fatal. She would obliterate the person's old identity and turn him into a runner, a fugitive she would guide to a place far away, where nobody knew him, and certainly nobody would ever think of killing him. She would give him a new identity and teach him how to be that new person for the rest of his life. By now there were people all over North America and Europe who bore names that she had made up.

She thought about her husband, Carey, the surgeon who spent every day of his life fixing and curing people. He had been her reward, the part of the world that she had taken for herself for no better reason than that she wanted him and he kept pestering her to take him. She loved him so much she could picture every centimeter of him with such clarity that she could feel him against her skin. She had lived a good life, but now she had to be ready to die to preserve the other people, the ones who had trusted her with their lives.

Jane let go of Carey's image and prepared herself for the next phase. The pain of torture was almost unbearable, but she had discovered it had other qualities, too. It set her apart from the rest of humanity. Each time the pain didn't destroy her was a failure for the enemy, a wall that had held against an attack. The cuts and burns were decorations of valor and at the same time proof of the torturers' unworthiness. The pain was the means of consecration, the welcome fire that proved the victim's nobility.

She would wait for the next torment, and if she got the chance she would use their implements as weapons. And when she couldn't do that anymore, she would use one of them on herself.

4

Jane waited several hours lying facedown on the bed. The young nurse had not scraped up the courage to call the police. Jane had made a number of excuses for her during the past few hours. Maybe she had not known the way here. No, she had come along with the doctor once, and she had come alone and left alone last night. Maybe she had felt she needed to wait for her boyfriend the doctor to return home so she could explain to him in private what she had seen and why they had to call the authorities. She had said something last night about wanting to talk to him.

The girl had said he was smart. That didn't mean he was smart; it meant only that he had persuaded her of his intelligence, and that he wouldn't have much trouble talking her out of helping Jane. That was the smart choice, the one that would probably keep them both out of trouble, preserve his freedom and his license to practice medicine, and let them forget they had ever seen her.

The easiest thing for them to do was to separate themselves from this unpleasantness. He had treated her bullet wound, and what had happened to Jane after that was not his business. He would use the girl's belief in his authority and her faith in his wisdom to smother her conscience.

Jane heard an engine, and then footsteps, and she lifted her face off the bed, straining to see. Even though she knew better, she couldn't help holding her breath, hoping the police had arrived. But a key unlocked the door. The door swung open and she could see the blinding yellow-white light of the morning sun slice into the room and illuminate it for a second. When the door closed, the same three men were standing in the room.

Jane could see there had been a change. They seemed to know something she didn't, and it had lightened their mood, as though they'd been excused from a big, unpleasant job. She felt a sick fear for Shelby. The man who had driven her here said, "Hey, Wylie. You going to tell her now?"

The tall man turned his head and glared at the driver. He said, "Yes, I am, Gorman."

"Sorry," the driver said. He looked at his feet.

Jane silently repeated the names to herself a dozen times. Wylie was the tall one, and Gorman was the fake cop who had served as the driver. She had an irrational fear that she would forget their names, even though she knew that this would be impossible. She would still remember them if she lived to be a hundred and the fresh burn scars on her back healed to invisibility. Wylie and Gorman.

Wylie stood over Jane with his arms folded on his chest. "Normally I'd kill Mr. Gorman for that, but it doesn't matter, because I've learned something I didn't know before. Want to know what it is?"

"No," Jane said. She was still in restraints and lying facedown on the bed. She turned her face away from him.

"I'll bet you don't." He undid the Velcro strips that held her wrists, and grabbed her hair so she had to turn toward him onto her side. He grinned, and she noticed how his mouth was twisted to make a smile that was really a snarl. It was as though the meanness behind his eyes distorted his expressions. "I started to get curious about you the first time I heard about you. A lot of people go through the jails and courts every day, but the only ones who ever get away seem to be the ones where some clerk screws up the paperwork or something. Nobody breaks out. So I started asking around. And you'd be amazed at all the people who are interested in you."

Jane studied the blue eyes and saw spite in them, and greed. But what she saw that was most disturbing was joy. He was celebrating a victory.

"What have you done?" she asked.

"In a way, it's good news for you. I'm arranging an auction for tomorrow. There are people who say they're willing to pay some really big money just for the privilege of meeting you in person for a leisurely chat."

Jane's stomach felt as though it had turned cold and heavy. She said, "Who?"

"The bidders are coming here, so you'll see them. And they want to see you before they hand over the money. One is named Barraclough. He's the younger brother of someone you had an altercation with years ago, I understand. He owns a security company. There's a private detective named Killigan, who represents Robert Eckersly. You apparently took Eckersly's wife away from him. There's a gentleman named Grady Lee Beard, a bounty hunter, I think, who says you gave him a knife scar that runs from his collarbone to his navel. He says you got him arrested in an airport only a year or two ago."

Jane turned away.

"Don't you want to hear about all the bidders?"

Jane thought, *Now I understand why you don't care if I know your name.*

"They all seem to have somebody they want to ask you about."

"I won't be telling anybody anything."

"No?" He sighed. "What a shame. I don't think I'll want to watch. You know, when they were asking me questions to see if you were the same woman, every one of them mentioned those blue eyes. I was relieved that I hadn't popped them out. That was coming up soon."

"Why didn't you?"

"You passed out. I'm glad I didn't do anything so they wouldn't recognize you. Now that I know how valuable you are, I realized I can't afford you. I have other ways to find Jimmy Shelby. He's got a sister, and he's a regular good old boy, who will probably make some dumb-ass mistakes and get caught. So tomorrow when the bidders get here, you go on the auction block." He turned to the others. "Maybe we ought to actually build an auction block. What do you think, Gorman? Maloney?"

The one who had shot her said, "Was that necessary?"

"Sorry, Mr. Maloney. Just having a little fun."

Now she had all their names. Wylie. Gorman. Maloney.

Wylie laughed, turned away, and went to the door. "I've got some stuff to do. You two keep an eye on her. A couple of those bastards might be smart enough to come early and try to steal the merchandise." He went out the door and locked it.

Wylie was gone all morning, so Gorman went out to buy hamburgers and french fries and milk shakes for lunch. Jane had been fed intravenously, and it had been days since she had eaten solid food, so the lunch caused cramps, but then, hour by hour, she felt better and stronger. Wylie didn't return by dinnertime, and Gorman and Maloney grumbled. Maloney went out to buy the food this time. They let Jane sit in her bed and eat without restraints. Jane ate quickly. She knew now that this was going to be her last night before these men sold her. Once she was in the hands of any of the likely bidders, her chance of survival would end. She saw

Gorman get up to throw away his trash, so she lay back in her bed. When Maloney went to the bathroom, she lay on her stomach and wrapped the Velcro restraint around her left wrist to tie it to the bed frame, then lay on her stomach. She put her right hand under the sheet so it couldn't be seen. She hoped that both men would glance in her direction and assume the other had made her secure. Then she arranged herself so she could open one eye a slit and see the rest of the big room.

After Maloney, Gorman, and Jane had eaten, the two men went to the steel door, looked outside, then locked it. She could hear them fiddling with something that clanked, but she closed her eyes. They were more worried about the bidders taking Jane than about her making an escape, and she had to keep them confident.

They came closer to her. Jane caught sight of Gorman's watch, so she knew it was ten in the evening when Gorman and Maloney made an agreement. Each of them would stay awake to keep watch for four hours. The first shift was to be Maloney's. He sat at the table near Jane's bed drawing pictures on the backs of some medical papers that the nurse had left. Jane could see the drawings were the sort that ten-year-old boys drew, fighter planes diving low toward a stronghold made of piled-up boxlike structures, strafing them with machine guns. A second wave came in higher, releasing large bombs from their bellies. After a while he obliterated the defenders with a couple of large, puffy explosions.

Next Maloney drew a few pictures of women, all with exaggerated breasts and bottoms, and impossibly thin waists. He wasn't very good at hands or feet, and when he got to the faces, he drew big, lipsticked mouths and cowlike eyes, but kept drawing bad noses and erasing them until they were gray smears. At last he tired of making art. He sat on the couch near Jane and stared at the closed door to the office where Gorman was sleeping, then at his watch. After a time his head tipped backward, his eyes closed, his mouth gaped, and Jane heard him snoring.

Jane waited. Gorman had retired to one of the offices along the side of the building, and he had been snoring for an hour. She knew she would move quietly but could not make herself perfectly silent. She had to let Maloney reach the stage of sleep that Gorman had already reached. If he heard a small noise now, his mind would try to remain asleep by incorporating the noise into his dream.

Just as Jane was about to move, Maloney stirred. He sat up, took off his coat, and tossed it onto the arm of the couch, then slipped off his pants and draped them over the coat, then lay down full length. He pulled the spare blanket that had been left on the couch over him and immediately went back to sleep. Jane waited for what seemed to her like an hour.

After a time Jane raised her head. Maloney was deep asleep now. She was so eager as her time approached that her breaths were becoming shallow and her thoughts were scattered, tumbling over one another. So many things had to be done before Wylie got back, and he could be stepping up to the door right now. She was badly hurt. Would she even be able to do those things? She clenched her teeth and thought. First she had to get out of the bed.

She slowly, carefully removed her single Velcro restraint, trying to muffle the *skritch* sound by pressing the pillow over it. Then she pushed herself up so she was on two hands and her left knee. She eased to her right, then lowered her tender right leg to the floor. It would have to hold her weight for a few seconds. If it collapsed, she would fall and wake Maloney. She shifted her weight to the right leg while her left was lowered to the floor beside it. The leg held. Then she was kneeling on the floor beside the bed.

Maloney had taken off his coat and pants to sleep. She touched the pants pockets for the gun, then searched the coat pockets. Where was his gun? The gun must be here where he could reach it. She reached out and slowly, gently slid her hand into the small space beneath the cushion he was using as a pillow and the couch. It wasn't there.

Jane began to crawl. Crawling was quieter and easier right now than putting all her weight on her legs. She crawled to the table where Maloney had been drawing. She lifted his paper slightly, and caught sight of a black, chunky object. She reached under the paper, encountered the cool steel and then the knurled handgrips of the Beretta M9F, and felt her face forming itself into a smile.

She had Maloney's gun in her hand. The gun was a huge step. She had accomplished a wonder. At the worst, Jane wasn't going to have to lie in bed helpless until the time came to let the next set of captors torture her to death. She could take at least a couple of the tormenters with her, and then end her own life. Her heart was pounding with exhilaration.

Jane crawled toward the door of the office where Gorman slept. When she was nearly there, she came to a steel support pole rising from the floor and used it to pull herself up to a standing position. She took a step with her injured right leg and realized it was much stronger than she had expected. The twinge she felt was bearable; and, even better, the leg held her weight.

She stepped to the steel door of the room and tested the knob. It turned smoothly. She held it. There was a raised circular dead bolt at eye level, with a key slot. She stared at it as she prepared herself to open the door. In a moment she would have to spot Gorman in the darkened room. She might have to fire and kill him before he found his gun and aimed it. She stood slightly to the side, held the gun in her right hand at chest level, and turned the knob the rest of the way until it stopped. She pushed the door inward and saw Gorman.

He was across the room lying on his side on a couch. Near him was a big wooden desk. He was still asleep, his mouth open and his jaw slack, breathing deeply. It would be easy to shoot him from here, but she would have to be positive he was dead, and that meant three or four shots, and then trying to make it back on her bad leg to a spot where she could shoot Maloney before he was awake, up, and dangerous. She had his gun, but she didn't know if there was another one in this building.

Jane took another step into the room, and then turned a bit to close the door behind her, but she stopped, staring at the inner side of the door. Right in front of her was the inner side of the dead bolt. It was a four-inch circle of brass exactly like the outer side. The dead bolt was the kind that had keyholes on both sides, and this side had the key in it.

She quietly extracted the key from the lock, backed out, and closed the door. She stuck the key in the lock and turned it to lock the dead bolt. Gorman was locked in. When he woke up he wouldn't be able to get out. She put the key in her shirt pocket and turned her eyes toward Maloney. He was still sleeping.

It took her a long time to walk to the couch, taking each step with care to be sure that it was silent and that it didn't strain her injured right leg. The time seemed to be passing too quickly. She must not waste her last chance by taking too much time. Wylie could be pulling into the parking lot at any second.

When she came near the couch she could see the items laid out on the table near her bed. There was the blowtorch they had used to heat the skewers; there were the bamboo sticks they had used to beat her, the skewers, a big pair of bolt cutters with two-foot handles, and a pair of big steel rings with screws attached so they could be embedded in a support beam and made to hang heavy objects. She saw a coil of rope and knew that the heavy object was to have been her. They must have planned to hang her up for the next torture session. There was a roll of duct tape, with a pair of scissors. She supposed they would have taped her mouth when the screams got too loud to tolerate. There was a set of handcuffs and a key.

Jane picked the handcuffs up and stepped to the spot between the couch and the bed. She touched the muzzle of the gun to Maloney's head and gave it a hard push. He flinched, and his eyes opened and focused on Jane.

She whispered, "If you move or make a sound, I'll kill you. Do you believe me?"

He nodded.

"Get on the bed and lie on your stomach." She kept the gun aimed at him as he moved from the couch to the bed. She closed one handcuff on his right wrist and the other on the steel bed frame. Then she used one of the Velcro restraints to fasten his left wrist to the other side.

She limped to the table, took the duct tape and scissors, then returned and wrapped the tape around his head and across his mouth three times before she cut it.

She went to the couch where he'd been asleep, and put on his pants. They were too wide and too long, but she cinched the belt as tightly as she could. Then she found her flat black shoes under the bed, and stepped into them. She bent close to Maloney's ear. "I'm not going to harm you or Gorman. I'm just going to leave. But don't ever let me see you again."

Her anxiety was shifting into hope. She had the two men locked up. She had the gun, and now she was taking steps toward the steel door at the end of the building. And then she saw the chain. There was a thick, heavy chain running through a bolt hole in a vertical I beam, then across the door, around the nearest support pole, and back. It was fastened there by a big padlock. She lifted the padlock and looked beneath it. There was no key. It was obviously intended to keep someone from forcing the door from outside, so there was no reason for the key to be gone. Where was it? She looked everywhere nearby—any sort of small ledge created by the structure of the building, or by the floors. She went into the bathroom and looked there, too.

For the first time, Jane's eyes began to water. She was so badly hurt, so weak and tired after the past few days. She had dared to feel some faint hope, and now this. *No. No weakness.* She blinked her eyes clear, gripped her pistol, and walked back to the table that held the tools they'd used to torment her. She put the gun in her belt and snatched up the pair of bolt cutters with the long handles. She brought them to the chain on the door and closed them on the shaft of the padlock. She squeezed the handles as hard as she could, but they made no impression on the lock.

She knelt and examined every link of the chain, looking at the weld that closed each oval. At last she found a weld that looked a bit thinner than the link, so it formed a small indentation. She fitted one blade of the bolt cutters into it, then tried to bring the two handles together to cut it. She kept trying, but she wasn't strong enough. She stopped to catch her breath and let her muscles relax. Sweat had made her hair damp and streaked her forehead. The various pains in her body seemed worse. She set down the bolt cutters and examined the weld of the link she'd been attacking. It did show some signs of wear, a slight distortion.

Jane got up, went back to the table, picked up the blowtorch and the plastic cigarette lighter, and returned. She struck the lighter and then turned the knob on the blowtorch. It hissed for a second and then ignited. She adjusted the flame to make it smaller, a deep blue point that was hot and intense. She set the bottle-shaped torch down so the point of the flame was on the weld of the link.

She waited for a long time, watching the link get hotter and hotter, then red-orange, then cherry red. She decided it was time. She lodged one handle of her bolt cutters against the wall of the building, opened its jaws, and set one blade in the red-hot weld. She stepped out of her shoes so her bare left foot was set against the floor, and grasped the other handle near the end with both hands. She pushed, hard. She used her strong left leg and her back and shoulders and arms. She thought she felt movement, but it wasn't enough to cut through. She knew she had to use her injured right leg. Even if it could exert only a hundred pounds of pressure, it would help. And if she died later tonight, she would know that she had used everything.

She used both legs, she pushed harder, and the blade cut through and the handles came together. She pushed the red-hot link against the hinge of the steel door and used the leverage of the bolt cutters to bend it, so the opening widened. A length of chain slipped through and fell to the floor. Jane pulled the bolt cutters away, turned off the blowtorch, and stepped into her shoes.

She walked to the door and reached for the knob. She was relieved that the knob turned and the door opened. She held on to the bolt cutters as she stepped through the doorway into the night.

The air was cool and moving, and she loved the sweet taste of it. There were no cars on the asphalt outside. The lot was shielded from view on three sides by other buildings sharing the same parking lot, and on the fourth by the building where she had been held. She had a bad feeling about limping along the street that Wylie would use to enter the lot, so she slipped between two of the buildings and stopped to listen. There seemed to be streets on two sides, with the whispery sound of cars passing, and ahead of her was the glow of electric light. Jane picked the street away from the lot entrance and headed for it.

At the end of the passage between buildings, she looked out and saw that the street she'd chosen had no pedestrians and only an occasional car. She looked down at her bolt cutters. One end was a pair of steel shafts with rubberized handles and the other was two steel blades like a parrot's bill. She knew the men had brought the bolt cutters here in case they decided to cut off fingers or toes. Now that she was outside in the air and could see sights that had the dull normalcy of any other city street, the horror of the men's plans struck her in the stomach like a physical sensation. She felt an impulse to drop the bolt cutters. No, she told herself. It was too early to feel, too early to allow herself any weakness. She must think only about what she had to do. The throwaway cell phone she'd had in Los Angeles had gone with her purse in the fight, and so had the false identification she'd brought. She had a sudden thought. Maloney and Gorman must have had cell phones, but she hadn't taken them. How could she expect to live if she didn't think of things like that? No, she thought. Taking them would have been foolish. If she'd called the police she'd go to jail forever. And she couldn't wait in Los Angeles for Carey to come and get her. She had to get moving away from this place.

The old warriors came back to her. If one of them ever managed, after the torture had begun, to see a second chance to fight, how precious that would have been to him. She must not waste this chance. She knelt and rolled up the bottoms of the oversize pants she had taken, pulled out her shirt to cover the gun in her belt, put her bolt cutters under her left arm, then stepped out onto the sidewalk.

Before her was a four-lane thoroughfare, with a traffic signal hanging on a wire in the center of the intersection, and a long row of industrial buildings and businesses. Across the street she could see a place that sold marble and granite to builders, a fence company, and farther down, a United Rent-all. None of the buildings had any lights on except a few overhead floods on their parking lots.

Jane kept to the shadows as she walked to the United Rent-all. She stepped to the side of the chain-link fence, where the light was dim, used her bolt cutters to cut five links in the fence, ducked, and entered the lot. There were a few cherry pickers for high work, a Caterpillar tractor, two plain white vans, two white pickups. The doors of the vehicles were all locked.

She looked at the front of the rental office, then approached and stared in the window. She saw a counter, a clock that said twelve thirty-five, and a door that led to a back room. She could also see an electric-eye alarm system at the doors and a set of metal alarm tapes in the windows. She moved farther back along the building and, in the dim light, saw that the back room was lined with shelves that held every kind of power carpentry tool she had ever seen, plumbers' equipment, and a few electronic boxes that could have been anything. Where was the dim light coming from? Overhead. She put her face close to the window and looked up to see that there was a large skylight above the storeroom.

She kept moving back toward the rear of the building. At the back was a roofed-in area that held a decorative fountain for fancy parties, a collection of lawn chairs and tables, and finally, a row of ladders of all sizes.

She came closer to the ladders. They were all locked up for the night with a chain running from a rung in the wall, through each of the ladders, and then padlocked to the last one. She fitted her bolt cutters to the chain, set her hands at the very ends of the handles, and cut it. She pulled out an aluminum extension ladder and leaned it against the roof of the building. With her injured right leg, she wasn't sure if she could climb. She tested herself, using her left leg to go up, then pulling her right to join it on the same rung, then holding most of her weight with her arms as she lifted the left again. It worked once, so she did it again.

With great difficulty she climbed the ladder to the roof. Each time her right foot rose to the next rung and she tried to make her right leg hold her weight, the thigh gave a stabbing pain that made her weak for a few seconds. At the top of the ladder she crawled onto the roof and looked down at the skylight. There were no conductive tapes on the glass, so she decided the frame must be what was on the alarm circuit. If she opened the latch and lifted the glass, she would set off the alarm. But with no tape, the glass itself wasn't wired. She used the butt of the gun to break a pane of glass, but no alarm sounded. She crawled back to her extension ladder, pulled one of the two ladder pieces out of the other, then lowered it down through the skylight. She rested a moment, then slowly went down the ladder into the room.

All around her she saw equipment of all kinds. But mounted on the front wall she found what she had been searching for. It was a large metal box that was nearly flat. It was held closed by a small lock. Jane looked around her, found a crowbar, fitted it between the box and its cover by the lock, and popped it open.

Inside there were rows of hooks with keys hanging on them. Each set of keys had a plastic tag on it. She selected a few sets that seemed to have license numbers on them, and put them in her pants pocket. She tolerated the pain and weakness as she slowly, patiently climbed back up to the roof, then climbed down on the other half of the extension ladder to the ground. She propped the half ladder along the side with the other ladders and ran the chain through them again, so her burglary wouldn't be obvious from the street.

She went to a small pickup truck, looked at its license plate, then sorted through her keys and found the right one. She started the engine, drove the truck to the gap she had cut in the fence, rolled back some more chain-link, and drove out through the gap to the street.

According to the clock on the pickup's dashboard, it was nearly two a.m. She drove straight until she saw a sign for the 101 Freeway. She followed the arrow, got on the freeway a few minutes later, and headed east. At the junction with the 134 she switched freeways, because she knew that the 134 became the 210 and met Interstate 15 a few miles ahead on the far side of Los Angeles. Interstate 15 North ran across the desert to Las Vegas, and then kept going north all the way to Salt Lake City.

5

Jane kept the pickup at ten miles an hour over the speed limit with a steady pressure on the pedal, trying not to slow down or apply the brake. She used her left foot because the right leg had been weakened by the bullet wound and hadn't been rested much tonight. When the sun came up just before six she was almost to Nevada on Route 15, and she had been successful in avoiding any traffic problems or slowdowns.

She had guessed correctly that the rental company would keep the gas tanks full so the staff could simply hand a customer the keys to any vehicle and tell him to bring it back with a full tank. When she left Los Angeles she had no purse, no money, no identification. She was wearing a man's shirt that had been put on her as a hospital gown, and a man's pants with the legs rolled at the ankles and the belt cinched tight. The only part of the outfit that was hers was the pair of flat black shoes she'd worn to the courthouse. Her only real assets were stolen: the truck, the loaded gun, and the bolt cutters.

She knew that the time was coming very soon when the police in California would receive the report of the stolen pickup truck. People who rented tools and construction equipment undoubtedly opened early. When she crossed into Nevada, she felt as though she had won an extra hour or two before a police car might appear behind her flashing its lights. It took time before auto thefts from other states got to the top of the list anywhere.

She drove into Las Vegas, took the Tropicana exit, drove east of the tall casinos on Las Vegas Boulevard, and pulled the pickup truck into the parking lot of a large chain drugstore. She put the gun and spare magazine into her pants pockets, tucked in the big shirt, and started to walk. She was in terrible condition, in pain and exhausted. At six thirty in the morning, the sun was low on the eastern side, but already strong. It always seemed to be either in her eyes or reflecting off every smooth, flat surface ahead of her. The pavement was already radiating heat that she could feel on her bare ankles.

The burns on her back and the bruises on her arms and shoulders and sides ached again, now that she wasn't sitting still in the truck. But the bullet wound was still her main worry. It was still angry and painful and made her limp slowly along the street.

The day was going to heat up rapidly, so she would need to get into some shade and air-conditioning. She had been in Las Vegas a few times before, staying in the big hotels on the Strip. She had noticed all the security cameras on the ceilings, and the mirrors placed in spots where they could only be for observation, and the many quiet, well-dressed men who appeared and disappeared, watching the changing crowds of people to be sure nothing disrupted the orderly flow of money from the customers to the casinos. She had found the security relaxing, because it took a bit of the pressure away from her. But she knew today was not a good day to try to enter any of the big hotels. A glimpse at her reflection in every window she passed showed her she looked like a madwoman. She wouldn't get more than a few steps inside the door before some calm, efficient functionary intercepted her and offered her help getting where she belonged.

She passed a tiny strip mall, where she could see two pay telephones on an outer wall. They struck her as almost impossible relics of the days before cell phones, but she could see that one of them had a telephone book that was intact. She went to the phone, opened the front section of the book, and, after some looking, found the address of a shelter for battered women.

A map in the front of the book indicated she had to walk east on Bonanza Road. She walked steadily, trying to get as far as she could from the pickup truck she'd abandoned, and hoping to be inside before too many people noticed her. The blocks were very long. She found that she could make better progress if she walked in the shadows of the big buildings and parking structures. After an hour she went into a gas station to use the ladies' room, wash her face, and then drink water from her cupped hands. She clawed her hair with her fingers to comb it. When she came out, an attendant was already standing in the shade near the pumps to satisfy himself that she was on her way.

By nine she was on the right street, and at nine forty-five she was at the front door. The shelter looked like a house, just another one-story bungalow among thousands. There was no big sign on the front, only a little wooden one that read "The Lifeboat" and an even smaller one beside the door that read "Please ring." She pressed a button on the intercom box and heard static. "Hi," Jane said. "I just got to town and I'm having a hard time. I wondered—" There was a buzz and a solenoid clicked a dead bolt open.

Jane stepped inside and saw that behind a counter to her left there was a young receptionist, with an older woman standing beside the receptionist looking down at some papers. The two looked up at Jane at once. The younger one smiled and said, "What can we—" but the older one interrupted. "Come in. Don't worry. You're in the right place. Come right in here with me."

The woman had white hair with a few remaining streaks of blond, so it looked a bit yellow, as though she had simply forgotten to make a decision about which color it should be. "This is the Lifeboat. We have everything you need right here. Come sit down in here." She led Jane into an office and let her sit on a soft leather couch. "Would you like some water?"

"Sure," Jane said. "I'd love some."

She went to a small office refrigerator, pulled out a pitcher full of water, and poured Jane a glass. Then she refilled the pitcher at the tap in the bathroom and put it back in the refrigerator.

"I'm Sarah Werth." She picked up a clipboard with a form on it from a table, and sat down in front of Jane in a desk chair. "Now, honey. Let's get some quick essentials."

"All right."

"How did you get here? Is there a car outside we need to move?"

"No, I walked."

Sarah Werth looked at her for a second or two, then returned to her form. "Do you need medical attention right away?"

"I need access to a first aid kit, but that's about all."

She stared at the gap where the two top buttons of Jane's shirt were open. "I can see somebody has been hitting you," she said. "Would you like to report a crime?"

Jane could tell she had seen one of the bruises. She drew the shirt closed and buttoned it. "No, I can't do that," Jane said. "I know what I need, so can I just ask?"

"If you want to do it that way, you can," said Sarah. "But I'll need to ask you the rest of the questions afterward."

"Fair enough," Jane said. "I would like another glass of water in a minute. I'd like a bath and then something to eat, and then a place to sleep for about eight hours."

Sarah waited for a couple of seconds, but nothing more came. "Those are easy." As she took Jane's glass and refilled it, she said, "We have about seventy women and children with us right now, most of them in secret, secure locations."

"What kind of locations?"

"They're mostly houses, single-family houses that are owned by the Department of Housing and Urban Development. We keep them occupied and kept up. If someone comes to us looking for a particular woman, we ask her if she wants to see him. If she does, she meets with him here. If she doesn't, we never heard of her."

"Sounds smart."

"Is someone looking for you that you'd like to avoid?"

"Yes. Anyone who comes looking for me is someone I'd like to avoid. But I don't think people can find me here, or I wouldn't have come."

"All right. Take this clipboard and fill in all the blanks that you can."

Jane took the clipboard and worked her way down the form. Her name was Melanie Kraft. She had no current address, but had last lived in Salt Lake City, and wanted to go back. She had been driven to Las Vegas a few days ago by a man she had known in Salt Lake City. But he had beaten her up and burned her, so she had stolen some clothes from him and run away.

She filled in all the spaces, but left out the wound in her thigh. In some places there was a law that people like social workers and nurses had to report all gunshot wounds to the police.

When Jane handed back the clipboard, Sarah said, "I can see why you're afraid. I'm a nurse. Would you mind if I looked at the burns?"

Jane turned away and raised her shirt.

"Oh, my God," the woman muttered. "Hold on right there. I'd like to take a picture of that."

Jane let go of the shirt. "No pictures. I'm sorry."

"You have to think ahead. Someday, a man like that is probably going to kill you. Even if you aren't up to charging him right now, you're going to wish you had evidence of what he did to you."

Jane said, "What happened is over if I can keep it over."

"If you won't do it for yourself, think about the rest of us. Now that he's out of your life, he's looking for somebody else right now. He'll do the same to her, or worse, unless you stop him. This thing we're doing here really works only if we all help. I can hide people from creeps. But the only one who can take him off the street is you."

Jane said, "I agree strongly with every single thing you've said. I can only tell you that this time it's a one-of-a-kind situation. I have no personal relationship with this man. I escaped the first second I could. Calling the police would only endanger me."

"Are you a sex worker? You didn't check it on your form."

"No. Please. Just listen. You can see I have injuries. I escaped with no money, no identification, not even my own clothes. I want to move on. As soon as I can get a job and earn enough to leave, I'll go. Sometime later, I'll send you a contribution that will more than repay what you invest in me, I promise. But please. I can't leave photographs of myself, or have any conversations with the police."

Sarah Werth stared at her for a few seconds. "I assume you've given me a false name."

"Of course."

Sarah Werth set the clipboard on her desk and stood. "Come on, and we'll get you bathed and fed and assigned to a bed."

In the bath Jane kept her bullet wound dry, but washed it in hydrogen peroxide from the first aid kit and rewrapped it with gauze and tape. There were no signs of infection, and the stitches had held. The rest of her body was a pattern of welts, bruises, and scars. Everything hurt, every surface was sensitive, but in the end she didn't feel as though any of the injuries but the bullet wound was deep enough to need much attention. She thought about Carey. He would know what to do about the injuries. But even if she'd had a phone, she couldn't call him from here. The number would be on the bill, and a phone number was as good as an address.

When she was finished, she was given a pair of black exercise pants and a T-shirt. She put them on and went into the bedroom she was to share with a woman named Iris. Iris was not in the room yet, so Jane got into the bed she was assigned and slept.

The escape from Wylie, Gorman, and Maloney; the burglary; the five-hour drive to Las Vegas; and the long, painful, limping walk to the shelter had left a deep exhaustion and a flood of impressions and images that gave her quick, bright, unsettling dreams. One was about walking through a city that had huge buildings without doors. Then it got dark and she could see that there was a man walking to overtake her. As he came closer and walked into a bit of light aimed downward from one of the buildings, she recognized him.

"Hello, Harry." As always he was wearing the gray-green coat, and this time he had a hat, a man's snap-brim like the one she had seen him wear the night when she had first taken him away from his troubles.

"Hi, Janie."

"I thought you'd be around soon."

"Do dreams come to you, or do you come to us?"

"That's too idle a question for right now. I'm in terrible trouble, Harry. I was captured and they tortured me. They lamed me so I can hardly walk."

"I know. I know the things you know because I exist only in your mind. The hurt was a revelation, wasn't it? Maybe it was supposed to change you."

"It made me weak and slow and afraid to be hurt again."

"Maybe Hawenneyu the right-handed twin needed you to be in one place and not another at a particular time, and the price of having you there was the wound. Maybe it made Hanegoategeh the left-handed twin think he had won and turn his head away for a moment. Or maybe what happened was meant to remind you that some people have been amazingly tough."

"The Grandfathers?"

He shrugged. "Every one of them was a relative of yours. When they were fighting far from home, and one of them decided to stay back and die, it terrified their enemies."

"My enemies aren't terrified. They can't wait to find me."

"You could just as easily have killed the last two in that building."

"If I had killed them, what would make me different from them?"

"Are you different from them?"

"I would never take anyone's life unless I had no choice."

"You're alone, hurt, and hiding. You may not have choices from now on. Everyone is a warrior, and every last one of us falls in the fighting. For now, one of the brothers has kept you alive. He must have had some purpose in mind. Be ready." He looked to the left, nodded to her, and then crossed the street. He hurried up the sidewalk, but when he stepped into a shadow, he never stepped out of it again.

Jane slept in dark, unremembered dreams for hours, then woke before dawn to find a woman standing in the doorway. The woman saw that Jane was awake. "Good morning," she said.

"Good morning."

She went to the other bed and gently touched the sleeping woman in it. "Iris, get up, honey."

The sleeping woman jumped, uttered a little cry, and held her forearms up in a gesture that Jane recognized as an attempt to protect her face from blows.

Jane said, "It's all right, Iris. You're in the shelter. You're safe."

Iris took in two deep breaths that were like sobs, then sat up and rubbed her eyes. "I'm sorry. I was having a bad dream." Jane got a chance to study her. She was about twenty-five, with very white skin and the kind of thin blond hair that looked like cornsilk. It had been cut short, but it looked uneven and jagged, as though she had cut it herself.

The woman who had awakened them said, "The dreams will go away, too. Don't worry. I'm here to take you two to another house. It's just across town, but I'd like to get going right away, because there's less chance of being seen before dawn."

Jane and Iris got up and put on the rest of the clothes Sarah had left on the dressers in the room—for each, jeans, a fresh T-shirt, a long-sleeved shirt to keep off the night chill. They didn't stay for breakfast or to put on makeup. They just gathered their few belongings and went through the office to the lobby that had once been a living room. Through the window Jane could see a small SUV with tinted windows waiting in the driveway. A middle-aged woman got down from the driver's seat and opened the side doors, but no light went on.

The SUV took them across the city to a quiet street in Henderson, and up the street to a small yellow-tan stucco house with a red tile roof that made it look as though it had been built in Tuscany. The van pulled into the open garage and Jane and Iris got out. Jane said, "Thank you."

"Stay safe," the woman said, and waited in the driveway to watch them walk to the back door of the house.

Jane knocked on the kitchen door, and in a few seconds a woman about forty years old, taller than Jane, came and opened it. She was wearing black capri pants and a T-shirt, as though she were up for the day and knew it would be hot. "Come in."

As they did, Jane said, "My name is Melanie. This is Iris."

"Hello," the woman said. "I'm Sandy. There are three other women here already—Beth, Michelle, and Diane. They're asleep, but they've got jobs that start around nine, so they'll be up before too long. I volunteered to let you in."

"Thank you," Jane said.

"I'll show you your room. Do you mind sharing?"

"No," Iris said. "It helps."

They followed Sandy into a back bedroom, where there were two narrow beds. Jane stepped close to the window and eased the curtain aside a half inch. The light was strong enough already so she could read the sign at the end of the street and the numbers on the houses. There were lights on in the kitchens of many of the houses, but very soon they wouldn't be needed. She said, "Come on, Iris. Maybe we can make ourselves useful in the kitchen. Before long it will be time for breakfast."

"Great idea. Let's get started." Iris hurried out of the room. She seemed to react instantly to fulfill any suggestion from anyone, as though on her own she had no idea what to do, or even what to want.

Sandy said quietly, "Do you know her story?"

"No. But it can't have been good. I figured keeping occupied might help her."

Sandy nodded. "It helps us all." They headed into the kitchen. As soon as Iris got there she began to work. As each new person came in for breakfast, she would nod and smile, but say nothing. Jane would introduce her and ask what each person wanted to eat, and Iris would duck her head away and go to work like a short-order cook, making the food as quickly as possible. There was a strange subservience about her, and Jane recognized that this was a person who had spent a long period buying safety with compliance. When the others left to get dressed for work, Jane cleaned the kitchen and did the dishes. She made Iris sit at the table and drink coffee "to keep me company." She praised Iris's cooking, and talked about what they could do to their new room when they'd found jobs and had time to earn a little money.

During the afternoon Iris kept to herself, going around the house dusting and vacuuming and polishing things that looked to Jane to be polished already. After dinner Iris took her turn in the shower and then lay on her bed with a transistor radio next to her head, turned on so low that a person five feet away couldn't hear.

Jane tried to get to know the other housemates. Not one could talk about who she was without referring to a husband or boyfriend who had at some point begun to hurt her, first by belittling, then by cursing, and finally by hitting. In the midst of the stories there were varying digressions about drugs, alcohol, other women, children. Jane didn't reciprocate. She said little, until a woman named Kyesha finally said, "And what about you? What are you doing here?" Jane stood, lifted the back of her shirt to show the angry burns and the deepening purple marks of the beatings, and then sat down again. "I don't think I'm ready to talk about it yet." Then she changed the subject to what jobs the women had found and where she might look for work, and the others seemed relieved.

Jane was trying to recover by getting as much rest and sleep as possible, so she excused herself at nine and went into the bedroom. Iris had fallen asleep with the radio on, so she turned it off. Within minutes she was asleep, too.

She slept deeply, until she awoke sitting up. She looked at the clock beside the bed. It was just after two a.m. She lay back in bed and closed her eyes again, listening to the night silence of the house. Had there been a noise that woke her? Yes. She heard it again—the scraping of metal on metal. She lay still, listening and evaluating the sounds, then decided that letting this kind of sound go uninvestigated would be the wrong thing to do.

She stood with some difficulty and put most of her weight on her strong left leg. When she stepped with her right there was pain, but she quietly moved toward the source of the sound. The sound was coming from the kitchen door, and it was so low that she could hear it only because the air conditioner had cooled the house enough to quit and leave absolute silence. Jane looked out a crack between the kitchen window curtains and saw the shadow of a man bent over, fiddling with the part of the door near the doorknob. He must be jimmying the lock.

There was a quiet creak, a cracking sound as the wood beside the lock was compressed by a tool, and the door moved inward a little. Jane turned and bent low, moving as quickly as she could on her bad leg toward the bedroom. She made it through the doorway, found her bed, and flopped onto it. She listened, and after a few seconds she heard the floor in the hallway creak.

A shadow filled the doorway, and a man's voice said, "I know you're awake." The level was conversational, not a whisper. "You can't hide in bed."

Jane sat up to face him, and turned on the lamp beside her bed so the room was awash in bright light.

"Iris!" the man said loudly.

Iris's legs jerked under the covers as though she were trying to run. She lifted her head, seemed to wake, and saw him. Her face appeared to collapse, her mouth hung open, and Jane heard a low moan that grew steadily higher, like a sob.

The man was tall, dressed in a pair of tight blue jeans and western boots. His black shirt hung loose like a Hawaiian shirt, and Jane suspected it was to cover some kind of weapon. She said, "Who are you?"

The man stepped toward Iris's bed without looking at Jane. "None of your business."

Jane flung her blanket aside and called, "Hold it."

The man's eyes involuntarily turned toward her voice, and saw that her hand held a gun that was aimed at his chest. He stopped in mid-stride.

Jane spoke quietly. "If you take a step toward her, you'll never take another one."

He turned his head the rest of the way toward Jane, and his shoulders squared. "I came to take her home." He glared at Iris for a moment, and his voice seemed to harden. "She asked me to come because she wants to go home." He turned to Iris. "Don't you?"

Jane swung her good leg to the floor, stood up beside her bed, and aimed the gun at him with both hands. "I know you can probably scare her into saying something that she doesn't want to. Now I want you to take a long, careful look at me. If you think I haven't fired a gun into a man before, or that I have even a slight reluctance to do it again right now, then go ahead. Try to get to me."

He studied her angrily, and seemed to see something he didn't like. His arms and shoulders lost their rigidity, and his knees straightened. He crossed his arms on his chest. "Why don't you let her decide?"

"She decided to go to a shelter instead of being with you. And after you found out where she was, you decided that the only way you'd ever get past the door was if you forced the lock. Is that about right?"

"You can say it like that, and I can't deny it, but it's not really like that. We had a little argument, like married people have, and she did something foolish. Now she's been waiting for me because she can't get home without me." He turned to Iris, and once again his voice became harsh, imperative. "Tell her."

Iris's voice was tremulous. "Please. Please." It was impossible to tell who she was talking to.

"There you go," he said. "See?"

"Please," Iris said again. "Don't let him take me."

"There *you* go." Jane stepped toward the end of the bed, where she had a clearer view of him. He wouldn't be able to take cover behind any furniture. "Take yourself back out the door where you came in."

"I'm not leaving without her."

"Of course you are," Jane said. "Just turn slowly and walk to the door." She advanced a step to adjust her angle so that when he stepped through the doorway, she wouldn't lose sight of him for even a second. "I'm going easy on you because I don't want to spend a lot of time going to your trial. Just leave, and that will be the end of it."

He took two steps, his head down and his body slouching, but the steps were too small. She saw him take a deep breath, then another. Then he leaped toward her, reaching out to grab for the gun. Iris screamed.

Jane stepped back, his leap fell short, and he snatched empty air as Jane fired. He sprawled on the floor, his right arm still extended. Jane stepped close to him, the gun in her hand. She said to Iris, "He's going to need an ambulance. Can you go to the phone and dial nine-one-one, please?"

"What are you going to do?"

"I'm afraid I've got to leave before they get here."

"No. Don't leave me alone with him, Melanie."

Jane looked up and saw the other three women venture cautiously into the room. Jane said, "There. See? The others are here. They'll take care of you and help you get through this. You'll get sent somewhere else where you'll be safe."

"I'll never be safe." Iris turned to the other women. "I divorced him, but he took me and made me stay with him for months, and he hurt me every day, until I got away and came to the shelter. He came here, too, but Melanie stopped him. She tried to make him leave, but he came after her."

"We've got to call Sarah," said Sandy, the woman who had met Jane and Iris when they'd arrived. "Don't do anything until I come back." She hurried into the living room.

The four women stood in the bedroom, as far from the wounded man as possible. None of them appeared to want to do anything to stop his bleeding.

He said to Jane, "Police will be here soon. You really messed me up with that gun. You're going to jail, honey."

"No, honey. I'm not," said Jane. "And if you do anything but lie there, you're not, either."

Sandy came back, still holding the phone. "She's on the way. She'll be here in a few minutes. She said don't do anything, don't say anything, just make sure he doesn't hurt anybody or get away."

A few minutes later, Sarah Werth and the young assistant pulled up in front of the house in two cars, and came inside. The young assistant knelt over the man. "Give me your arm." She snapped handcuffs on his wrists. Then she stood.

Sarah Werth beckoned to Jane. "Come out here with me, Melanie." Jane stepped into her shoes and followed her into the kitchen.

Sarah looked at the door. "Is this where he came in?"

"Yes. He jimmied the lock with something. We'd better see what, because it's still on him. He came in to get Iris."

"And you shot him after he jumped to get your gun away. Is that right?"

"That's the short version."

"We don't have much time." She reached into her purse and produced a folded wad of money with a paper clip on it. "Take this."

"But—"

"This is no time to be coy. We have minutes." She put the money in Jane's hand and added a set of car keys. "Take the black car that's at the curb. Get as far away from here as you can. When you're safe, leave it somewhere sensible, and mail me the keys and a note saying where it is."

"You can't do this," said Jane. "You'll get in terrible trouble."

Sarah Werth said, "He found her, broke in, and tried to kidnap her. When I intervened, he tried to attack me, so I shot him. I have a damaged door, five eyewitnesses, a registered pistol, and a lifetime of good behavior. I can take the heat without any effort. You can't. Now I need time to fire my own gun so there will be powder residue on my hands and a bullet missing. So go. You saved Iris's life tonight. Go save your own."

Jane leaned close and kissed Sarah's cheek. "You're like an angel."

"So are you. Good for us. If we're mistaken, I'll be proud to spend some time with you in hell. Now get out of here." She pushed Jane toward the front door.

Jane slipped out into the night. She put the gun into the waistband of her black exercise pants, limped to the small black Honda at the curb, got in, and started it.

She turned her head to look back at the safe house, but as she did, she saw Iris. She was running down the front lawn toward Jane, a look of terror on her face. She was carrying the backpack she'd brought with her. Jane could only imagine that somehow the man had gotten loose. She opened her car door and started up the lawn, but Iris reached her, clutched her arms, and said, "Please, Melanie. Take me with you."

Jane said, "Iris, honey. I can't do that. Where I'm going, it will be more dangerous than it is here."

"You have to. He's hardly hurt at all. He'll never stop looking for me. When he finds me this time, he'll kill me."

There was the muffled sound of a shot from inside the house. It had to be Sarah firing her pistol. It wasn't loud, but Jane could see that a couple of lights had gone on in upper windows of houses along the street. Jane heard, far off, the sound of sirens. She knew before looking at Iris's face that she was telling the truth about the ex-husband. He would never stop, and there was no chance the women in the safe house could stop him. She looked back at the house just as the young assistant stepped out on the porch. She waved at Jane frantically, urging her away. "Get in."

She drove toward the bright lights of the Las Vegas Strip and Interstate 15. The Strip was so big and bright that it threw its impossible smear of color into the sky—blue, green, gold, red—and tore a gash in the night. Her car rose onto the overpass above Route 15 and, for a moment, was part of the light.

Iris crouched in the passenger seat as Jane went over the bridge down the ramp and onto Route 15. She drove up the wide interstate out of town and into the darkness, keeping at the speed limit every second, never letting up at all. She was heading north, as the signs reminded her after every entrance ramp, and she drove with the sensation that every mile she put behind her was making her and Iris safer. It was another few minutes before she thought to take the pistol out of her waistband and hide it under her seat.

Jane said, "I'm going to Salt Lake City." She looked at Iris beside her, but there was no visible reaction. "Since you're with me, that means that's where you're going too. Is Salt Lake City all right with you?"

"I guess so," Iris said "I've never been there, and nobody there knows my name."

"What is your name?" said Jane.

"Iris May Salter," she said. "It used to be Hampton, but I had my maiden name restored in the divorce."

"Iris Salter is your real name?"

"Real? Of course. It never occurred to me to change it again, but maybe that's a good idea."

"You might want to consider it. I find it never hurts to make things a little harder for people who want to hurt you."

"Steve—that's my ex-husband's name—seemed to think he had a right to hurt me."

"People who like to hurt you can always tell you why it's your fault."

Jane drove along Interstate 15, trying to put as much road as possible behind them. It was nerve-racking to be on such a major highway, the most obvious way out of Las Vegas. If the police listened to Iris's ex-husband and thought they needed to hunt for the woman who had really fired the shot, they would be on Interstate 15, too. They already were on Interstate 15, all day every day, all night every night, because Interstate 15 wasn't just a river of money coming into town. It was the route of an invading army of troublemakers and screwups. Jane couldn't afford to be pulled over by a cop for some minor infraction tonight. The authorities in Los Angeles had already had three days to take frame grabs from the security cameras in the courthouse and distribute them to cops along the obvious escape routes, and Las Vegas was the most obvious escape route of all.

As Jane drove, she tried to decipher and untangle her predicament. She was hurt. She had promised Jim Shelby she would meet him at the hotel in Salt Lake City, and she was already three days late. Crouching in the seat beside her was a young woman whose will seemed to have been beaten out of her.

Jane said, "I think we should talk."

"Okay. What about?"

"I wasn't planning to take you with me. When you came running out, I thought something else had happened, and then you were in the car and we had to leave. For a lot of reasons you don't know yet, that might not have been your best move."

"I had to get away."

"Getting away from a man like that is a good idea, but that's not the point. The point is that everything you'd seen about me was an indication that I had a few problems that existed before I met you, and might put you in worse danger."

"I know," said Iris. "I saw your back after your bath. And I saw the bandage on your leg. And the giant bruise around it."

"You saw that?"

"I wanted to meet you, so I went into our room, and I saw you weren't there. I went toward the bathroom, and you had finished your bath and opened the door a crack to get rid of the steam. When you reached up to clean the steam off the mirror with your towel, I slipped aside so you wouldn't see me in the mirror and think I was spying on you. But I saw."

"Seeing the marks shouldn't have made you want to risk going with me. I couldn't even protect myself."

"I could see you were someone who understood what it's like. Your burns are from metal that was heated up. You can see that on my back, too. When Steve did that to me he used a bunch of big nails. He heated them in a frying pan and dumped them out on my back. And I could see where somebody hit you with a switch, too. In some ways that was the worst for me, even though it hurt less than the burns or the punches. It was humiliating, like a child being whipped for doing something bad. I'm sure you know."

Jane said, "I'm not much like the person I've been pretending to be. Let's try to figure out what you can do, and where I can take you."

"I'm not the way I seem, either. I'm a normal person. I never even knew people like Steve. I met him at a club in LA.

He carried himself like a bad boy, and I thought that was dark and mysterious and sexy. He was very male, always in charge. And there was an edge to him, sort of a repressed anger that I took for toughness. I fell for him—or for the man I had invented. That's the right term—fell for him, like you fall for a hoax or a fraud. I married him. A few months after that, he started to work on me. I was young and naive, and to him that was the same as being stupid. I wasn't a poor kid, brought up in the backwoods somewhere, and I hadn't raised myself on the streets, so I was weak. I liked pretty clothes and things, so I was spoiled. After a while I was sad. It was hard to live with his contempt and be happy. I told him I didn't like being treated that way, so I was a nasty bitch. After a while he was watching everything I did, but without ever looking at me when he spoke to me. I was an enemy, and the minute he got up in the morning he started noticing things about me that weren't right. The day after the hitting started I left. I slipped out and went to my parents' house in Sherman Oaks. I filed for divorce from there. My father was a doctor, and we had a nice house with my old room and everything, but he told me the best thing for me was to go to another city until the divorce was final. I should get a job and meet nice people my age and do some thinking about the future I wanted."

"That sounds smart. That's exactly what I'm trying to get you to do now."

"I went to Boston. I only came home for the final decree, then went back. And then my father died. It was the last thing in the world I expected. He was always very fit and healthy, and he seemed so young that I always forgot his age. He had a massive heart attack and died, and then I realized I hadn't actually been seeing him. I'd been looking at him and seeing him as he'd been fifteen years younger. When he died, my mother was all alone."

"So you came home to be with her."

"Yes. She was alone, after being married for over forty years. He was the sort of person who just quietly took care of everything. She never seemed worried about anything, because he was this big, reassuring presence. Now she was lost. So I moved in. I don't know how he found out, but Steve knew immediately that I was living there. He showed up at the door a few days after the funeral and said he wanted me back."

"Did you fall for it?"

"No. I told him there was nothing at all left between us, and that he should go away and never come within a mile of me again. He, of course, wanted to stay and argue about it."

"But you didn't give in?"

"Not then, and not the next fifty times. He called at all hours, showed up when I went to work and stood in front of my car, sent presents I didn't want and apologies. He said he hadn't ever wanted to be mean to me, but I had forced him. Surely I understood that."

"Iris, honey. I've heard this story before. I don't blame you for any of it. But you need to think about tomorrow and the next day. We need to make a plan for how you're going to spend the next month or two."

"Please," Iris said. "I've got to tell you, so you'll understand."

"All right."

"I got a restraining order. He violated it about three times before the cops or the judge or someone persuaded him he couldn't prevent me from going to work or wake me up in the middle of the night. A few months after my father died, my mother got sick. It was a heart problem, too. And then she died. I heard afterward from a lot of people that this kind of thing happens quite often with couples who have been close. The one who was left didn't take long to follow the one who died."

"What did you do then?"

"I was alone, and I saw the world a little more clearly. The house that had been the symbol for me of safety and security since I was a baby had changed. Without my parents, it was just an empty, sad building. There was no help or advice or companionship, or even safety there anymore. There was a sadistic, crazy man out there somewhere, and the house suddenly seemed so fragile and insubstantial that he could walk in through the walls to get me. I mean, it was a one-story, sprawling ranch-style house with big glass windows everywhere. All he'd need was a rock. I went to a realtor and told him to estimate what the house was worth, price it twenty thousand cheaper, and sell it fast. The house sold, I deposited the check, packed up, and moved out in a hurry. I put my parents' furniture in storage, rented a one-bedroom apartment in a duplex, and moved in. Steve waited until one day when the people in the other half of the duplex had gone to work, and came and got me."

"Just like that?"

"Pretty much. He kidnapped me—put tape over my mouth and wrists, then dragged me out to the back door into a van, taped my ankles, shut the doors, and drove off. He's big and strong; I was small and weak. That's all it takes. He drove to a place he had leased in Nevada. And then it began. Being his ex-wife was about being punished for being a failure as his wife, and for leaving him and divorcing him, and for not coming back when he told me to. There were no illusions about a romantic relationship. It was him getting even and teaching me a lesson. I was a person who had done him grave injury, and now I'd pay for it. He had me for five months before I got away."

"How did you accomplish that?"

"He went grocery shopping. A couple of times when I'd gone with him I'd tried to get people to call the police, but they never had. Still, he kept his hand on my wrist after that. This time, he couldn't take me with him, because my face didn't look too good. So I waited until he was gone, and slipped out of the chain he had on my wrist. I had been preparing by not eating for a few days. He put the lock on the same link as always, but it was too big this time. I didn't really know where I was, but I knew it was Nevada and the sign on the highway said, 'Las Vegas, 146 miles.' I hitchhiked to Las Vegas, but if I hadn't been picked up, I would have walked. I stopped when I found the shelter where I met you. I know I should have kept going, but I needed food and rest. But now I'm out, and I'll have a big head start on him, thanks to you."

"You're welcome," Jane said. "I'm glad you're okay. But I have something urgent I need to do when we get to Salt Lake City. I'll leave you as much money as I can, and get you checked into a safe hotel. But then I have to go. If you'd rather I leave you somewhere else, I'll try to do that."

"With you," Iris said. "I want to go with you."

"I can try to come back for you."

"Why can't I help you do whatever you're doing?"

Jane took a deep breath, and then let it out slowly. "I know how this is going to sound, but I guess I have to say it and hope your gratitude or your ability to recognize me as a friend will keep you from ever repeating it. I'm running. I'm being hunted by some men who will kill me if they catch me, and they plan to take a long time letting me die. The reason I couldn't hang around to wait for the police in Henderson is because the cops are searching the country for me, too. And I'm in no shape to protect you. That bandage you saw around my leg is covering a gunshot wound. Just about the most dangerous place in the country you could be right now is with me."

"Please," said Iris.

"Are you even listening?"

"Sure. I can repeat it all if you want."

Jane could see sincere fear in Iris's eyes, and the profound sadness of abandonment. Jane drove on, trying to make as much distance as she could. The next three times that she looked, Iris's eyes were still on her, unchanged. The fourth time, the eyes were closed. Iris was asleep.

Jane sped out of the lower slice of Nevada and kept going across Arizona. She knew she was driving through some of the most dramatic places in the country, but the deserts consisted of the two cone-shaped beams of headlight illuminating a road that seemed straight and infinite beyond her sight, and the mountains were a steep, winding ribbon of pavement that sometimes made her feel as though she were flying up, down, left, right like a plane in a dogfight. She could see the North Star in the clear black of the sky in the unlighted places she drove through.

She passed towns—Saint George, Cedar City, Beaver, Elsinore, Scipio, Nephi. The sun began to rise on her right, in time for Spanish Fork and Provo. When she came off the interstate at Salt Lake City she was glad she had told Jim Shelby to meet her here. By her reckoning she had driven 430 miles in about six hours. She was far enough from the West Coast so the escape a few days ago from the courthouse in Los Angeles would be little remembered here.

The Residence Inn where she had told Shelby to wait for her was four blocks east of the interstate, across the street from Pioneer Park. It was already eight thirty in the morning, and the traffic was steady, full of people going to work. As she approached the address, she recognized the big, low, brick building that looked like a huge house in a green space with a sidewalk jutting from the building to the street, and broad parking lots on both sides.

She scanned the lots for the new Camry she had left for Shelby in the barn near Riverside, California. But she had chosen the car well. There were probably thirty cars she could see that looked enough like it so she would have to go around on foot, examining each one closely.

Iris woke and sat up. "Is this where we're going?"

"Yes. I'm going in alone. That will give me a chance to be sure everything's okay. I'll be back out in a while."

She pulled into the nearest lot, then drove to the part that was at the rear of the building and got out. She walked the length of the parking lot before she found the car she had left for Shelby. When she had scanned the rest of the lot to be sure nobody was watching the car, she approached it and looked inside to see if she could detect any damage or any signs that it had been opened by force. It seemed all right. She walked to a back entrance, went down a long hallway lined with rooms, and went to a small table in the lobby with a white phone on it. She picked up the receiver and heard a ringing signal. A female voice said, "How may I direct your call?"

"Can you please ring John Leland's room?"

After two rings, Jim Shelby's voice said, "Yes?"

"Hi," she said. "It's me. What's your suite number?"

"Two-sixteen."

"I'll be right up."

She went to the elevator just off the lobby and rode it to the second floor. As she stood there she felt distaste, then realized she was remembering the last elevator, the one that had brought Wylie, Gorman, and Maloney into her life.

The doors opened, the hallway was empty, and she walked out into the corridor. The door marked 216 opened, and Jim Shelby stood in the doorway. She slipped in and he shut the door, locked it, and bolted it. "I heard the elevator arrive," he said. He turned and stared at her. "What happened to you? Why are you limping?"

"I got shot," she said.

"Jesus. Who shot you? One of the men at the courthouse?"

"Not the ones we both saw. These came along later—one named Gorman and one named Maloney. They pretended to be cops, so I went with them. When I realized they were just more thugs, I tried to get away, and Maloney shot me. The one in charge is named Wylie. But that's all over. I'm here, and so are you. Tell me how it's gone so far."

"The way you said it would. No surprises."

"You were careful to be sure nobody followed you here?"

"I'm positive. It was a long drive through open country. If there had been anybody following, I'd have seen him."

"You made stops and turnarounds to be sure?"

"Yes. About four times before I got out of California, and then once every hour after that. I even got off the interstate and drove in the opposite direction to the last exit twice."

"Good," she said. She looked around her. "This is a nice place. I wish we could stay for a month and try to get over some of the things that have happened to us."

"We can't?"

"No. What I'm worried about is your sister. When the hunters are looking hard for a fugitive and the trail goes cold, they go find the nearest relative. The day before I broke you out of the courthouse, I called your sister and told her to close up her house and get out of Austin. If we didn't make it, she could come back in a couple of weeks. If we succeeded and got you out, she would be the next way to get to you, so she had to stay away. She said she'd do it."

"Where did she go?"

"I don't know yet. I told her to call the person who acted as go-between to get her in touch with me. I'll call the woman now and see what she knows. Have you seen a pay phone around here?"

"There's one downstairs in the lobby."

"Good. I don't have a cell phone. Or any identification, or much of anything. Do you have any change?"

Shelby emptied his pockets, then went to the dresser in his room and returned with a handful of coins. "I'll show you where it is."

"No. Show yourself as seldom as possible. I'll find it." Jane took the change and set off. She held herself with a stiff determination, ignoring the pain. When she reached the phone she dialed the number, put in the amount the recording demanded, and waited.

The voice that answered was a receptionist. "Legal office."

"I'd like to speak with Allison, please. This is Jane."

"Please hold." The receptionist's line was silent for a few seconds, but when she came back she said, "I'll put you right through."

The next voice was Allison's. "Jane. You're a celebrity in certain circles. Best jailbreak in memory."

"I've been in those circles. They can keep their award."

"And Kristen Alvarez sends her congratulations, too."

"Thank her again for letting me destroy her reputation."

"Not only does Kristen Alvarez have a reputation that's too good to ruin, but she's honored to have you borrow her name for a jailbreak when you do such a good job. I'm delighted that you let me in on it, too. Some of the things I've done for you are legally the worst things I ever did, but they're the ones I feel proudest of. When I fall asleep at night, what I think about isn't the nine-hundredth plea bargain. It's that I had the guts to—well, we both know, so there's no need to repeat things."

"Right. Did our mutual friend Sarah call yet with an address?"

"Yes. It's 3592 Dryden Road, Ithaca, New York."

"Ithaca?" Jane said. "You're joking."

"I'm not. I suggested it. You know Ithaca—it's pretty remote, but with lots of new people coming and going for the university."

"True. If she calls again for any reason, tell her I'm on my way."

"You're going there? I could take a couple of days off and fly there. We could have a nostalgic lunch at Cornell or something." She laughed. "Coffee in Willard Straight Hall."

"The people who framed Sarah's brother will be trying to get to her now. She's all they've got, so this trip could be kind of tense."

"God, Jane. I wouldn't have your life for anything." She paused. "I'm sorry. That didn't sound the way I meant it."

"Yes, it did. And for the moment, at least, you're right. But I'm hoping things will look up shortly. Thanks again. See you."

"Good luck."

Jane hung up and walked back toward Shelby's suite. Allison was a woman she'd met when they were students at Cornell. After they'd graduated, Allison became a lawyer. A few years after that, she had unexpectedly come to see Jane at her house in Deganawida, New York. She explained that she had an innocent client who was about to be convicted, and she was positive that once the verdict was read, he would never get out of prison alive. She had spent the past two days meditating on her responsibilities as an officer of the court, a defense attorney, and a human being. She was aware that years before, when they were in school, Jane had made a friend and classmate disappear. Could she do it one more time?

On the day of sentencing, Allison was in court, but the client was not. Since he wasn't violent, she got the judge to grant him an alternative court date, but he didn't turn up on that date, either. An all points bulletin was issued, a warrant for his arrest was circulated, and his picture and description were added to the displays on various police department bulletin boards. The particulars were still in the NCIC system, although nearly twenty years had passed and the fugitive student was pushing forty. Jane had met Kristen Alvarez years later, and had done a favor or two for clients of hers.

Jane went to the front desk in the hotel lobby, and waited for the young man in a sport coat to acknowledge her presence. He looked at her and raised his eyebrows.

"Hi," she said. "My name is Carol Rosen. I reserved the room for Mr. Leland, two-sixteen. I wondered if you have a second room available for me for the next week."

"For seven days?" He went to the computer, and from the way he looked at the screen and typed, she could tell he knew he had one. "Yes," he said. He typed in some other mysterious information. "And how would you like to take care of that?"

"You can put them both on the same American Express card," Jane said. "It's the one that ends in 65951, right? Carol Rosen?"

"Uh . . . yes. Do you happen to have it with you?"

"I'm sorry, but I left it with my purse upstairs. Can I just stop in later and you can take another impression?" She gestured toward her leg. "I've got a bad sprain, and I . . ."

"Well, sure," he said. She could tell that he didn't feel comfortable and wasn't supposed to do it, but was determined to be nice to her. She was obviously a good customer. He produced a card with the number of the room and the usual address and phone number information. "Just initial here and here, then sign here."

Jane did, and he said, "It's vacant right now, so you can have early check-in. How many keys will you be needing?"

"Two."

He produced two key cards, stuffed them into a folder, wrote Room 392 on it, and handed it to her.

"Thanks," Jane said.

"You're welcome, Mrs. Rosen."

Jane limped off to the parking lot. She got into the black car and shut the door. Iris sat up. "Sorry to keep you waiting."

"That's okay," said Iris. "I guess you need me to get out of the car, right?"

"Not in the way you mean it. Here," she said. "I brought you a key card for your room. It's on the third floor, 392." She handed the little folder to Iris, and kept one of the two key cards. "It's vacant, so you might as well go right in."

"Oh, Melanie. How am I going to pay for it?"

"You're not. It's charged to the American Express card of a woman named Mrs. Carol Rosen."

"Is that you?"

"Sometimes it is. Tomorrow you can be Carol Rosen, except with the desk clerk on duty this morning. Get a look at him. You can sign for meals and charge them to the room. Also laundry. And I haven't explored the hotel, but I think there's a shop or two in there, so feel free to charge some clothes, too. Signing for things won't help anybody find you. There's no trail. Everything is in Carol Rosen's name, and I always pay the bill when it comes. I have a ride, so I'm leaving you the car. If something changes so you don't need it anymore, leave it somewhere safe, like an airport lot, call Sarah at the Lifeboat, and she'll send somebody to pick it up."

Iris leaned over and hugged Jane. "Thank you for everything. Are you leaving right now?"

"No. I need to get some sleep first. Don't worry. I'll be back for you in a week or so. In case I'm late, here's the cash that Sarah gave me before we left."

"But then—"

"I'll have what I need." Jane put the money in her hand. "If for some reason you can't be here when I get back, call Sarah at the Lifeboat and let her know where I can find you. All right?"

"All right."

The two women got out of the car, and walked toward the hotel. "See you," Jane said. She walked to the end of the building, then turned the corner and stopped to look back. She watched Iris hesitate for a few seconds, standing outside the building and looking aimlessly in one direction, then another. She was afraid to go in and pretend to be someone else, afraid to drive away, and afraid she was attracting attention by standing where she was for too long. Finally, she lowered her head and stepped in through the double doors.

Jane watched the doors close. *Good. One foot in front of the other. You'll make it.*

6

That morning it was hot in Austin, Texas. Gorman drove the rental car with the air-conditioner fan blowing hard while Wylie sat in the passenger seat beside him looking for the right address. Maloney announced the house numbers from the back seat. "Eighty-nine seventeen. We're close. Eighty-nine twenty-one. There it is. Eighty-nine twenty-nine. The white one up there."

"I see it," Gorman said. "Want me to go around the block to park?"

"Hell no," Wylie said. "Just park."

Gorman made the Lincoln Town Car swoop to the curb behind a parked SUV.

"I'll go get started with one of the neighbors," said Wylie. "You two stay here, but watch the front door."

He got out of the car and went to the house to the left of 8929. He rang the bell, but nobody appeared. He knocked, but there was still no answer. He walked down the sidewalk and went to 8929. He rang the bell, knocked, looked in the front window. The place appeared to be deserted. He looked back at Gorman and Maloney in the car, and moved his index finger slightly to point to the house on the right, then walked to it. This time, when he rang the bell a woman opened the door a few inches. He could see that she was thin, about fifty years old, with long auburn hair, and that she was wearing blue jeans and flip-flops.

She looked at him suspiciously, as though she were planning to slam the door if he moved toward her.

He didn't move. He smiled and said, "Hello, miss. My name is Bobby Simms. I'm an old friend of Sarah Shelby. Actually, I'm more than that, because I'm a distant cousin, too. I just drove here all the way from New Orleans. I called her a few times on the way, but I haven't been able to reach her. I'm a little worried. Have you seen her in the past few days?"

The woman behind the door frowned. "Are you a reporter?"

"A reporter? Me? Lord, no," Wylie said, and then gave a surprised laugh. "I've never been accused of that before. Why would you ask that?"

The woman's brows knitted, as though she had forgotten her suspicion and was concerned about him. "You know about her brother, right?"

"I haven't kept up. I haven't seen either of them in a few years. What's wrong with Jimmy? Is he sick or something?"

"I'm sorry," she said. "I can't really go into their personal business. Sarah left town about a week ago, and I'm not sure when she's coming home. If you'd like to leave a message for her, I can give it to her when she's back."

"Well, then, what about Jimmy? Do you have a number or address for him?"

"No, I'm afraid I don't." She looked distinctly uncomfortable. "I'm sorry, but I've got some things to do." She began to push the door shut.

"Wait," he said, and she left the door open about half an inch. "Is there anyone else in town who might be able to give me a number or address?"

She pulled the door open a few more inches to answer. "I honestly can't think of anyone. She left without telling me anything, but I'm sure there isn't anything wrong. She just said she was going on vacation for a while, and to keep an eye on her house."

The woman had a tell, a small mannerism that revealed when she was lying. It was a habit of looking in the upper right corner of her field of vision whenever she was forming the answer to a question, instead of looking into his eyes. He had been watching her do this since he'd first spoken to her. He sighed and turned to look in the direction of his car, as though he were straining to think. He suddenly hurled his body against the front door.

The heavy wooden door flew inward, struck the woman, and knocked her onto the living room carpet on her back. She was so stunned that she lay still, trying to fathom what had happened. Finally, she took in a deep breath.

Wylie closed the heavy door and took two swift strides, dropped to his knees beside her, and grabbed her throat, choking off the scream. "You're lying to me," he said. "Lying to me is about the craziest thing you could do."

The front door opened again to admit Gorman and Maloney. Wylie looked up to acknowledge them. "This lady has decided to lie to me instead of answering my questions."

"That would really be stupid, ma'am," Gorman said. He pulled his jacket aside to show her the badge he had used in Los Angeles, and made sure the woman could also see the gun he had in a shoulder holster. "Obstructing police officers in a murder investigation is about as serious as it gets."

Wylie kept his left hand on the woman's throat as he used his right hand to drag her to a sitting position. "I always heard that Texas cops didn't put up with this kind of crap, so you should know better. We came all the way from the city of Los Angeles hunting a dangerous escaped killer, and sure as hell won't go home just because somebody tells us lies. Now tell us where Sarah Shelby is right now."

The woman was beyond terror now. "Are you really police officers?" She didn't see Wylie's hand move before the slap on her left cheek spun her head to the side. She cringed and tried to look away, but the open hand slapped her again. "I'm sorry," she said. "I didn't mean anything."

She was shocked, but not hurt. She made the assumption that Wylie had finished. She seemed to relax for an instant, but then Wylie slapped her face several times, harder each time, then stopped and moved his face close to hers. She was trembling and a low moan escaped from her throat.

"I'm helping you get used to your new world. As of now you aren't somebody who can keep the bad things out just by shutting your door. You just gave that up. Sarah Shelby is off aiding and abetting the escape of a murderer. A wife killer. You know that already, because you're obviously a friend of the family. But you don't seem to realize that anybody who helps a murderer get away is going to share his fate."

"I didn't do anything, and she didn't tell me anything. She just went away."

He didn't hit her, just clutched her arm. "Here's all the education you'll need, all in one afternoon. If you lie to the police when we come around trying to find a murderer, you're as much a criminal as he is."

"Are you going to arrest me?"

"What happens to you is up to you. It's a kind of race. If you talk before Jim Shelby kills another innocent person, and before somebody else tells an officer what we need to know and he's captured, you'll do okay. If you don't, things will go hard." His head was behind the woman's, so she didn't see him nod to Gorman.

Gorman said, "Jesus, chief. She makes me sick. Why don't we just take her out and shoot her now? You gave her a chance. Now the offer is expired."

"Not just yet," Wylie said. He took her head in his hands and turned it so she had to look at him. He studied her for a few seconds, then released her. "Okay. Put the cuffs on her."

Gorman stepped forward and grabbed the woman's wrists.

"Wait!"

It was her voice, drastically different from before. "She did leave an address and phone number, just in case something happened here."

"What is it?"

"It's written down. I folded the paper and put it inside one of the books in the bookcase. The one over there that says *Cats of the World.*"

Maloney stepped to the bookcase, pulled out the book, flipped the pages, and found the folded sheet. He opened it and read it. "3592 Dryden Road, Ithaca, New York. And there's a phone number. Seven one six—"

"Save it," Wylie said. He picked up a pillow from the couch, unzipped the cover, and pulled the pillow out. He put the pillow cover over the woman's head, zipped it tight to her neck, wrapped the pillow around his pistol, and held it up to the woman's head.

"Please, please," she said. "I helped you."

He fired one shot. The sound was muffled, but the woman's head jerked to the side. There was a splatter of bright red liquid soaking the pillow cover, and the woman's body followed the head, tilting to the right and falling to the floor.

"Not bad, eh?" he said. "No blood spatter all over, and only one shot in case one of the neighbors came home. They hear one shot and they stop what they're doing for a second, listening. If they don't hear another one, they figure it was nothing—a firecracker, a backfire, a door slam. A squirrel fell on their roof."

"Yeah, and when he hit the shingles, his gun went off," Gorman said.

Wylie looked out the front window, craned his neck to see up and down the street. "Let's go. We'd better get started." He opened the door, and the three men walked across the street to their car. "We've got a long drive ahead of us."

7

Shelby was waiting for Jane when she returned to the hotel room. She stepped inside and closed, locked, bolted, and chained the door. She smiled. "There's some good news."

"What?"

"Your sister listened to what I told her. She left her house in Texas, and drove to Ithaca, New York, to wait this out."

"Thank God." His legs seemed to give out and deposit him on the bed. "Is she going to meet us here?"

"I'm afraid not," she said. "If she gets on an airplane, the people who are after you might be able to trace her, and the police certainly will. We'll have to drive up there and get her."

"When do we leave?"

"I drove here from Las Vegas for most of the night. When I wake up, we'll talk some more."

She took the spare pillow from the closet shelf, lay on the couch, and slept. When Jim Shelby saw the process, he was intrigued. She seemed to move from a state of hyper-awareness to deep sleep in less than a minute. He had found the couch reasonably comfortable, but she had no blanket, and she didn't undress or make any other preparations. This was something he had noticed about her from the beginning. She had control over herself. Her movements were always economical, never aimless or nervous. When she looked at anything—a person, a building—she seemed to pick out instantly the part that was important. When she had looked at the crowd at the courthouse, she had instantly separated the bystanders from the enemies, and both from the police, and had begun to act before anyone else. Her mind was always focused—looking, thinking, noticing.

He intuited that part of the reason she allowed herself to sleep at the moment was that he was here to watch over her. He knew that she had no illusion that while he was still recovering from a knife in the back he could protect her from an intruder, but he could delay one, and he would fight hard enough to make a lot of noise. He understood what she was feeling, and he knew that what she wanted was for him to find something to do that wasn't noisy, look out the window occasionally to check for the men who had caught her in Los Angeles, and stay with her.

He lay on the bed reading the magazines the hotel had left on the coffee table. They were almost entirely ads for women's clothes and jewelry, and for the restaurants where women could wear them. He still couldn't quite imagine ever again having money to spend on a woman, but for now being out of prison was enough. Every surface in the prison was designed to be harder and rougher than a man's bones and skin. It was as though the authorities wanted prisoners to see how small and weak they really were. It was as ugly as they could make it without letting on that they were trying—light green paint over uneven, chipped surfaces of walls and barred windows. Ugly brushed concrete floors.

He dozed at some point. He didn't remember a last impression. The magazine was at his side, his fingers still on it.

The woman was across the room, sitting in one of the chairs from the small, round table and staring out the window. He sat up. "How long have you been awake?"

"A half hour or so."

"I'm sorry to make you wait. I didn't expect to fall asleep."

"It's fine. Now that I've rested a little, I've been able to think."

"There's something I've been wondering about," he said. "When you came to the prison, and even at the courthouse, you were Kristen Alvarez. I assume that isn't who you are."

"No, I'm not Kristen Alvarez. I just borrowed the name of a real lawyer."

"Now that we're out of the courthouse, do you mind telling me your name?"

"That depends," she said. "Whenever I take on a runner, I've got to know certain things that are dangerous to you—your new name, your address. But I will die before I reveal them. If I tell you my secrets, will you do the same for me? Will you die before you'll tell anyone else what I tell you?"

He looked at her for a moment. She was leaning back on two legs of the chair, both feet resting on the sill.

He said, "The knife I got in my back was just the first attempt. I would be dead by now if you hadn't taken me out. I owe you a life already."

She met his eyes and nodded. "Jane Whitefield."

"Pleased to meet you."

"I'm glad you're pleased, because we'll be spending some time together."

"We will?"

"There are tricks to changing who you are and living as a new person. I've got to start getting you ready to live a nice, quiet life somewhere as John Robert Leland. It takes preparation to do it well, but we didn't have time for that."

"Are you warning me that I'll get caught if I try to do this myself?"

She looked at him thoughtfully. "Not getting caught is partly luck, partly attitude, and partly premeditation. But it depends mostly on who's looking and how hard. There are something like twelve million illegal aliens in this country right now. Nobody finds them because nobody's looking. Men convicted of murders are on the other end of the spectrum. Lots of people are searching, and they tend to be the last people you'd want after you—experienced homicide detectives, federal and state agencies, and all the miscellaneous invisible security companies that protect credit cards, give people ratings, make sure nobody runs out on debts."

"What do I do—stay in this room?"

"We'll try to stay invisible as long as we can, but not here. Most people called escapees have walked away from work-release programs. The ones who actually break out are usually caught within hours a few miles from the prison. You've already lasted longer than most. But if you stay in a hotel too long, the staff people get curious about you because you're not behaving like an ordinary customer. You have to either give them an explanation that satisfies them and doesn't raise other questions, or go. We need to pick up your sister, so we'll leave as soon as we're ready to travel."

"What do we do?"

"First we work on our appearance."

"You mean change?"

"There are lots of things that help. The clothes I left in the car for you at the courthouse were all expensive and neat—tailored pants, dress shirts, sport coats, a couple of good ties in subdued patterns. When people picture an escaped convict, they think of a guy with a three-day growth of beard, dirty, torn clothes, and a haunted expression. So we play against that expectation. You have short hair, and we can't lengthen it, but we can dye it. Your hair is blond, and most of the men in the country have brown hair. You can't shave it, because a shaved head practically screams prison. We want the observer's mind to see you and automatically think, 'Respectable, prosperous.'"

"What if somebody has seen my picture?"

"People are far more likely to see someone who looks a bit like you, but isn't, and turn him in. Whenever there's a famous fugitive, the police get thousands of calls. What we want to do is make sure none of them is about you. We make people's expectations censor their vision."

"That works?"

"More often than not. The first part of the game is adding one layer after another of changes, all designed to make you less like you and less like a convict. The second is making a plan for the day when something goes wrong."

"If the police find me, then they'll come for me in a way that won't let me just talk my way out of it."

Jane said, "If the police who find you know you've been convicted of murder and you've escaped from a courthouse, give up and go quietly. If you're just stopped by a cop, don't assume he knows anything. Lie. Show him the John Leland identification I left in the car for you. Try to fool him to the end. Don't worry. We'll work on all of it. Where are the keys to your car?"

He got up, took them out of a sport coat he had hung in the closet, and handed them to her. "Are you going somewhere?"

"Shopping. I'll get us some dinner and a few things we'll need for the next phase. Anything in particular you'd like?"

"I've been in prison for three years. I'm not too picky. Should I come with you? I'm good at carrying heavy bags."

"Thanks, but not yet," she said. "For now, I'll be the one to show my face. I'll be back in less than two hours. When I knock, look in the peephole before you open the door. Don't open it and look. Oh, and I seem to be out of money. Can you give me a few hundred from the money I left in the car for you?" He pulled a wad of money out of his pocket and handed it to her. She walked to the door, and then she was gone.

Jane went to his car, got in, drove the perimeter of the hotel grounds, and then made a circuit of the neighborhood. There were no vehicles parked in sight of the hotel with people waiting in them, no loiterers across the street in Pioneer Park.

She drove to a large plaza dominated by a supermarket. She parked near the back of the lot, and selected a cart that someone had left far from the rack. She found that she could use it like a walker to take the weight off her healing right leg. She bought a cooked chicken, salad, and vegetables for dinner, and then bought food they would need on the road—bottled water, cookies, nuts, fruit. She loaded it all into the car, and then went to the Target store beside the supermarket. She bought hair dyes, an electric razor, a pair of scissors, and a hand mirror. She found makeup that lightened her complexion a bit, and some tanning lotion. She bought sunglasses, hats, polo shirts for Shelby, sweaters, pullovers, and pants that would cover her bruises and burns. The last item was a small suitcase.

When she had finished her shopping, she drove along the boulevard until she saw a gas station that had a pair of pay telephones on the wall outside. She stopped and filled up the tank, then went to the telephones, put in five quarters, and dialed the number of the old stone house in Amherst, New York.

"Hello?"

"Carey. It's me."

She heard the huff of air leaving his lungs, then heard the breath of air he took and she could picture him, standing in the kitchen. "Are you all right?"

"I'm okay. It's been a little hairy, so I couldn't call before now. I just wanted to let you know that the hard part seems to be over, so you shouldn't worry about me too much from here on."

"I'll try to worry exactly the right amount. How much is that?"

"I'm sorry," she said. "It was stupid to put it that way. Don't worry at all."

"I assume you can't say where you are or who you're with. Can you say when you'll be home?"

"Not yet. I would guess it will be at least a few more days. There's a lot to do this time. I wish it were now, but it can't be. I miss you so much I could cry. In fact I guess I am."

"And I miss you."

"What have you told people about me?"

He sounded weary. "I told them you've gone back into the consulting business because you missed the excitement, and you're helping a company change its supply and distribution systems to survive the hard times. They think you must have gone back to work because we've lost our savings in the market, so they just look at me with sympathy."

"That's very well done."

"Thanks. I've become an amazing liar—an undiscovered talent."

"I'm sorry," she said. "Look, I've got to go. I'm not sure when I can call again, so don't think anything has happened if I don't. I love you."

"I love you. If everything is okay, why are you crying?"

"The usual reason. Because I want to be with you and I'm not." She sniffed. "I'm sorry, Carey. But I've got to go. Bye."

She hung up the telephone, went to the car, and drove off. She hated these telephone calls. They were always from pay phones, always rushed. "I'm sorry" and "I love you" and lies to him to make him think that what she was doing this time was safe and easy. None of it ever fooled him. He had learned over the years to pretend he believed, because that made it possible for both of them to get through the conversation. During their first year together, they had fought a couple of times during these calls. Since then they had learned to pretend.

Everything was a half-truth or an evasion. She couldn't say anything that was true or real; she could never say where she was or whom she was with, just in case someone somewhere in the miles between them was listening. At times she had sensed that he wondered what purpose it served for her to call at all. But when she hadn't called, they'd both felt awful.

On her last trip she had been taking an advertising executive named Stephen Noton out of Massachusetts and trying to relocate him in a safe place in the West. He had been an innocent bystander, but that hadn't protected him. There had been a would-be whistle-blower in a giant soft drink company who had documentary evidence that some divisions in the company were smuggling narcotics in certain large shipments of sugar and tea and tropical fruit. The company's security men had already intercepted his first attempt to get a copy out, had cut off his access to his computer, and were searching the building for him. He had noticed a large envelope in someone's office that was about to be sent by messenger to the advertising company—specifically, to Stephen Noton. He slipped his document into the packet and got back to his office just in time to be dragged away. Before long Stephen Noton had the document, but the company knew it. Once he'd read it, the company was determined to kill him. By the time he had made his way to Jane, Noton had survived two attempts on his life, including a nighttime raid of his home. When Jane had told Carey she was going to help Stephen Noton, Carey had said, "This is an innocent man. Surely the police can take care of somebody like him without your help." She had stopped calling until Noton was settled.

Jane reached the hotel and repeated her drive around the block to see if there were any signs of change in the parking lots surrounding the building or Pioneer Park. When she was satisfied, she parked near the side door so she didn't have far to walk.

She took her two bags of groceries and supplies and walked into the hotel. When she reached the door, she knocked and then stood in front of the peephole. She saw it darken, and the door opened.

Shelby took the bags and she relocked the door.

He stared at her. "Have you been crying?"

"Me? No," she said. "I guess my eyes are still watering from the dry air in the West. They'll be better when we go east."

"When is that?"

"It's almost six now. We can probably be ready by midnight. First we have some work to do. Bring a chair into the bathroom in front of the sink."

Two minutes later, Jane joined him in the bathroom, opened the box of hair dye, and laid out the materials. When she had finished, she said, "Have you ever had your hair dyed before?"

"No."

"You'll be amazed at how much it helps." She pulled his head back above the sink and applied the noxious-smelling chemical to his hair. "Now sit still and relax for fifteen minutes, and then I'll do a few highlights. Nobody's hair is all one uniform shade."

"I suppose not."

"I know you're skeptical of this stuff, but believe me, it's worth the effort. Anything you can change about yourself, you change. Some changes are hard. This is one of the easiest ones. You want all the cosmetic stuff done right away, before you go out where you'll be seen. And soon you'll have to rent an apartment somewhere. You don't want to show up looking dark, and then be light. Men don't do that very often."

"Let's do whatever we have time to do."

Jane patted his shoulder. "You're learning fast."

"A few years in a state prison gives a person great perspective."

She finished the dye, and then mixed the small amount of blond for the highlights, and brushed it on select strands. "We'll give it a few minutes, and then you'll get to see the final effect."

When the hair was done, she held the mirror so he could see himself. "What do you think?"

"Hmm," he said. "I look really different. Maybe even better."

"Glad you think so. That's what we want. I like it, too. Any change you make is best if it's an improvement." She took all of the cellophane and packaging and disposable parts of the kit and put them into the shopping bag. "This is another precaution. If you do something like dyeing your hair, don't leave any of the materials in the trash. It's always possible that one of the chasers will get a tip or make the right guess. If you leave the dye or the box, they'll know you dyed your hair and the exact color."

"I understand."

"Good. The next thing is your skin. I've got a tanning lotion here that will change the shade of your skin. You won't be that pale prison color."

"Don't those things make you look orange?"

"I've experimented with just about every version that's on the market, and this one is the most natural looking. It looks like a mild tan." She handed the tube to him. "You don't have to do it."

"I'll do it."

"I'll get you started. Take off your shirt." She applied it to his face and neck and ears, his shoulders and back and chest. "You'll notice I'm wearing gloves, because I don't want to turn the palms of my hands dark. There. I'm finished with that part. Take a pair of gloves and go into the bathroom to do the rest. Do every part that the sun would tan if you were on the beach, including your feet and the tops of your toes. Then take a shower to get the lotion off."

When he returned, fully dressed, she said, "Very good. You look natural."

"How long does it last?"

"A few weeks, but it fades gradually, so it's possible to stop using it without suddenly looking pale. Or you can keep using it as long as you want. We're thinking in small increments of time now—how we can give you tomorrow and the next day. Anything that can disguise you for weeks is pure magic. Just keep reminding yourself that change is good as long as it doesn't attract attention. Here," she said. "I bought you some glasses. Try them on."

He picked up a pair of frames with faintly tinted gray plastic lenses, and put them on.

"Those are pretty good," she said. "The frames are like regular glasses, and they look expensive. That gives you the right kind of appearance—professor, not drifter. And they obscure the color of your eyes. Try the dark ones."

He put on a pair that wrapped around his face. "I like these."

"They're the right choice for sunny days. Take them off when you go inside. I try to do it before I open a door because I don't like that moment of near-blindness when I step into a building. I want to see everybody who can see me. Since the glasses you replace them with are nearly clear, you'll be able to take one step and stop to put them on, but use the time to survey the place. If you don't like what you see, you're already at the door."

"All right," he said. "What next?"

Jane looked at the clock beside the bed. "It's getting late, and that's a good time to travel—there will be fewer people on the road. Now we pack up and clean the apartment. What we do after that is get your sister out of her hiding place and take her with us into a better one before somebody finds her."

She went to the desk at the side of the room, turned on the desk lamp, found the pen, and filled in the quick check-out card. She put his key card into the envelope with it; then she took a twenty-dollar bill from his wallet and left it for the maid.

She took a hand-towel from the rack and went around the room wiping things off—doorknobs, the television set and remote control, the surfaces of all the furniture, the thermostat.

When Shelby emerged from the bathroom and put his razor, hairbrush, and toothbrush into his suitcase, she used her towel and wiped off every surface in the bathroom, too—mirrors, drawers, drawer pulls, faucets, tiles—rinsed the glasses, and dried them.

"You're pretty thorough," he said.

"There's no reason to make it easier for the chasers. If they find this room, they'll have to do a thorough job of fingerprinting to know it's yours. And maybe if we work at it, they won't find anything."

"That would be good," he said. "If they even get this far."

She stopped and looked at him. "I'm afraid this is what it's going to be like. You leave as little trail as possible, and you take the extra few minutes to give the chasers a chance to make a mistake or miss something. If they do, you've won for this day. You get to go on living until tomorrow."

"It doesn't sound like victory, does it?"

"No, because it isn't. Nobody comes to me until all his other options are gone. Your sister made it clear to me that yours were."

"They were. I was buying one day at a time by fighting off the inmates who had been trying to kill me in the yard or on the cellblock. The stab in the back came on a work detail. One guy came up to distract me while the one with the homemade knife came up behind me. Another one tried while I was still in the hospital. I don't mind precautions."

"Okay. Make sure we have everything."

He took his suitcase and hers. "Ready."

"Are you sure you can carry both of them?"

"Having both keeps me balanced."

She let him out into the hall and wiped the doorknobs, then tossed the towel inside and shut the door. They went to the first floor and put the envelope in the box at the end of the cashier's desk on their way out.

Jane walked to the gray car she had bought for Shelby. "Put the suitcases in the trunk and drive." She got into the passenger seat. "Circle the hotel, and then head toward Route 15."

Shelby drove around the block where the hotel was, and Jane studied the traffic, the cars parked in the area, and the people visible on the streets. Then Shelby came past the front of the hotel along the route to return to the interstate. As they drove past, Shelby pointed. "Look at that."

There were four police cars at the front entrance to the hotel with their lights off, and another unit on each side, near the residential wings.

"It looks as though they may have gotten a report that there were a pair of fugitives living on the second floor," Jane said. "I'd say they haven't gone in after them yet."

Shelby looked stunned and frightened, but he drove on.

"Stop at the light," Jane said.

"Sorry," he said. "It's hard to do anything but floor it." He pulled to a stop at the red light. It changed to green in a few seconds, and he continued up the street.

"There. That's good," she said. "You don't want to run a light right now. There will be more cops, probably." They went under the overpass where the street met the interstate, and there were two more police cars parked beneath it with their lights off.

"How did you know?"

"I guessed. Just before they go after somebody who's armed and dangerous, they block the streets so nobody walks into the middle of it."

"What should I do?"

"Keep going. When you're past the interstate and out of sight, I want you to swing around the next block and come out near the hotel. Let me off in the park."

"Let you off? Why?"

"I don't have a lot of time to tell you the whole story. But I left somebody else in that hotel, a young woman I picked up on the way in Las Vegas who had been abused by her ex-husband. I shot him. I'm sure he'll try to use the police to get back at her—get her arrested for the shooting, and so on. If she gets held long enough for him to catch up, he'll kill her."

"My God. How did you ever get involved in that?" He turned the corner and drove along a street parallel with the interstate.

"I guess I have a knack for making friends. Just let me off in Pioneer Park, and I'll take it from there."

"I can't believe you're going back for her," he said. He turned again and went under the freeway to the street behind the hotel.

"I think I may have made the mistake of assuming the cops were after the two of us—you and me. But maybe they're looking for the two of us—her and me."

He pulled to the curb and watched Jane get out. She leaned back in. "If things go badly in there, take the next street over to get on the interstate. Don't go past the cops again. Get on the highway just as we planned. Pick up your sister and do the best you can."

Jane walked across the parking lot, trying to make her limp less pronounced. There was a lock on the side door that was engaged at night, so she took out the key card she had retained from checking Iris in, swiped it in the slot, and entered the building. She went haltingly up the stairs near the door and came out on the third-floor corridor. She was relieved to see there were no police officers waiting in this hallway, but just as she found Iris's room, she heard the elevator give a faint ding, and the doors rolled open. Jane inserted her key card in the lock, the lock gave a green light, and she tried to open it. The handle wouldn't budge. The dead bolt must have been set from the inside.

She knew that if the police were in the next corridor, they would hear her knock. So she put her ear to the door and used her fingernails to scratch the door. It sounded a bit like a dog trying to get in. She scraped and scratched quickly and without stopping. If Iris was asleep, she didn't want to let her roll over and forget she'd heard anything. After a few seconds she heard something moving inside. She stepped back so she would be in the light if Iris looked out the peephole in the door.

The door opened, and Iris was smiling, about to say something. Jane held a finger to her lips and slipped inside past her, then closed the door. She whispered, "I came back for you. There are police in the parking lot, and I think they're on some of the upper floors. I don't know if they're looking for my client and me, or for you and me because I shot your ex. It probably doesn't matter, because I paid for both rooms with the same card. Get your things."

"Okay." Iris looked terrified, but she scurried around the room collecting the few items she had brought and stuffing them into her backpack, while Jane took a hand towel from the bathroom and repeated her routine of wiping off all the obvious places Iris might have touched.

Suddenly there was a knock on the door. "Police."

Jane put her face close to Iris. "Let them in. Don't lie about who you are. Maybe they'll want to see your identification. Fine. Just say you're alone."

Jane lay down on the floor beyond the bed and listened while Iris opened the door.

"Hi," Iris said. "What's going on, officer?"

"Are you alone in this room, miss?"

"Yes, why?"

"We were called because someone thought they saw a man and a woman who are wanted, considered armed and dangerous, at the hotel. The man is six feet even, light hair, and about one-eighty. The woman is tall and thin with long black hair. Have you seen anybody like that?"

"I don't think so," she said. "I just checked in today, and I haven't been out."

"One of the other officers thought he heard a stairwell door open on this floor, and then a room door opening and closing. He thought it might be your room. Was it?"

"No."

"Did you hear it, too?"

"If I did, it didn't make an impression," she said. "Doors open and close all the time."

"I know. Sorry to bother you."

"That's all right. Good luck." The door closed, and Iris clicked the dead bolt shut. Iris turned toward Jane, but Jane sat up and put her finger to her lips again and shook her head.

They both stayed still for at least thirty seconds, and then heard the two sets of heavy footsteps moving off along the hallway. Jane whispered to Iris, "You seem to be okay for the moment, but before long, somebody will notice the same card was used for both rooms. We need to get out to the car Sarah lent us before that happens."

"How?"

"You have to leave right away. Put both room keys in the folder and leave them in the automatic checkout box at the front desk, then walk out to the car. I'll try to be there, too. If the cops stop you, fine. You don't know anything, and haven't done anything. You're leaving because the cop told you there might be armed and dangerous people in the hotel."

"I want to go with you."

"All right. Just do as I say for now." Jane practically pushed her out the door.

Jane thought for a few seconds. There was no way out by using the elevator or going down the stairs to the lobby. It would have to be up. She went out to the hallway into the stairwell, then climbed painfully up one level to the fourth floor. She knew that there was a pool on the fourth level, and she could see the door at the end of the hall. She went out through the door, and saw the lighted water moving gently, throwing a reflection on the white stucco wall. There was a sign that said, *Lifeguard on Duty 8:00 a.m. Until 5:00 p.m.* Beyond the sign she saw what she had hoped for. On a rack next to the lifeguard's elevated chair there was a circular life preserver with a long nylon rope attached to it.

Jane stepped to the side of the pool and looked over the low wall at the parking lot below. On this side were the four police cars parked in front of the entrance. She walked to the opposite side of the roof and looked down. There were two more cars, to watch the rear entrance. There was only one more side, and she went there, looked below, and found herself looking down at a flat roof. It was a one-story wing of the hotel that jutted out a bit from the main building. On it were various vents and ducts, and what looked like a big central air-conditioning unit. Beside it was a large enclosure with a high fence, and inside were two large Dumpsters.

She took the life ring and lifted its rope from the hook on the wall. She walked to the side of the pool above the lower wing, tied the rope securely to the iron railing, and slipped the life preserver over her head and shoulders so her arms were free. She took a last look down, then gripped the rope, wound it around her right forearm, and lowered herself over the railing. She rappelled down the wall of the hotel, pushing off and landing with her left foot only, taking it deliberately to keep from making noise or swinging too far out from the wall. She managed to lower herself about forty feet, but then there was no more rope. She looked down. She judged that the remaining distance was only about six or seven feet, so she carefully slipped her body out of the life ring, held on to it with both hands, then touched the roof with her toes. She let go, and her right leg gave a painful twinge.

She took a few seconds to verify that she had not injured herself, then walked to the edge of the roof and looked over. There was a set of steel ladder steps attached to the brick wall, so she sat down, lowered her feet to the first step, and descended cautiously. The steps stopped at the top of one of the Dumpsters. She stood on the closed steel lid and looked out over the fence at the lot beyond. She could see Jim Shelby's car out on the street, and she could see Iris in the black car in the parking lot. Iris was closer. Jane went around the fence and moved along the side of the building until she was far enough, then limped to the row of cars where Iris was parked, and continued up the row until she reached Iris.

She opened the door and sat in the passenger seat. "Drive," she said. "Go out to the street at the exit over there. Go no more than ten miles an hour."

Iris drove slowly and cautiously. Jane watched the hotel

entrance, the police cars, and the cars in the street, but she saw no reaction, except one. As Iris pulled out into the street, Jim Shelby's car started.

"Good," said Jane. "He sees me." After they had moved off a hundred yards, Jane watched through the rear window while Shelby pulled out and followed.

Jane said, "Okay, my runner is following us. We'll keep going for a few minutes to be sure we haven't been spotted. Then you're going to have a choice."

"A choice? What is it?"

"The man behind us was convicted of murdering his wife a few years ago in California. I know he didn't do it, so about a week ago I broke him out of a Los Angeles courthouse where he was supposed to testify about another crime. He and I were the ones the police were looking for tonight."

"Oh, my God."

"There are also some other men paid to kill him, because it will close the case and nothing will ever happen to threaten the real murderer. They're the ones who shot me and then tortured me."

"Oh, my God, Melanie."

"Jane. Call me Jane."

"But what am I choosing?"

"You can take this car and drive someplace where you will start a new, quiet life and try not to get found by your ex-husband. That would be the most sensible thing you can do."

"What's the other choice?"

"You could go with us. Park the car in a lot somewhere, and then send the keys to Sarah at the Lifeboat, so she can send someone to pick it up. Then get in the other car with us. I'll try to get him settled somewhere, and then do the same for you. That's what I do professionally. So I might be able to make you better at disappearing. But it's a very harsh trade-off, because being with us is very dangerous.

You would also have to protect my secrets and my runner's secrets, even if it kills you." She added, "And it might."

"I'll go with you."

"You're not giving yourself time to think."

"I know what I'm doing. There's no question in my mind that Steve will find me again. He's very good at these things. He used to work as a private detective—got a license and everything—but he got fired. If he finds me, he will give me all the pain and suffering he can while he's killing me. You got away from the police, and from the people who want to kill your friend. But I know I can't get away from Steve. I need your help."

"All right," Jane said. "Get onto the interstate and follow the signs to the airport."

Iris drove the black car to the long-term parking lot, and Shelby waited outside in his car. Jane and Iris walked out to the street and got into Shelby's car. Shelby drove off toward the interstate.

Shelby glided onto the entrance ramp and accelerated. He merged onto the right lane of the highway, then moved another lane to the left. Jane turned and stared out the rear window for a full minute before she faced the front again and settled comfortably in her seat.

"Jim, this is Iris. Iris, Jim."

"Pleased to meet you," Iris said. "Thank you for letting me come along."

"Nice to meet you. But don't thank me. Jane made the decision and took all the risk."

"I'm sorry," Iris said. "I'll do my best not to contribute to the risks. I just have to get away from my troubles and start over."

"Me too," he said.

"Jim," Jane said. "When you checked in at the hotel, did you have to write down your license number?"

"No," he said.

"Have you driven this car since you arrived?"

"No. I made one quick stop to buy some food and supplies at a supermarket on the way, in Provo. I didn't want to have to go out and show my face here, so I figured I'd take one chance and then stay in until you caught up."

"Good. This car is probably still safe for the moment. If people recognized us, they didn't connect us with this car."

"What do we do to be sure?"

"We can't be sure," she said. "What we can do is keep moving. We'll take turns driving and sleeping. Every day or so we'll steal new license plates and change them. We'll pay in cash for the few things we need, and use the restrooms at gas stations. We'll get to your sister as quickly as possible."

"Agreed. I don't mind driving the rest of this shift," said Shelby. "You can go to sleep."

"Are you sure?"

"I've been restless, waiting to get on the road. It feels as though we're making progress, not just waiting for them to catch up with us."

"As long as we're moving, we're okay. Wake me up if you get sleepy. We've got nothing to do but drive." In a minute, Jane was sound asleep. A short time later, so was Iris.

8

It was late night in Chicago. Wylie lay on one of the two big beds in the hotel room, watching a rebroadcast of a baseball game. He didn't care at all about the fate of the Chicago Cubs, but he was too tired to keep pressing the remote control to search for something better. He supposed watching the Cubs lose was the price for watching them play.

Maloney seemed nervous tonight. He was standing on the balcony, staring out over the parking lot, waiting for Gorman to get out of the shower so he could have his turn. Maloney wasn't a good traveler. The constant motion and long hours seemed to make him tense, and it took him a long time to unwind before he could sleep.

There was a quiet knock on the door, and Maloney charged across the room to answer it. He squinted to look through the peephole. "It's Mr. Martel." Maloney moved his head back and forth to see if their visitor had brought anyone with him, but he realized that looking gained him nothing because he would have to open the door anyway.

He pulled the door open wide and said, "Welcome, Mr. Martel." Martel was about forty, but he looked younger, with smooth, unlined skin that was always so evenly tanned it looked almost unreal; thick, dark hair; and a tall, fit body.

Martel brushed past him into the room, then turned and closed the door himself, as though he didn't trust Maloney to do it. "Turn that off."

Wylie sat up and clicked the remote control, and the screen went black. Maloney closed the big sliding window to the balcony, then the curtain. Next he went to the bathroom door, opened it a few inches, and called, "Mr. Martel is here." After a couple of seconds the shower stopped. While they were waiting for Gorman to appear, Maloney seemed to feel he had to fill the silence. "I was watching the parking lot but I didn't see you pull in."

Martel looked as though he had never before realized what a moron Maloney was, and the realization was painful to him. He went and sat down in the armchair in the corner of the room. It was the only place in the room for a person to sit with any sort of dignity, so Maloney stood. After a few more seconds a damp Gorman emerged from the bathroom wearing a white terry-cloth bathrobe with the hotel's logo embroidered on the chest. He sat on the bed beside Wylie.

Martel said, "I understand that you discovered that the woman who got Shelby out of the courthouse is worth something."

"Yeah," said Wylie. "We were amazed. As soon as we realized she'd pulled it off, we grabbed her off the street. Maloney and Gorman pretended to be cops. We figured she could tell us where Shelby had gone."

"So?"

"She wouldn't. First she jumped out of the car screaming for help, so all Maloney could do was act like a cop and shoot her in the leg. After the doctor patched her up we started working her over to get her to talk. We beat her up, burned her, shocked her, got ready to cut her, and she said nothing. Zero. I was curious about her, so I sent out some e-mails to guys I know, describing her and saying what she'd done. I got two answers right away, and two more a day later."

"What guys?" Martel said it with a hint of irritation.

"I never let anybody know who I was working for, or what we were doing."

"I asked what guys."

"One is a private detective, only he lost his license. His name is Jack Killigan. He still works for some of his old clients, and he's done some searching for people. He gets so he knows who's worth finding. Another is Van Springer. He works as a go-between who buys things for people. One time it will be a clean car or a few guns, another time it's something else. Sometimes he gets asked to find somebody in particular. Another is a guy named Hosper, a bounty hunter."

"Okay. I get the idea. What did they say?"

"That when we got this one we hit the lottery."

"Really?"

"Yes. We just wanted to know where Shelby would be headed. When she wouldn't talk I thought if we found out where she was from, we could look there. But both these guys said they had clients who would pay seven figures for her. About five hours later, two more were sniffing around. Then I got an e-mail from a guy I didn't even know. He runs a big security company."

Martel said, "This is really interesting, Wylie. You amaze me sometimes. Most of the time you don't. When were you going to tell me about this woman?"

"I did tell you."

"You told me after she got away. You had already started negotiating with all these buyers. You were going to sell her yourself."

"No," said Wylie. "I wasn't. I was just trying to find out what we had on our hands, so I could give you the whole story."

Martel stared at Wylie for a few seconds, not glaring, but looking at him calmly and evenly. Then he said, "We have a different situation today. You don't have him or her, and I want them both. They're probably together again by now. I assume they don't know that we've got his sister's new address—or even that we know he has a sister."

Wylie looked uncomfortable. "Well, yes. The woman knows that we know there's a sister. When we had her, I said if she didn't talk we'd get the sister to talk."

Martel slowly shook his head. "Then if you know where the sister is right now, why the fuck are you in a hotel in Chicago instead of on the way to her?"

"We've been on the road for days, after cleaning up the place where we had her, and we were tired, dirty, and hungry for a decent meal. We'll do better if we feel better."

"Wylie. I want you to remember that the reason you're chasing around the country is that you fucked up. Repeatedly. Now you know the address, and here you are, resting up. I'm astonished. I'm sure you know that if you go up there and get Shelby and this woman, there will be a big payday for all three of you. I want her alive, and him dead. If you don't succeed, I'm done with you. I'm giving you a way to fix your mistakes."

Martel sat in the armchair staring at Wylie. Then he slowly moved his head to look at the other two. "Are you waiting for something?"

Wylie said, "You want us to leave now?"

Martel said, "Can you possibly think I don't?"

The three men hurried around the room picking up clothes they had thrown on the floor, filling their pockets with keys, wallets, and change they had left on the furniture.

"As soon as you're ready you can just go. Leave your room keys and I'll check out for you."

He waited in silence while they finished putting their belongings into suitcases and headed out the door. When they were gone he stood up, went to the window, and waited until he saw their blue Crown Victoria pull away from the building and drive to the exit from the parking lot onto the highway. He put the three room key cards in his pocket and went to the door.

It was these small, day-to-day decisions that made the difference between them and him. They avoided extending themselves if there was any discomfort, let themselves be distracted, stopped trying the minute they felt they'd expended exactly as much effort as they had to.

It depressed him that he had to pay men like these to solve problems for him. Eleven years ago he had started his business with the idea of never doing anything that would attract the attention of the authorities. That would allow him never to hire criminals. But here he was, years later, with not only these three but nine more on his payroll—a dozen men who were engaged in applying various levels of force to protect his interests.

He'd had the simplest sort of business plan. He had started a medical supply company and given it a name that sounded old and established. In order to have merchandise, he would induce a young salesperson from a pharmaceutical company to sell him medical drugs. He specialized in the obvious ones—Oxycontin, methadone, morphine, Vicodin, Valium, and a few others that were in such high demand he could charge huge markups and sell them instantly. For eleven years he had been an enormously successful drug dealer without ever having to step on a dark street or deal with anyone who used drugs.

He always paid the pharmaceutical company's bill on time. That kept the salesperson in the clear and the pharmaceutical company happy. He would produce paperwork that listed small resales to a large number of genuine hospital pharmacies, clinics, medical groups, and universities. The government looked closely at every prescription written for drugs like these. The prescription had to be written by an MD personally on a numbered prescription slip that carried the doctor's medical license number. But no prescriptions were ever written. In theory, the drug just stayed locked up in these institutional facilities for years. The hospital pharmacists had never ordered or received any of these drugs, so they never wondered where the drugs went. The drugs never got onto an inventory, so they were never reported missing.

Martel's companies never had his name on them. The officers and managers were all doctors. One of his brilliant observations that made his business possible was that it was absolutely futile to go to mature, practicing physicians and present them with a scheme to make extra money. They had money. And the ones who were corruptible were already working schemes of their own and didn't need a partner.

Instead Martel sought out very young doctors, men and women still in medical school or interning. Some were still paying tuition or huge student loans. If they agreed to be on the board of one of his companies, they would receive good pay for doing very little. They might notice at some point that their names appeared on other papers—on the letterhead of company stationery, or even as a signatory of a letter. But they would not know that their credentials were being used to get the company licensed to handle narcotics. After three or four years, the young doctor might move on to another part of the country and forget the relationship, but Martel's companies would not forget him.

Martel had operated some of the companies for as long as eleven years without raising much suspicion. The only way the authorities might find discrepancies was by comparing sales data from the giant pharmaceutical manufacturers with the records of the hospital pharmacies to which Martel supposedly had sold small amounts of a drug, a form of check that seldom happened. When it did happen, he could produce receipts or drugs on demand. He knew that given the tiny amounts of drugs involved and the age of some of the orders, the authorities would see no point in an investigation.

Whenever it seemed to him that questions were about to be asked, he would dissolve the company or have another company he owned buy it and take over. On some occasions he had even made a show of turning over unsold drugs to the local authorities to be destroyed. When he did that, the bottles were full, but not necessarily full strength. At times he had such quantities of narcotics going through his companies that he could have made a fortune just diverting the number of bottles and pills that would constitute normal breakage from shipping that never took place.

He loved the business. It not only had made him rich but it had also brought him women. Pharmaceutical sales reps were nearly all young, attractive women. To them he was a very important customer. Unlike many of their other customers he was male, unmarried, only slightly older than they were, and unfailingly interested in them. He also traveled from city to city, where he met lots of other women who knew only that he was a rich, handsome man who had something to do with medicine.

Today he had changed his itinerary to stop in Chicago because he had sensed Wylie and the others needed to be reminded to be afraid of him. He had sent them out to kill Shelby—to finish killing him, really. Shelby was only a mild concern, but Martel hadn't forgotten him. Martel had made sure Shelby was convicted of the death of his wife, but having him in a jail cell was simply not enough. Every year criminals were released on appeals, new evidence was found, lawyers were declared incompetent. There was no reason for Daniel Martel to live with that risk—or any risk. Shelby was like a bee that had been swatted but hadn't died yet. More than one bee like that had staged enough of a recovery to sting.

This woman was something else. Wylie didn't seem to have fully understood what he'd had, and he'd gotten careless enough to let her escape. If there were four people who didn't know each other but knew who she was and wanted to bid millions for her, then there might be eight, or twenty. But Wylie was a man of action—another term for a fool. He had acted to get an auction going without first thinking through all of the implications.

Martel left the hotel and drove toward Midway Airport. He felt depressed when he had to think about men like Wylie. Having just two or three of them was enough to keep all of the pharmaceutical reps and interns and bookkeepers from becoming troublesome. But he had learned that he couldn't stop there. He'd had to hire a second set of three to serve as a threat to the first set. Then he'd needed to hire another six to counter the first six. He had forced himself to stop at a dozen. But he sometimes implied to each of them that there might be another dozen, or an unknowable number, waiting for them to cause problems and be annihilated.

9

Jane woke at three a.m. leaning against the passenger door and sat up. She looked at Shelby beside her, then at Iris lying behind her on the back seat. "Time for my turn at the wheel," she said. They traded places and she drove for a time, then looked at Shelby. "This is a great time to sleep. In a couple of hours there will be bright sunlight coming through the windshield."

"It's taking me a while to wind down. There are too many days behind me when I would have given anything to be outside and watch the telephone poles going past."

"Iris is asleep. Are you in the mood to talk?"

"Sure."

"I'm sorry about bringing Iris without giving you a chance to refuse. Iris is a good person in a lousy situation, and she needs a little help. And she'll help us, too. Unlike us, she can walk in any door without fear of being recognized."

"I understand," he said. "If you trust her, I do. Things happen, and we have to adjust."

"Things happen is right. I had expected that you and I would have to elude the police. I didn't imagine that the people who framed you would be there, too. Tell me what you know about them. Who are Wylie, Gorman, and Maloney?"

"I have no idea. I know the names Wylie, Gorman, and Maloney because you told me. I can only guess they must be friends of the man who killed my wife."

"What about him—the man who killed your wife?"

"Almost nothing. I know that he was living with her for a while. I saw some of his clothes left in a closet."

"If you don't know about him, let's talk about your wife."

"I met her in college. The University of Texas at Austin. She was beautiful. Long, honey-blond hair, a great smile, a body like a goddess."

"I have an unpleasant question. If I'm being insensitive, please forgive me. But your sister told me Susan cheated on you even then, right after you met her. Is it true?"

Jane watched him shrug, and then stay silent for a few seconds. "At the time, I would have sworn she would never cheat. She could have just dropped me and had somebody she liked better. But in the light of what happened later, and what I think happened, I'm not so sure. An attractive woman always has men looking at her. Any day she's inclined to, she can bring the whole thing on and have it over with in an hour or two, including a bit of flirting ahead of time and putting on fresh makeup afterward. There were plenty of times when she could have, and catching her at it would have been the last thing I was thinking about."

"So you proposed and she accepted, and you married. What did you do for a living?"

"I was a beginning executive at Cole and Castor, the office supply wholesaler. They started me as a trainee account manager and then moved me around a bit, so the departments and I got used to each other—sales, advertising, inventory, purchasing. Sue was in pharmaceutical sales at Megapharm, working mostly with hospitals and medical groups."

"And when did the problems start in the marriage?"

"About two and a half years into it, I sensed that she wasn't quite right. First she was working late and tired all the time. I would get home around seven and she might show up at ten or eleven. She always dressed up with high heels and expensive clothes. She would come in and shed all that stuff on the way into the bathroom to wash off her makeup. When she came out she was in a pair of sweat pants and a big T-shirt. She would hardly talk to me while she had a snack and went to bed. Then we'd get up in the morning and start over."

Jane waited. He was talking steadily, moving in the direction of the crime, the moment when all of these details had made sense to him.

"Then she started having to go to medical conventions to lobby the doctors there to prescribe her company's products. This kept her away for three or four days at a time, with part of it being the whole weekend."

"When did you have time for each other?" Jane asked.

"As she got busier, we were together less. Sex was practically nonexistent. She was gone so much, and then when she was home she was always too tired to even think about making love. I tried to be patient with all that. Then I thought I should say something, ask whether there was something I could change to make things better. She said no, the work would all pay off in the long run, and so I should be patient. I told myself she had a right to her career, and if working all those hours would get her somewhere, I should support her."

"So you dropped the subject?"

"She said she loved me. We're all brought up to think we have to talk about everything, and that's all that matters.

It isn't. What people *do* is the truth. If she doesn't have sex with you, she doesn't love you. If she isn't with you, it's because she doesn't want to be."

"How did it end?"

"It took a while. I still thought that I was seeing things clearly. Then I happened to notice some new things. The first was while she was away at a weekend convention in Atlanta. She had left on Thursday morning. A notice came on her e-mail Friday that said her flight to Atlanta on Saturday morning was going to be delayed about fifteen minutes. I didn't see the e-mail until Saturday afternoon. The e-mail carried the six-digit confirmation number, so I looked up the reservation on the airline's site. Sure enough, the flight was Saturday morning, and the return flight was Sunday night. The flight wasn't charged to her company. It was charged to a credit card in her name, and it was a credit card I hadn't known about. The billing address was her mother's house. Naturally, I was wondering what she had been doing from Thursday morning until Saturday morning, and where she had spent the nights."

"What did you do?"

"I called her, but everything went to voice mail. I went to visit her mother, to ask her if she'd heard from Sue. When I asked what she knew about the credit card, she seemed surprised. First it was 'What card? What do you mean?' Then it was 'Oh, that card. When you get married, plenty of things still come to you at your mother's house.' I could only pretend to shrug it off. I went home. When Susan came home on Sunday night I didn't say much about any of it. I just looked for signs. I noticed she didn't unpack that night. We both left for work the next morning, and I came back and opened her suitcase. She had a couple of tiny little bathing suits, but she loved to swim, and was at a big hotel, so it meant nothing. She also had business clothes and a cocktail dress, and jeans. Nothing conclusive."

"Did checking the suitcase help set your mind at rest?"

"The opposite."

"Why?"

"When I found myself sneaking around and searching my wife's suitcase for evidence, I felt I had come to a low point. I wanted to know once and for all. I also didn't want to know. Maybe it was a brief fling and it would end, and she'd learn she loved only me, and she'd be a great wife forever. I hated myself for having that thought, and for wishing I could be protected from the truth until the ugly part of the truth went away. I hated myself for suspecting her, and I felt self-loathing for ignoring the signs for so long. Some nights I was ready to confront her with the whole mess, and then I'd wake up in the morning and start wondering if I was just putting bad interpretations on innocent facts. It was horrible."

"So you did confront her?"

"No. I came home from work as usual one night, and she didn't. That wasn't unusual. But I had a funny feeling. I noticed something was different in the living room. Things seemed to have been moved. No, I realized. They were missing—a couple of pictures, a vase or two. I went into the bedroom and opened her closet. There was nothing left in it. Her dresser drawers were empty, and the drawers in the bathroom and the medicine cabinet. Usually the bathroom counter looked like a cosmetics store, but all the bottles and jars and tubes were gone. I went to the phone and called her cell number, but her phone was off. I called her private office number and it went to voice mail. I texted her—'Where are you?' I figured if she was checking any e-mail it would be her office address, so I sent a careful e-mail, so I wouldn't embarrass her. I just said to please call me as soon as possible. And I waited up all night, but there was no response. At around five a.m. it occurred to me that I should check on some other things. I called the number for our bank, and punched in the account numbers for our accounts. The checking account had a hundred dollars, and the savings account balance was zero. She had moved away and cleaned us out. At seven I called in to work to take a sick day. At eight I called her mother."

"What did she say?"

"That Sue wasn't with her, and her leaving town was my fault. She couldn't even go home to her mother, because I was too close by and wouldn't have left her alone. She had left Texas entirely."

"Did that make you think about backing off?"

"No. I was frantic. I just wanted to know what went wrong. Was she in love with somebody else? Was I just too repulsive to stay with for another minute? Was she mad about something? I looked for her. I finally went to see a lawyer, and while I was telling him the story I mentioned the whole money issue, because I couldn't pay him a lot of money until after payday. Right away he told me I didn't have a prayer of ever seeing the money again, but it was an adequate pretext for finding her and asking her for an explanation. He hired a skip-tracing company, and they found her new address, which was in California."

In the back seat, Iris stirred and sat up. "Hi," she said. "Where are we?"

"We're still on the interstate, getting ready to make a stop for gas," Jane said. "It's a good time to use the restrooms and get a cup of coffee."

"Great idea," said Iris. "You two can just head for the restrooms and come back to the car. I'll be the one to show my face and buy the coffee."

Jane said, "Good idea," and looked at Shelby.

Shelby got the hint. "Thanks, Iris," he said. "It'll make stopping a whole lot safer for us."

Jane pulled off the interstate at a large gas station and bought gas, and they all used the restrooms. When Iris returned to the car with the coffee, Shelby was asleep.

10

Jane still drove with her left foot so she could rest the muscles of her right thigh and help it heal. She had been trying for all of this time to keep her mind on Jim Shelby's troubles and off her own. But as she drove through the last dark stretch of night on the interstate, the thoughts and feelings came back to her.

She had been shot, captured, and tortured. She had not allowed herself to think about the horror and the brutality of the torture right away, because the memories and images might weaken her. She'd had work to do to get herself away from Los Angeles to Las Vegas and on to Salt Lake City, and then to get Shelby back in motion. But the darkness and the solitude brought her own experiences back.

The three men had done her terrible harm. She was afraid that she wasn't healing quickly enough, and that she and Shelby—and now Iris—would be killed because she couldn't run and couldn't fight, and her limping would make them stand out.

Now that she was beginning to heal, and the car made her injuries undetectable, she had a new concern. Now she was feeling the loss of the beautiful, strong, smooth body she'd had. She had always been a runner, a member of the track team at Deganawida High School and then at Cornell. Over the years she had kept running, and also done tai chi and practiced aikido each day, but she hadn't thought much about how it made her look. Now she knew that beauty had been more important to her than she had ever admitted to herself. What would Carey think when he saw her?

Her mind moved deeper into the experience. The captors had not raped her. She supposed that since she had been shot right away, rape would not have happened until she had recovered. And then their priority had been to find out where Jim Shelby was, so they weakened and marked her further. But she had expected that sometime soon she would be raped. If they'd had the chance to complete their auction, then she would have been at the mercy of men who had been hunting her for years, hating her for outsmarting and outrunning them, but most of all for freeing their prey. She would have suffered everything they had been wishing they could do to her. Rape would have been only the beginning.

Jane checked her rearview mirrors, as she did every minute or two. There was a set of headlights that had been behind them for a few minutes. When she went faster, the other car sped up, too. When she slowed down, the other car didn't pass. Instead, the car slowed down, too, hanging back just far enough so she couldn't get a look at what was behind the headlights. She accelerated sharply.

Shelby sat up. "What's going on?"

"I'm just trying to figure that out," she said. "There's a set of headlights behind us that's been there too long."

He turned in his seat and stared out the rear window. "Could it be cops?"

"I can't say no to anything, but usually if cops get curious, they speed up and take a closer look at you. They run your plates on their computer. If they're still curious they pull you over."

Suddenly the car behind them pulled out into the left lane. Jane caught a clear silhouette of the approaching car in the headlights of cars behind it. "It's a cop," she said. "I can see the light bar on the roof. He's going to pass us. Sit tight." She slowed down.

The car moved steadily up to their left, accelerating all the time. It slid past them, and the cop in the passenger seat glanced at them but then let his eyes focus on the next car ahead. The police car was moving fast now, and its red taillights gradually diminished into the distance. "I guess we're not the ones he wants."

"That's a relief," said Shelby. "Want me to drive for a while?"

"Not yet. Feel like talking some more?"

"About what?"

"When I've taken people out of the world in the past, all of them had somebody chasing them. But I can't recall any who were already serving a life sentence in jail and still had enemies trying to get at them. Why do you?"

"I don't know. They sent me to prison for life. They should have been satisfied."

"I keep thinking it has to be something about the murder. If we can figure out what happened to your wife, maybe we'll know what these people are so afraid of."

"My sister told you the essentials, and I've told you most of what went on between Susan and me."

"You said she moved to California. What was there?"

"Supposedly it was to be able to start a new life without interference from me."

"'Supposedly?'"

"Her mother said that. After I found out where Sue was,

I called her mother to ask if I could come over and talk. She said she thought that might be a good idea. She said to come over to her house at seven, and we could have a real conversation."

"Did you tell her you knew where Susan was?"

"No, I didn't," he said. "I didn't feel as though she had ever been on my side, and I certainly didn't that night."

"And nothing new happened the weekend Susan went away? No argument, no big fight stands out in your memory?"

"No fights. The only thing that stands out is that I'd found out she had concealed a lot about her business trips, and I had asked her mother about the credit card. The next thing that happened was that she was gone."

"About the money—"

"I didn't care about the money."

"I believe you weren't motivated in any of this by money. The victim often isn't. The thief is. Otherwise she wouldn't steal. How much was in the account she emptied?"

"About two hundred thousand. What I'm saying is that she didn't decide to leave me to get my part of the money."

"Why do you think she left?"

"Embarrassment. Humiliation. I had evidence that she'd been having an affair, and evidence that her mother had known and helped her. They had both lied to me. As soon as her mother told her I'd found her reservation and the credit card number, she knew what our next conversation would be about, so she decided there wouldn't be one."

"Was she afraid you would do her physical harm?"

"She couldn't have been. She'd known me since college. I've never done anything violent. I just wanted to talk, so I could either close the door on the whole marriage, or know what to do to save it."

"But you decided to start with her mother?"

"Yes. If I was polite and respectful, I thought she might give me an idea of what to expect from Sue. I even thought that if it went well, she would tell Sue I was being reasonable and deserved an explanation."

"How did it go?"

"I went to her house at seven, and she opened the door. When I stepped inside, I saw she wasn't alone."

"Who was there?"

"Her brother—Sue's uncle Dave—and his two sons, one they called Little Dave after his father, and Cody. When I walked in, they were all sitting in the living room scowling at me."

"How did you react?"

"It didn't look good, but I thought I had to try. So I said, 'All right, then. We can all talk. Here's the situation I'm in. The wife I've loved since freshman year has taken off and left me without saying a word. She took with her our savings, about three quarters of which came from my paychecks, and a new car that belonged to both of us. I had been planning to ask her about her last business trip, when she left home two days early and came home a day late. She charged the trip to a credit card that I didn't know she had, and it is billed to this address instead of ours. I'd like to hear her explanation of all of this. Since she's gone, I thought you might be able to help me understand what she was thinking.'"

"What did she say?"

"Her mother said, 'I can't believe you've come into my home and in front of my family accuse my daughter of adultery and theft.'

"I said, 'I didn't come here to call her names.'

"'Why did you come, then?'

"'I'd like to know if she has plans to come back to me. I'd like to know if she's found somebody else, and if she plans to file for divorce. If so, we'll have to get some legal help and make an agreement about how to proceed.'

"The one to answer was Uncle Dave. He said, 'You came in here with an attitude. You accused the lady of conspiring with her daughter to steal your money and then helping her daughter to whore herself out to other men. Now, it's time for you to get yourself out of here.'

"I said, 'I'll leave in a moment, but first I'd like to say something to Mrs. Owens.' And I turned to her. That was a mistake. The two boys were on me from behind. The pair of them were grappling with me and throwing punches at once. As soon as I was fully engaged in fighting them off, the father got up and started throwing hard punches from the outside. A few of them landed. Pretty soon I was worn out from struggling with the boys and bleeding from the punches. The only satisfaction I got was watching them wreck the house doing it. They threw me out on the lawn and locked the door."

"Did you just go home?"

"I went home the long way. They called the police, who got there in a minute. There were two of them, an older one and a young one. The older one explained the situation. When they're called out on a domestic disturbance, they have to arrest somebody. There were four witnesses on one side, and one on the other. Guess who got arrested."

"Couldn't the cops see who got the worst of it?"

"Of course. What the older cop said was that I had obviously been hit in the head a lot, and since this was about my absent wife, I was obviously living alone at that time. It was better not to leave me alone, since there might be a concussion or something. So I was going to spend the night at the station."

"I suppose that makes sense."

"The problem was that it gave me a record. I had been arrested for domestic violence."

"They released you. What happened next?"

"I flew to California, to the place where the skip tracer had found Sue. I drove straight from the airport to her apartment building in Santa Monica. I had no idea how long it would take to wrap this up, so I'd taken a week off work and bought a one-way ticket."

"What did you do first? Did you sit in the car and watch the building to see if she was alone?"

"It never occurred to me. It was a first-floor apartment in a big stucco building that was one of about seven buildings on the block, mostly condos. I just figured I'd go talk to her."

"Was she there?"

"It was around midday, between twelve and one, and I figured she couldn't have found a new job to go to this quickly. And she didn't need to, because she had all our savings. But when I rang the bell, nobody answered the door. I knocked, stood around, looked in the underground garage to see if our car was there. The spaces were just about full, but ours wasn't one of the cars. At this point I was wondering if I had the wrong address. I went to the side windows to peer in. But when I got to the side window, I saw a plant in a pot on the ledge outside. Susan was one of those women who didn't have much self-discipline, so she found ways to make up for it. She set her alarm clock fifteen minutes ahead to fool herself into getting up. She bought candy, but froze it so she couldn't eat it on impulse. And she always hid a spare key outside so she wouldn't lock herself out. The pot looked to me like the sort of place where she'd hide a key, and I didn't see any others, so I poked my finger into the dirt and found the key. I unlocked the door and went inside."

"Did you learn anything?"

"It was the right address. The first thing I saw was the vase that used to be on our mantel—blue and yellow glass melted together in swirls. It was on a coffee table next to an issue of *Maxim*."

"The men's magazine?"

"Yeah. There were things of hers—or ours—around the place. I would say exactly one carload of them. And there were other things that belonged to a man. The place had leather furniture, a big-screen TV. I noticed that on the kitchen counter there were two coffeemakers, and one of them looked exactly like the one from our house in Texas. The bedroom had a king bed, two dressers, and two nightstands, and on one of them the alarm clock was set fifteen minutes ahead. I sniffed the pillow on that side, and it smelled like her hair. I went to the closet. About half of it was taken up by a man's clothes—sport coats, shirts, jackets, baseball caps, a panama hat, lots of sneakers and shoes. The other side was full of clothes I'd seen Susan wear. There was also a really short, sheer red nightie that she had tossed toward the laundry basket, but the basket was full, so it was draped over the rest. For years she had been wearing T-shirts and sweat pants to sleep in."

"What did you do?"

"I went back to the living room. I sat by the coffee table and looked at the mailing label on the corner of the magazine to see what his name was. The label said 'Megapharm,' which was the name of her company, but the address was on Wilshire Boulevard in Los Angeles. I started looking in drawers and things to find something—bills or other mail that would at least give me the name of the guy she was living with. But after a while it occurred to me that I was being stupid. I was in a place I had no legal right to enter. The marriage was over. So I took a sheet of paper from a notepad by the phone and wrote her a note. I said, 'When you're ready for the divorce, get in touch. You know the address and phone number. Jim.'"

"After all that, you just wrote a note and left?"

"I turned in my rental car at the airport, then waited about three hours for my flight. I remember wondering if

I should go back to try again, but I couldn't think of anything that would accomplish. I had my cell phone on all that time, but she hadn't called. I even checked the voice mail at home in case she left a message for when I got home. When I boarded my plane I turned off the phone and that was that."

"That was that?"

"As far as I was concerned, she was out of my life. I went home and went to work for a month or so. I did my best to stop thinking about her. I started to date a woman I knew from work. I suppose it was nothing serious. We had known each other for years and both kind of wondered what it would be like. She'd been divorced for a year and a half, and now I was separated from my wife, so we found out, and it was pleasant. Then, about three weeks later, Sue was killed. The day after they found her body there was a knock on my door. The California police had asked the Texas police to find out just where her husband was."

"Standard procedure."

"Well, they woke me up, and with me was the woman I'd been dating. That went into the record—that I wasn't a grieving husband, but a guy who had already replaced his wife. Then there was the domestic violence arrest at her mother's. At that point I learned that both of them—Sue and her mother—had gotten restraining orders against me in both states, saying I represented a danger to them. Sue's death was settling on me just about the time the police started telling me why I was a great suspect and trying to get a reaction on tape."

"Did they tell you the details of the murder?"

"She was found in the apartment by the building manager, who wanted to talk to her about why her rent check had bounced. He couldn't get her to answer the door, so he opened it, and there she was. She had been hit with a heavy metal object several times, and then stabbed. They didn't have a time of death, and it was impossible for me to provide an alibi to account for every possible time."

"Did the cops give you any useful information?"

"I learned pretty quick that I was the only suspect. What I didn't know yet was that the man who shared the apartment in Los Angeles with her was gone. He had moved every single thing of his out of there. Then he had given the place a careful cleaning. My prints were on a few things, but his weren't. The apartment lease was in her name. The note I'd left proved I'd been there. I hadn't put a date on it, and so the guy who framed me left it on the counter as though I'd been there in the past few days."

"Tell me about the trial. At least some of the men who have been after us were there. Did you see them?"

"I was in Los Angeles County Jail for ten months before my case came up on the docket. My sister told me there were men going around in Austin scaring off people who might testify for me, but I never saw them. Once the trial got going, I got the rest of my education. I was a man with a history of domestic violence, a person who broke a restraining order to get to his ex-wife. Everything the prosecutor could say I'd done was against me. But he also brought out everything bad Sue had ever done to me, and that was against me, too. The fact that she'd cheated on me and stolen our savings didn't make anybody sorry for me, but it was a convincing motive for murder. They brought her mother, uncle, and cousins to testify I was crazy with anger. Sue had supposedly even said something to some woman at work about how, if she was murdered, it would be me. I'm sure the woman was paid to say that."

"How long did it take the jury to convict you?"

"They had a verdict in three and a half hours. They put the cuffs back on me as soon as the verdict was read, and took me back to the county jail. A week or so later they got me out to hear my life sentence."

The voice from the back seat startled him. "You poor thing."

He turned his head to look at Iris. "I thought you were asleep."

"I woke up. I hope you don't mind that I heard." She put her hand on his shoulder.

He shook his head. "There aren't any secrets. It was all in the papers and on TV at the time. It probably is again right now, so everybody knows what kind of man escaped."

"Nobody escaped," Jane said. She glanced at Iris in the rearview mirror. "Neither of you escaped. Those people don't exist anymore."

11

They stayed on the road as long as they could, and stopped only to change drivers and buy necessities. They paid in cash for everything they bought. The long, straight highways in the middle of the country gave Jane time to begin teaching the others how to stay difficult to find. "Every time you deal with anybody, there is information to protect, and misinformation to plant. Even here on the road."

"On the road?" said Iris. "You mean we lie just for the sake of lying?"

"We hide the truth, or anything that could lead anybody to the truth. The fewer people who see Jim, the smaller the chance he'll be recognized. I was photographed at the courthouse, so I'm a potential problem, too. So we have you do most of our talking, and if only one person needs to show her face, it will always be your job. We want to protect the car, and have as few people as possible associate it with us. That's why I try to park it where it's not easy to see, and there are no cameras to leave a record of the license number. If we talk to anyone in a station or restaurant, always lie. If we're going north, say south. Any misdirection might save your life."

When it was Jane's turn she drove hard, staying at or slightly above the speed limit for each three-hour shift, pushing it when the rest of the traffic was fast, and then keeping the needle glued to the speed limit when the rest slowed down. She didn't accelerate or touch the brakes for long stretches of road, because keeping a car moving at the same speed used the least gas and put the least strain on the car's parts.

They drove for almost three days, over nineteen hundred miles from Salt Lake City to Delaware Avenue at Gates Circle in Buffalo, and they arrived at one forty-five p.m. When Shelby began the arc that would take them halfway around the circle, Jane said, "Keep going north for a few blocks, then pull over wherever you can do it safely and we'll change places."

He pulled over a few blocks farther on, and Jane took the wheel. She went around the first block, then came back south on Delaware and into the center of the city.

Shelby said, "Where are we going?"

"To a place where you'll be safe while I pick up your sister and bring her back."

"She's my sister. I should be with you."

"She and I have met, remember?" Jane said. "This is the best way."

Iris said, "But what's the point in splitting up?"

"Anybody who knows where Sarah is will be waiting near her, trying to get Jim. When I was in Los Angeles, one of the men who held me there told me they knew about her and that she'd be the next one if I didn't tell where Jim was. She'll be a priority for the police, too. They always expect fugitives to turn to a relative, and most of them do. The reason we've been tearing across the country is to get to her before anyone can figure out where she is."

"But we could all do that together."

"If you stay here with Jim, he doesn't have to go out and be seen. You don't fit the description of the woman who helped him escape, so you make him safer. There's only one person looking for you, and he's in a hospital or a prison cell for now."

"But you're still hurt."

"I'm not planning to do anything strenuous."

"But—"

"Don't bother," Jane said. "This is something I'll do better alone."

Jane called from a pay phone on the way to reserve a room, then drove them to the Hyatt Hotel in downtown Buffalo as though she were a friend who had picked them up at the airport. She paused at the entrance and watched them go inside with their suitcases. As Jane had instructed her to, Iris went to the desk with a credit card of Jane's to register while Shelby disappeared into a men's room in a corner of the lobby. Jane had seen enough. She drove off.

The drive to Ithaca was exactly as she remembered it from the years when she was a student at Cornell. There was a very long stretch of the New York State Thruway, and then the exit at Waterloo, and the long drive beside Cayuga Lake to the southern tip. She stopped in a gas station in Tompkins County near Ithaca to fill the tank, then went into the ladies' room to change the bandage on her leg again. For the whole trip she had been careful to keep the dressing fresh and clean, and she had used her left foot on the pedal when she drove, so her injured right leg was improving rapidly. Jane found her way to Dryden Road just after seven in the evening.

This was farm country, but most of the property this close to the university was no longer planted, and the only domesticated animals seemed to be dogs and a few horses. She had to read the house numbers stenciled on the sides of galvanized-steel rural mailboxes at the side of the road, but the long gravel driveways led to suburban houses, a lot of them probably owned by professors at Cornell or Ithaca College.

When Jane found the address she was looking for, she got only a second or two to glance down the driveway at the house. She saw a flash of lighted windows, and that was all. She drove on for a few hundred yards before she found a place to pull over. She looked in every direction, then saw that the nearest farmhouse was old, and apparently whoever owned the land didn't live there. She backed her car into the orchard and parked it.

Jane sat in the car for a few minutes and watched the traffic while she thought. There was something that bothered her about what she had seen at the house where Sarah was staying. At the end of the driveway was the house, and beside it a two-car garage. That looked fine. The garage door was shut, and there was no telling whether Sarah's car was there or not. But there had been a lot of lights on in the house, and no blinds or curtains shut. There was something inviting about all the lights, but it didn't feel like a house where someone was trying to wait quietly. Maybe Sarah was one of those people who felt safe only if every bulb in a house was blazing, but she had not struck Jane that way.

Jane reached under the seat and picked up the pistol she had brought with her across the country. She released the magazine and made sure the fourteen rounds she remembered were still there. She clicked the magazine back in, pulled the slide to cycle the first round in, and flicked on the safety. But the gun didn't make her feel better. Something was wrong.

Jane opened the glove compartment. She found the plastic pack of razor blades she had used to scrape off the dealer's stickers on the windows. The blades were the old-fashioned kind with one sharp edge and one thick and blunt, used mostly for linoleum cutters and paint scrapers. From the drugstore bag on the floor she picked up the roll of adhesive tape she had used whenever she changed the bandage on her thigh. She took off her shoes and socks, taped one razor blade to the top of each foot, and replaced the socks and shoes.

The house was about a quarter mile back up the road, so she began to walk. The right leg was still weak, but the pain had subsided over the past few days. She kept to the shoulder of the road, but when a car came along she diverted her path into the orchards and bushes where the headlights would miss her and she wouldn't be seen in the dark. She walked back to the mailbox, but she went more slowly up the outside of the driveway, where the view was complicated by trees, then slipped across to the side of the house.

It was a single-story house with a high, pitched roof and narrow clapboards painted the dried-blood color of a barn. She looked in the first window and saw the dining room. There had been an attempt to furnish the neat little house with authentic early-nineteenth-century furniture. The dining table and chairs were bird's-eye maple, and in the part of the living room she could see were a couple of red cherrywood tables and short cabinets. There were built-in bookcases along the far wall.

For all the lights, Jane could hear no sounds inside, and saw no people. Before she went to the front door and knocked, she wanted to reassure herself that Sarah Shelby was here, and alone.

Jane walked farther between the driveway and the side of the house, and around to the kitchen window in the back. She had to go up the first step of the back porch to see in the window. There was a counter, and in the sink she could see pots and pans that Sarah must have used to prepare her dinner. She pulled herself up a little farther and peered in at the kitchen table. There were four dirty plates, four glasses, and four sets of silverware. Everything was pushed aside or piled, as though dinner was over and four people had eaten. It was too many. Who could Sarah Shelby know in Ithaca, New York?

Jane walked to the garage and looked in the side window. There were two cars inside. One would be Sarah Shelby's. Jane had an awful suspicion about whom the other might belong to. She tried to assure herself that if someone were trying to ambush Shelby when he came to meet his sister, he wouldn't leave his car in the garage. But she couldn't prove that to herself.

Jane moved to the front of the house and crouched among the shrubs. She was careful not to touch the clapboards and not to make a sound that could be heard inside. Slowly, carefully, she raised her eye to the corner of the front window.

Sarah came through the living room, but right behind her was Maloney, the man who had shot Jane in Los Angeles. Sarah was carrying some beer bottles that someone had left in the living room, and Maloney was carrying something, too. As Sarah went through the dining room into the kitchen, Jane could see she was hobbling, as though her ankles were tied with a short rope to keep her from running.

Jane moved with her along the outside of the house, then saw her in the kitchen starting to wash the dishes in the sink. Then Jane saw Maloney step in. This time Jane could see that what he was carrying was a short-barreled pump shotgun. The sight of it made Jane sick. She knew what he would do with it if he met resistance. If Sarah tried to run, or if someone tried to drag her away, Maloney could hardly miss. There wouldn't be much chance of her surviving.

Jane couldn't see a simple way to get Sarah out of the house without getting her killed. If Jane got the right angle, she could probably shoot Maloney in the head and kill him before he killed Sarah. But then Sarah would still be in the kitchen when Gorman and Wylie raced in, guns drawn.

Jane walked carefully along the side of the house, moving from window to window to determine exactly where Gorman and Wylie were. She had to make whatever move she was going to make before Sarah finished with the chores. When she was done, they would almost certainly make her more difficult to rescue—maybe with the shotgun and maybe by tying or chaining her to something immovable, with someone close enough to kill her.

At least they didn't seem to have harmed her yet. She looked all right. Jane thought carefully as she searched for Wylie and Gorman. If she could find them in one place close together, she might be able to take them both out. She could fire without warning, take the first one through the head, and then immediately fire several rounds at the other, who would be a moving target by then. If she got the second one, she could move around the corner of the house to the kitchen window, and maybe shoot Maloney from behind as he stepped to the other room to see what had happened. Sarah had seemed smart when she had visited Jane. She could only hope that Sarah was also alert enough to know that when shooting started she should duck and run from a man with a shotgun. But Jane knew it was a terrible plan. It depended on so many unlikely breaks. She craned her neck to see if anyone was in the living room to her left.

"Hold it." The voice was Wylie's terrible Texas drawl.

Jane turned her head slowly in the direction of the voice. She could see him at the corner of the house to her left. Only his right arm and gun hand and his right eye were visible. Jane was standing in front of a lighted window, her body not even turned far enough toward Wylie to see him clearly, let alone take her gun out of her pocket, aim, and fire at him. Her right leg was still weak from the wound in her thigh, and she couldn't hope to run fast enough to avoid getting shot.

Jane threw her body backward between the bushes, rolled and pushed her gun into the center of a thick, dense yew bush, then kept crawling back away from the house and the light.

Wylie fired once and hit a tree, exploding particles of bark above her. Then he fired low and to the side, missing her again and spattering dirt in the air. "Last chance. You've got no place to go."

Jane's heart beat harder with anticipation. That was exactly the impression she wanted him to have—that she was unarmed and helpless. She stood and raised both hands in the air.

"That's right," Wylie said. "Much better." In the corner of her eye she saw him come slowly around the house. His gun was still aimed at her, but his body was fully visible now. "Let's walk slowly to the front door."

Jane took two steps forward, and that brought her up to the low yew bush where she had hidden her gun. In a moment she would drop to her left knee, snatch her gun from the bush, turn, and fire. One more step.

"Not that way." It was a second voice, coming from the opposite direction. It was Maloney. "Over this way toward the light."

They had her in a cross fire. Maloney was aiming his gun at her with both hands, and he had a perfect view of her back, with nothing to shield her. Jane's heart dropped to her stomach. She had told herself she would never let herself be taken alive by these men again. The reason she had taken such a foolish risk was that she didn't want Sarah to be in their hands as she had been. Now they had not only Sarah, but her. She should have shot Gorman through the window as soon as she'd seen him, and taken her chances with the others. If she picked up the gun now, they would kill her in a second.

"Come on. What's it going to be?"

Jane stepped past the yew bush toward the light, her hands in the air. She had just thrown her life away, and probably Sarah's, too.

The front door opened before she reached it, and Maloney came up behind her and put his hand in the center of her spine. He pushed her in. Jane saw Sarah across the room, standing with her back to the wall with Gorman, who held the shotgun on her.

Jane stared straight ahead so she could hold all three men in her peripheral vision and detect any sudden movement. She would get another chance, she told herself. She only had to be ready to take it. And her gun was still a secret. It was in the yew tree with its safety off and a round in the chamber so all she had to do was grasp it and pull the trigger.

The next few minutes were unbearable. It was worse because this time she knew all of it before it happened. Wylie and Maloney searched her together, roughly and with no restraint. Jane made sure to seem as weak and injured as possible, to be barely able to stand. When she thought it was over, Wyle knelt and lifted her pants legs to be sure she didn't have a boot knife. He ran a finger around the inner elastic of her socks to be sure there was nothing else, then stood. She knew that as soon as they had reassured themselves that she had no weapons, they would begin with, "Where's Shelby?" They would go on from where they had left off in Los Angeles. She knew every painful sensation that was coming, every stifled wave of fear.

"Where is Shelby right now?" Wylie asked. "I'm sure Sarah would like to hear about her brother."

"I don't know," Jane said. "I was supposed to meet him in Salt Lake City. Because of you, I got there late and he had already left. I thought this would be the first place he'd come." She braced for a punch.

Wylie grasped her shoulders so hard she winced from the pain, and looked into her eyes as though he were searching for the truth. Then, surprisingly, he shrugged and pushed her. She fell, as though she could barely stand.

"What?" Jane said.

"You're probably right. He seems to be the sort of guy who will travel across the country and end up here at some point. I'm not surprised that you're faster at it than he is. He's not a pro like you."

While Maloney watched her, Wylie stepped into the kitchen and returned with a length of rope and a roll of duct tape. He tied her wrists in front of her with rope, then wrapped duct tape around the wrists and covered the knot so she couldn't untie it or slip out of it. Then he knelt and took a second length of rope and tied it around her ankles, so she could take a stride of only about a foot.

He stood and looked at her. "That ought to do it. With that bullet hole in you, I guess you won't get in too much trouble."

Jane gave him a frightened, defeated look, but she was elated. He had missed the two razor blades taped to her feet under her socks.

Wylie said, "You're wondering why I'm not worried about Shelby anymore."

She looked as though her immediate predicament left little room for caring. "A little."

He put his face close to hers. "Because he's practically dead already. The cops will get him in the next few days, probably, and if they don't, we know he'll turn up here eventually. You're the one we're thinking about. Now that we've caught you, we'll be able to take the next few years off." He turned. "Hey, Gorman. You're the best kiss-ass we have. Give our esteemed employer a call and tell him what we've got."

Gorman pulled his cell phone out of the pocket of his jeans and walked out of the room through the short hallway into the kitchen. His voice could be heard muttering and mumbling through a conversation that took place mostly on the other end.

Wylie said, "This is going to be about you."

"What about me?"

"It's the auction I was trying to get arranged when we were in Los Angeles. As soon as he gets the bidders here, we'll go ahead with it. Since you showed up, Jim Shelby is a minor worry for him."

"I thought you said you weren't interested in Shelby anymore, and you'd let the cops arrest him. Why is he a worry at all? You could let Sarah go, and forget trying to trap Shelby. He can't harm you."

"We can't just drop it, because that's the way our employer is. It's what made him rich. He doesn't leave things to chance; he makes sure."

"Why Shelby?"

Wylie moved close to her ear and said quietly, "Because our boss is the one who killed Shelby's wife."

Jane heard Sarah Shelby's indrawn breath. She must have heard what he'd said, even though it was close to a whisper. Jane kept her face expressionless. "What for?"

Wylie shrugged. "Beats me. He wanted her for a while, and then I guess he didn't." He smiled. "That's just an observation. He doesn't talk about his love life to me."

Gorman came back into the living room, putting his phone back in his pocket, and Wylie stepped away from Jane.

"What did he say?" asked Wylie.

"He's happy. I think he's going to have a party or something. He kept saying we'd get part of the take."

Wylie took Jane into the bathroom. "Stay in here for a few minutes. Don't try anything, and don't come out until I let you out." Jane stood in the bathroom, her ear to the door.

"How much?" It was Wylie's voice.

"He didn't say anything you can get a grip on. He said half, then he said, 'You'll get a slice,' and then it didn't sound like enough, so he said, 'a big slice for the three of you.'"

"Shit. Sounds like ten percent," said Maloney.

"Sounds like ten each," Wylie said. "If we got a million for her, we'd keep a hundred grand each. That's not bad."

Jane considered trying to say something that would undermine their confidence, but she sensed she would only make them angry. She wanted them to see her as weaker and more debilitated than she was. The best she could hope was that their greed and their distrust of the boss would offer some opportunity later.

Maloney said, "When's this auction going to be?"

"Tomorrow night," Gorman said. "He doesn't want her on our hands for too long."

Wylie said, "I'm pretty sure we can handle that."

"If you disagree, call him. He's not afraid we can't hold on to her. He's afraid if the word gets out, people big enough to kill us might take her for their own auction. If she's been at this for long enough, she could have pissed off just about anybody."

Wylie paused for a moment. "All right. There's not much point in arguing with him."

Jane was beginning to feel more anxious. If the auction was going to happen tomorrow night, there was very little time. She had to find an opening and get herself and Sarah out of this house.

Then Wylie said, "I want to keep the women separate. Let's keep this one in the living room. I'll go tie Sarah in the bedroom where she's been sleeping. Whoever's awake on the next shift can come and check on her every hour or so. I don't want anybody messing with her, though."

Gorman chuckled.

"I'm not kidding," Wylie said. "We've got people coming tomorrow, and then we've got to ask her some questions. One thing at a time."

"I agree," said Maloney. "What we ought to be thinking about is if somebody shows up early to take the other one away from us."

A few minutes later, Wylie opened the bathroom door and let her out. Jane was never alone. There was always someone sitting within a few feet of her, and she was always secured to an immovable object. Now and then, when one of the men had to use the bathroom, they would untie her wrists and let her go afterward. She would get there in an exaggerated limp, as though her leg were useless. On the first trip, she got the razor blade out of her right sock and retaped it to her back just below the belt, but she didn't try to escape. There was always a rope tied around her neck and draped out the door, so she couldn't get out a window. When she came out, they would tie her wrists to the free beam above the living room.

Hours passed, the sky brightened, and then it was too late to think of slipping away into darkness. Jane was tired, but the men all seemed to be fresh and alert. She knew the impression had to be an illusion, but it made her more wary. The men would not free Jane's hands even for a few minutes to help Sarah, who had to do all of the cooking and serving and cleaning alone. There was no chance to speak with her. As the day went on, the three men became more tense and nervous. They were always up, standing by a window to look out, checking their guns, or going out to the road to watch for suspicious cars.

And then, slowly, the sun went down again. Jane had remained quiet and watchful all day, and never had a chance to make an escape attempt. Then, at just after nine in the evening, Wylie's cell phone rang. He spoke a few sentences in a low voice, his face turned away from her. But finally he said, "I'll see you in a few minutes." He pressed the disconnect button and called out, "The first one's here. Get ready, everybody."

Gorman sat Sarah on a kitchen chair in the living room and untied her wrists so she could serve drinks if they were needed. Her ankles were still tied about a foot apart so she couldn't run. Maloney and Wylie moved furniture so all the seats faced the front of the living room.

Gorman took the shotgun and went out the back door of the house. Jane knew he would take up a position among the trees outside so he could guard against someone taking Jane by force. After a short time, Wylie's telephone buzzed again, and he had the same kind of conversation. "Come ahead. We'll be ready to start within a half hour." Several more times in the next few minutes, he received calls. Each time, Jane felt her chances to escape fading.

There was a knock at the front door and Maloney went to answer it while Wylie pulled Jane out of the living room into Sarah's room. He sat on the bed and let her sit, too.

"Why are we in here?"

"A little suspense might jack up the price. You need to make an entrance."

They sat in silence and listened to the sounds of men arriving, coming into the living room, and being seated by Maloney. Jane thought she heard him say "Welcome" about eight or nine times. A few minutes passed, and then Gorman appeared at the bedroom door. "They're all inside, all gathered in the living room. It doesn't look like anybody's prepared any tricks ahead of time."

"Good," said Wylie. "Go back and keep an eye on them, and we'll be there in a minute." He sat on the bed beside Jane, studying the floor in silence. She assumed that he was trying to think of a safe way to divert some of the money from the auction. Finally he stood. "Let's go."

He clutched Jane's arm and pulled her roughly up the hall into the living room. She limped as though her right leg were paralyzed and as if she were in terrible pain. While they had been out of the living room someone had brought a low, thick-legged round coffee table that was about a foot and a half high and set it under the free ceiling beam. Wylie saw it and said, "Up there." He could see she could never do that with her ankles tied, so he took the rope off her ankles and half-lifted her onto the table, but her hands were tied behind her. She stood there, looking ahead at the far wall. There was a loud wave of murmuring and whispering. She looked down, first at Wylie's sardonic smirk, and then let her eyes rise a bit to survey the audience.

Ranged around her on three sides she saw men whom she recognized. Near the front was Rhonda Eckersly's ex-husband. She hadn't seen him in fifteen years, but he looked at her with eyes that seemed almost inhuman, eager and hungry. There was Phil Barraclough, the brother of the man she had killed in the snow outside the deserted factory. He looked like his brother, but his face was unmoving and pitiless, just a mask of patient hatred. She looked away to keep track of her captors. There was Maloney, who was watching the door, and Gorman, who seemed nervous and eager to be finished with her and gone.

Wylie lifted his arm up and gestured at her. "There she is, gentlemen. She's the one you've all been searching for, and we have her once again. I'll bet when you first learned about her, you all thought you were hunting for someone else who had run away from you. But by now you know that she's the one you really should have hunted. The people you wanted didn't hide themselves. She did it. She knows their new names and where they are right now, because she made up the names and took them there."

"Come on, Wylie," said Gorman. "The sooner you start the bidding—"

"What's the hurry?"

"Every cop in the country is looking for her. So let's get her sold and on her way before we all get put away."

Wylie frowned at him, but seemed to relent. "Gentlemen, I'd like to hear some bids."

She saw the bidders lined up before her, and it was like an inventory of her nightmares. She looked at Rhonda Eckersly's husband, and felt a wave of nausea. Rhonda had tried to leave him because of his cruelty. He was from an old southern family with lots of money and influence, so when she ran away, he simply reported her car stolen, and the police brought her back. He had put an iron ring in the floor of their living room and kept her chained to it by the neck. When he was tired of hurting her, he invited some like-minded friends and let each of them have a turn. Jane had taken her out of the world at least fifteen years ago. She had a new name, was married to a man who cherished her, and had two boys and a girl who were growing up fast. Every year she sent Jane an unsigned card that had something to do with "Indian Summer" from a different city to let her know she was still safe.

Eckersly looked old now, his cheeks sunken like an unwrapped mummy. He said, "A million."

Wylie frowned. "The bidding has begun at a million. And all the bidder wants is a chance to convince this woman that she made a mistake. Remember, everybody. She knows where somebody you want is hiding. But she also knows where somebody *he* wants is." He pointed at Eckersly. "And where somebody *he* wants is." He pointed at Phil Barraclough, the brother of the man she had shot.

Barraclough raised his hand. "Two million."

"I hear two million," said Wylie. "I want to remind everyone that all bids must refer to cash money. No checks, real estate, stocks, bonds, or precious stones; no gold or business partnerships." He looked around. "If you outbid

Mr. Eckersly and Mr. Barraclough, you know they'll each pay you a couple of million to get the use of her, and find out what she did with someone they're hunting for. And you'll still have her."

The bidders looked at each other, as though each were trying to assess how much the others might pay. Grady Lee Beard said, "Three million."

Jane said, "You don't have that much."

Wylie's right arm straightened and he hit her, a punch on the jaw. The punch knocked Jane to the side, so she fell off the table, but Gorman leaped forward to catch her before she hit the floor in the midst of the bidders. Wylie shook his hand and blew on the knuckles as though they hurt him.

Grady Lee Beard said to Jane, "I'll have that and plenty more after I get you. I know a dozen guys like these who will pay big for a chance to talk to you. They just don't know we've got you yet."

"I've got a bid of three million," Wylie said. "You bidders might also think about the fact that she doesn't just know about somebody you're hunting for. She knows about *you*. She knows whatever her client knows about you—anything you might have done that wasn't strictly legal, and even what we're doing now. You can be sure she never tells any secrets that could put you away. Buying her is the only way to buy your safety. Her new owner will get every one of your secrets. What will it cost you to be sure that Mr. Beard, here, guards those secrets?"

"Four million," Eckersly said.

"Four million to you, gentlemen. This is a slave market. Once you own her, you can do anything you want with her. If you hate her, you can show her how much pain can be inflicted on a person before she dies. Or you can find out what you want and then resell her to the next customer for a profit. Whoever wins the bidding tonight reaps the benefits, because she'll only get more valuable. Any more bids? Do I hear five?"

There was silence. Some of the men in the room stared at Jane, as though they were trying to read her mind and determine how much the contents of her memory were worth. She refused to let them make eye contact.

"The last bid was Mr. Eckersly at four million. Final offer?"

The silence took on a resentful, shamefaced quality, the bidders looking down at their shoes rather than at Wylie. "Mr. Maloney, call our employer and see what he thinks of four million."

Maloney dialed a cell phone and spoke into it. "Hello, sir. The bidding is now at four million, and no counterbid. Is that an acceptable price?" There was a pause while he listened. "Thank you, sir. I'll tell them." He put his phone in his coat pocket. "I'm sorry, gentlemen. At four million the price is not high enough. Our employer has submitted a token bid of eight million dollars. He's going to give you one final chance to do better. If nobody beats eight million, he'll take her off the market."

Phil Barraclough said, "I thought the rule was that you had to bring your stakes and pay off at the end of the auction."

"That's right," Wylie said.

"You're telling me that you've got eight million here in this house?"

Wylie shook his head. "We brought the merchandise for him. She's worth eight million."

"That's just bullshit," said Barraclough. "He's wasting our time. He's not going to sell her."

"If that's how you feel, I can't say I blame you for dropping out. If anyone wants to go on with the auction, the bidding will start again at eight million."

"When do we have to hand over the money?" asked Beard.

"When we get the cash, you'll get her. But we've got to be gone in twenty-four hours, so it'll have to be before then."

Beard looked around him at the others. "All right. I want to be in on this. There are people I've been looking for, and she knows where they are. I have two million in cash in this backpack. If a couple of you want to go in with me, we can get together and make eight million."

The other bidders were silent. Two million was clearly not a big enough percentage to make them risk an ongoing partnership with Grady Lee Beard. He was tall and rangy, with very light skin that had the ability to hold scars as raised pink lines, so the history of his dealings with others was written on his face.

Wylie said, "Our employer doesn't care how you get together, or who contributes what. All he wants is that we go home with upwards of eight million, and somebody else goes home with the woman."

A few of the bidders whispered together and there were muttered expletives, but no deal seemed to be concluded. There were frustrated scowls in parts of the room, as several bidders whose pitches had been rejected looked for each other in the crowd.

"Eight million and one thousand."

The whispering and murmuring stopped. One by one, the men in the room found the source of the words. Jane felt sick.

"Is that a bid?" asked Wylie. "I believe we have a bid. It's eight million, one thousand dollars. Does everybody hear the bid?"

The murmuring increased again, and this time Jane could see that the men were talking faster. There was some desperation as they tried to cobble together instant alliances to beat the bid. After a few more seconds, the side conversations died out and the men's attention was on Wylie. "Mr. Eckersly has bid eight million one thousand." Wylie was much more animated, and Jane could tell he must be delighted. His cut would be eight hundred thousand.

"Let's get our boss on the phone," Wylie said, looking at Gorman.

Gorman leaned into the alcove that led to the kitchen and talked into his phone rapidly, with his free hand covering his ear so he could hear above the hum of side conversations. He nodded and said "Okay." He held the phone up so his boss could hear, and called out, "The bid is in range. He doesn't want to beat it."

This set off some more conferring as aggressive bidders tried once more to put together partnerships.

Wylie let it go on for a few minutes, until the voices began to die off. "I have a bid of eight million and one thousand. Do I have any other bids? Does anyone want to beat eight million and one thousand? Any bids for the woman who has hidden so many people for so long?" He stood tall, moving to look over the heads of the nearby bidders who had been walking around to talk to others. "No bids? Then it's going . . . going . . . gone! For eight million one thousand to Mr. Eckersly."

The men who were still seated all seemed to pop up at once and mill around the room talking to the others. Between two of them Jane could see Eckersly sitting in his chair with a smile just barely lifting the corners of his lips. He suddenly seemed to be aware of her, and his eyes turned to settle on her and the smile broadened. The effect was like looking into an open coffin and seeing the corpse open its eyes and the face powder at its mouth wrinkle and crack as it smiled.

Jane knew terrible things about Eckersly. Rhonda had been twenty-five when Jane had taken her away, and Eckersly had been in his late forties. Now he was in his mid-sixties, but he looked ancient. The people in this room probably all thought that he was an astute speculator who would make a profit by forcing her to betray the people Beard and Barraclough and the others wanted, and then kill her for simple revenge. Jane knew him better than that. After all these years he wanted Rhonda back. He wanted to drag her to the same room and renew her torment where he had been interrupted, and then he wanted to do the same to Jane. He was a sadist, and simple murder would not be enough after fifteen years of waiting. He would prefer to keep them both alive for months, maybe years.

Jane saw a few of the bidders begin to leave. Some seemed angry at particular men who had not seen fit to join an alliance. Others looked merely tired and frustrated. She saw Wylie and Gorman make their way through the group to talk to Eckersly. She hoped there would be a delay, a problem of some kind with the cash. He had a large hard-sided case that sat between his feet. Was it big enough to hold eight million dollars?

Wylie and Gorman were obviously thinking the same thing. Jane looked around her for Maloney, and she found him near the front door, watching the bidders filing out. As she watched, she saw Ronald Hanlon stop at the door, give her a smirk, and then blow her a kiss.

She looked away as he stepped outside, and she had to keep herself from shuddering. She hadn't thought about him in years. When she had crossed his path, he had been a trafficker in women from eastern Europe. His business was buying groups of them from a fake employment agency based in Kiev, and promising them jobs in the United States. In order to get into the country they had to sign loan papers for his high fees, and then swear to false answers on what they thought were immigration papers, but were just requests for tourist visas. When they arrived he kept them in isolation and forced them to work as prostitutes for two or three years until they paid off his fees. One of them who had served her indenture had come to Jane to ask for help to get her sister away. Jane had managed to get a dozen other girls out with the sister and into new lives. Hanlon had apparently been waiting for a chance for revenge.

As the rest of the bidders left, Jane looked at each one and remembered. It occurred to her that in this small house tonight there had been only a few whom she didn't know to be killers. The few faces Jane had never seen before had simply been speculators in misery, professional hunters who had heard of Jane's existence and shown up to see if she could be had for a reasonable price.

Now the bidders were all outside, and Maloney stood beside the front door looking out the small window set into it, with the shotgun in his hands. He was watching to be sure the disappointed men really were getting into cars and driving off. She looked at Wylie and Gorman, who were still occupied with Eckersly and his suitcase. Jane did her best to look weak and in pain. Finally she stepped down from the low table and then sat on it. Wylie noticed, but it didn't seem to worry him. It didn't matter if she couldn't stand up on the table anymore, because the sale had been made. He looked down at Eckersly and listened to something he was saying.

"You can't seriously expect me to sit here all night watching you count my money."

Wylie said, "What we're going to do is count out a hundred thousand in hundreds and weigh it. Then we're going to weigh the rest of it, a bunch at a time. And we're going to look at it while we do that. So if there's something wrong, tell me now."

"There's nothing wrong with it," Eckersly said. "This is four million. The other four million is in Jack Killigan's car. He's sitting up the road waiting for my call, and he'll bring in the rest of the money anytime you want."

"I'm just giving you fair warning. If we find a one-dollar bill, you'd better be able to make it a hundred. If we find blank paper cut to dollar size, we'll kill you. Got it?"

"You have no reason to talk to me like that. I came here and bid in good faith."

"If you pay in good faith, too, you've got nothing to worry about."

Jane felt the tension building in her chest. She had been waiting for a chance, an opening, an opportunity, for two days, but Wylie and his friends had never seemed to lose their interest in watching her. She had always been in their sight, tethered and hobbled by ropes. But now she sensed that her chance was coming. The men weren't watching her now. They were watching each other.

Jane's eyes moved to Gorman, who was at the front window with his hand on his pistol. She saw the watchful look on his face, then looked at Maloney, who was still standing at the front door. He had the same stern look, almost squinting to be sure he missed nothing that was going on outside. They were on guard, but not guarding Jane anymore. Then she realized that they were right to be anxious.

The house had just been visited by fifteen or twenty men who had killed people and were engaged in trying to find other victims who had eluded them. All of them knew that each of the others was carrying a lot of money—enough to bid in a million-dollar auction. Somebody was going to be attacked for that money, and it had to happen in the next few minutes, before the bidders dispersed. Jane retrieved the razor blade from the waistband of her pants and sawed through the rope that held her hands. She kept the hands together behind her.

Jane focused her eyes on Sarah Shelby, and Sarah understood that it was a summons. She edged close to Jane with her hobbled legs. Jane whispered, "In a minute there will be gunfire. When it happens, I'll be running. You'll have to stick close to me."

"How can—"

"Sit."

Jane put the razor blade behind her on the table, where only Sarah could see it. Sarah sat on the table beside her, picked up the blade, held it behind her back while she adjusted her grip on it, then bent to tie her shoe while she sliced through the rope that held her ankles close together to prevent her from running. In one motion she sat up and set the blade behind her near Jane.

Jane picked it up, keeping both hands out of sight behind her back.

Suddenly all thought was obliterated as the world seemed to explode into deafening noise and flashes of light. Glass from the dining room window blasted into the house and peppered the hardwood floor. There was thumping as someone ran up the hallway near the back of the house. There was firing outside, but it was impossible to tell who was shooting at whom.

Eckersly half-rose from his chair and then collapsed to the floor, bleeding. There was random fire from the direction of the dining room as someone emptied a magazine in the general direction of the men standing near Eckersly's suitcase. Wylie and Gorman drew their pistols and fired a half dozen shots each at the opening in the window.

Maloney raised his shotgun to his shoulder and flung open the front door, then fired into the night. He pumped the shotgun and stepped back as Jane hurled herself toward him. Instead of letting go of the gun and fighting his much smaller attacker, he tried to swing the barrel around to shoot her. She was less than a foot away from him when she slashed the razor blade down the side of his neck, just below his jawbone. He dropped the shotgun and grasped his throat with both hands as though he could hold it together and save himself, but the blood spurted out between his fingers while Jane moved past him to the front door.

He collapsed to the floor as she ran out into the night with Sarah beside her.

Jane ran to the yew bush where she had left her gun, knelt and grasped it, then raised it in both hands and spun around just in time to see Gorman come out the front door after her. She fired at his chest. He jerked backward, but still stood, so she fired twice more. The second shot went high through his throat, and the third hit the center of his chest. Jane could hear volleys of shots from somewhere up the road. The bidders must be fighting each other for the cash they'd brought.

She turned to look in the front window of the house, but she saw only Eckersly lying on the floor. She pivoted and followed Sarah to the left front corner of the house. She had not seen Wylie yet, and she couldn't go anywhere while he was alive. "Stay here," she whispered, and cautiously made her way along the side of the house to the back corner. Lying there was the body of Ronald Hanlon, probably shot through the dining room window by Wylie or Gorman. She stepped around it and aimed at the back steps by the kitchen door, but the door was already wide open and there was nobody to be seen. She advanced toward the garage quickly, trying to get there in time. She heard a car start, and knew she was too late. She heard the car squealing out of the garage, then kicking gravel up from the long driveway.

Jane hurried past the house to the driveway, and saw the big blue Ford Crown Victoria speeding down the narrow drive with its lights off. She used both hands to steady her aim, and fired four times. She punched a hole in the trunk, then the back window shattered and the car wobbled from side to side, but it didn't stop. The car reached the end of the driveway, swung out onto the highway, and drove out of her sight.

The gunfire out on the road had stopped. Some sets of robbers must have triumphed and left, and the losers were probably dead. Jane stepped to the kitchen door. She moved carefully down the short hallway to the living room, and found what she had expected. Maloney was lying by the door. The blood that had pumped out through his severed carotid artery had run all over the hardwood floor into a pool, then stopped when his heart did. Outside the front door she could see Gorman's body on the porch. Eckersly was sprawled on the floor where she had seen him fall. His suitcase of money was gone. And so was Wylie.

12

Jane drove south out of Ithaca, heading for Route 17, the Southern Tier Expressway. Sarah sat beside her for a few minutes in silence, then said, "I can't believe we're alive."

Jane said, "We did what we could do, and didn't make any mistakes, so here we are. I can only hope it lasts. We're going to have to be very careful, and find a place where you can stay put for a while."

Sarah didn't seem to hear. "And now I know who murdered Susan."

"Yes. The man Wylie and his men were working for, whoever that is. It was pretty obvious before, but Wylie admitted that much."

"But I know the name. Right after they broke into the house and captured me, Wylie told Gorman to call the boss and tell him. When Gorman called, somebody else answered, and Gorman asked for Daniel Martel."

"Are you sure about the name?"

"Yes. Absolutely. I could never get that wrong, and I'll never forget."

"Now that you've told me, neither will I."

Jane brought Sarah into Buffalo, and then to the Hyatt hotel. She parked a short distance up the street near the convention center, because there was a pay telephone on the outer wall. She got out and called the hotel room. After a few rings, Iris answered the telephone. "Hello."

"Hi, honey. You know who this is."

"Yes," said Iris. "We've been worried about you. What happened?"

"It took longer than I thought."

"What time is it?"

"It's about three a.m. I've got Sarah with me. What I want you to do is wake Jim if he's asleep, and get the two of you packed up. Then I want you to wipe every smooth surface of the room for fingerprints. When you're satisfied, fill in the quick checkout card, put the key cards in it, and drop it in the box. Don't forget to wipe off the key cards and the checkout card. Then come out to the street."

"Uh, okay. Jim? Time to get up."

"Good. Get going." Jane ended the call and looked at Sarah, and she was glad Sarah was standing by the car and she'd had the phone clamped to her ear so Sarah couldn't hear. At three a.m. Iris had been asleep so close to Jim that she'd only needed to speak a bit above a whisper, and probably touch him.

Jane got back in the car and made a circuit of the block before she pulled to a stop a few yards up the street from the hotel where she could see the front entrance. She thought about her decision to leave Iris and Jim alone in a hotel tonight. In retrospect, it seemed obvious that she was leaving them in a position that was likely to lead to intimacy. She decided not to tell Sarah anything.

In fifteen minutes, Jim and Iris appeared just inside the hotel entrance, and Jane started the car and began to move. As the two came out the glass doors, her car pulled up the driveway and stopped under the overhang. Jane popped the trunk lid, and Jim put the two suitcases in the trunk.

The two got into the back seat, and Jane began to move. Jim said, "Sarah. I'm so glad to see you."

"I'm glad to see you, too. It's the first time in years when I saw you wearing regular clothes."

"This is Iris. Iris, this is my sister, Sarah."

Sarah looked at Iris for a moment, made a decision to smile, and said, "Pleased to meet you."

"Me too," said Iris. She decided to smile, too.

Jane drove out the driveway and down the street, and headed south away from the center of the city of Buffalo.

Jim said, "Where are we going?"

Jane said, "I'd like each of you to think for a moment. Is there any good reason why any of you can't live in Pittsburgh?"

"What sort of reason?" Sarah asked.

"You didn't go to college there, or have a favorite aunt who lives there. You didn't once have a job there, or have a former fiancé who lives there. Nobody who looks closely at your past will find any reference to Pittsburgh."

"Not me. I don't know much about the place, really," said Jim. The others looked at each other, but said nothing.

"Perfect," Jane said. "We'll go take a look. We'll be there in a few hours."

"What are we going to do there?" asked Iris.

"We'll find a nice house, probably in the suburbs, and then we'll begin the next phase."

"What's that?"

"Trying to create a new normal. Pittsburgh may not be the place you stay for the rest of your lives. But it's the real thing, a city where there are jobs and everything a person needs to live a good life. There are over three hundred thousand people in the city itself, and two and a half million in the general area around it. You've gotten used to using new names and being alert. We've changed your looks a little. Now you live. When you get good at it, and your permanent ID catches up with you, then you'll be ready for anything—finding jobs, making a few casual acquaintances. We'll take all of this slowly."

"How long will it take?" Sarah asked.

"A few months. Six, probably, to get you settled. Of course, you always have to be ready to get out fast, if something makes you nervous. Then we'll replant you somewhere else and start over."

"What makes you think we're ready for this?" Shelby said.

"You've all got the basic tricks, and you've practiced a bit. You don't break character, and you never forget you're in danger. The part that's important is to remember that you can never go back to being the people you used to be, even for a minute, and you can never drop your guard. The rest is refinements."

"Like what?"

"Pay attention to appearances, always. If you must meet people, you smile. If people like you, they're not suspicious. You keep yourself in places where you're relatively safe. You go to plays and chamber music concerts, not sports events where there will be a thousand cops and fifty TV cameras. Every step is slow. You aren't in a hurry. Every day you're alive and unnoticed moves the odds over to your side a tiny bit. For the moment, let Iris be the one who deals with strangers, with Sarah as the backup. As time goes by and you get more settled, Jim can get out more."

Jane, Iris, and Sarah checked into a big hotel in Pittsburgh, then went to search for apartments while Jim stayed in the hotel out of sight.

After two days of searching, they drove to a residential neighborhood on the outskirts of town, where several sets of duplexes had been built. There were perfect, thick lawns that they could see had been laid in as sod like strips of carpet. There were two trees per lawn, roughly fifteen feet tall, planted with a backhoe that moved from building to building, all landscaping completed in an afternoon.

They toured the model duplex, and Jane, Sarah, and Iris were intrigued. The hardwood floors were perfect blond wood, the crown moldings were eight or ten inches to give the ceilings a vaulted look. The counters were all granite, and the cooking island was exactly like the ones in the home magazines. The master bathroom had a deep tub with jets, and the shower was surrounded by glass and had multiple heads, as though a team were going to use it.

Jane told the rental agent that she and Sarah and Iris would have to think about it. As they drove off, Sarah said, "Is that kind of place a real possibility?"

"It's leading the league right now," Jane said. "It's upscale, the sort of place that won't have lots of surprise police visits—or worse, surveillance. The place is so new you can smell the paint, so everyone will be a stranger, and nobody will be suspicious if you don't know your way around Pittsburgh."

"Let's talk to Jim."

They took the apartment. They paid the first and last months' rent with an electronic transfer from a Chicago bank account Jane held in the name Heather Gollensz.

Jane helped Iris and Sarah shop and decorate the apartment. They registered a sale of the Honda in the name John Leland, and got Pennsylvania plates. Other electronic transfers gave the Lelands a bank account, and Iris another. On the fifth morning in the new apartment, when Sarah emerged from her room on her way to the kitchen, she saw that Jane was sitting in the living room, fully dressed, with her suitcase at her feet.

"You're going?"

Jane nodded. "It's time."

"I guess I felt it coming."

Jane said, "I left the things you'll need on the counter in the kitchen—a lot of cash, another gun, and some ammunition I brought with us from Ithaca. As soon as the permanent IDs and things show up in my post office box, a man will call me, and I'll pick them up and send them to you. Remember, the best way to keep from making a mistake is to stay scared."

There was a short, tentative honk of a car horn.

Jane stood up and moved the curtain aside, then let it drop. "That's my cab. I was going to say good-bye to Jim and Iris, too, but you'll have to do it." She hugged Sarah. "I'll see you before too long." She took her suitcase and went out the door. Sarah watched her get into the cab and then saw the cab moving off down the street toward the highway.

13

Dr. Carey McKinnon had performed his first surgery of the day at seven in the morning. It had been a relatively routine removal of a gallbladder with no complications, and as of his evening rounds, Mr. Gryzkowski and all of his other patients had been recovering well. He had completed four surgeries today, five yesterday. If he kept up this pace, he would probably catch the attention of the Medicare people who looked for false billings.

For the two weeks since Jane had left, he had been fully scheduling his mornings with surgeries, then spending the afternoons seeing patients in his office. He ate his meals in the hospital cafeteria and went through his rounds in the evening. Then he left to drive to Amherst and put his car in the old converted carriage house next to Jane's car, and then walk up the driveway to enter his dark, empty house. Each night he did exercises for an hour, showered, and watched the news on television before he collapsed into bed.

Staying busy was the best thing he could think of to do. There was no question that the tall, dark-haired woman on the television news who had freed a convicted killer from the Los Angeles courthouse was Jane. It hurt Carey to know that she would do something crazy and audacious now. It meant that she not only was willing to risk her life but had been willing to risk his, too—or at least his chance for happiness.

What she did was illegal—buying or making false identities; obtaining and carrying unlicensed guns; operating imaginary companies to commit mail fraud, wire fraud, money laundering. But what kept him in a constant state of anxiety was the danger. The service she offered was to put herself between killers and their victims. He could understand some of this as part of her family history and traditions—the glorification of the warrior, the horror of incarceration and confinement, the contempt for fear, the peculiar Native American notion of changing names to fit new circumstances, the well-founded distrust of government. He understood all of these things and their origins. But comprehending the logic of a situation was not the same as accepting it. He hated this.

The idea that his beautiful wife had for years before their marriage harbored and transported fugitives had always made him sweat with retroactive fear for her. The fact that she was doing it again made him frantic. She helped fugitives out of a kind of idiosyncratic public-spiritedness. To her, saving people from danger was just something a person did, if she happened to have the skills.

The difference between public duty and personal responsibility was utterly lost on her. The idea that only duly sworn peace officers were supposed to save people from criminals struck her as absurd. She had said, "Fine. I'll do it only when they can't, or won't." The only difference she could see between herself and the authorities was mere legality, and she had no regard whatever for legality. When she heard someone talking about "obeying the law," it was as though he had announced he lived his life according to the rules of mah-jongg or gin rummy.

He loved her. He was never going to end the marriage, and everything else was empty chatter. He had not even asked her to quit. She had simply promised. It was just before their wedding, maybe two weeks. She had been on the road, and come home safely. She said to him, "Well, that's over. I'm through being a guide. If I'm going to marry you, I can't do that anymore."

She had stopped. She had turned her attention to the sorts of things that surgeons' wives did. She helped raise money for the hospital. First she took her turn serving on committees where her job was to fold letters and type envelopes, and slowly moved up to chairing committees and putting on benefits. She became active on the Tonawanda reservation and taught an after-school class in the Seneca language for middle-school students. Jane had become the ideal middle-class married woman of two generations ago. He had tried to talk to her about her decision, but she didn't seem to be sensitive about it. She said, "I took a lot of people out of the world and made new people turn up in other places. I'm glad I did. Now the last person I have to make disappear is me. There is no Jane Whitefield. I'm Mrs. Carey McKinnon."

After three years, she had announced it was probably safe to have a baby. Nobody had found his way to the house in Deganawida, nobody had arrived from some faraway place asking for Jane Whitefield, and no word had come that one of her old runners had been found. She had chosen the room next to theirs in the big old stone house that would be the baby's room. They had painted it a pale yellow with bright woodwork and crown moldings, and bought furnishings, and even a few stuffed animals. She had gone to the attic in the Deganawida house and brought back an antique cradleboard. She had taken it from a box and unwrapped its paper wrappings and shown it to him before she'd hung it up. It was made of a frame of half loops of bent hickory like ribs, and had a few wooden hoops at the top like a canopy to protect the baby from sun and rain. The frame was covered by a skin of beadwork. The background was black, with a pattern of green stems and leaves topped by forest wildflowers in white, red, and yellow. Carey could see it was very old, too old to be anywhere but a museum, but he said nothing except that it was beautiful. She hung it on a wall with a picture hanger, a substitute for the way a seventeenth-century ancestor had hung it in a longhouse while she was inside, and on a low tree limb while she worked in the fields or orchards.

They had tried to have a baby for two years, but so far, it hadn't happened. After a year he'd had a colleague do workups on both of them, but they learned nothing. Their infertility was unexplained: everything was working perfectly but had not resulted in conception.

A few months later, a pregnant twenty-year-old girl had shown up looking for Jane Whitefield. One of Jane's old runners had been the girl's teacher in a San Diego high school. The girl's much older former boyfriend, a small-time criminal, was trying to find her so he could take the baby. Jane had put the girl into her car and driven off. But months later, when Jane had come back from wherever she'd taken her, she had seemed different. After she'd been home two days, she took down the antique cradleboard, carefully rewrapped it, put it back in the attic, and then closed the baby's room.

Since then, Jane had gone out with runners twice. One was an advertising man named Stephen Noton who had somehow gotten his hands on a document about drug smuggling, and was being hunted for it. The third runner Jane had taken on since she'd quit was James Shelby.

Tonight Carey was tired. The loneliness, the obsessive brooding on where Jane must be at this moment, got much worse at night, and he couldn't fight it by staying busy. He looked at his watch. It was after midnight. It was Friday, so it wasn't as bad as it could be. He could sleep until noon tomorrow if he wanted, and then go in for hospital rounds at two or three in the afternoon.

He went to the kitchen without turning on the bright light, opened the cupboard, and took down the bottle of Macallan twelve-year-old single malt Scotch. He set a heavy crystal glass on the counter and poured, then held his glass under the faucet and gave it a small squirt of water.

"Doc Holliday, I presume?"

He turned toward the kitchen door and there she was, standing in the dim light just inside the doorway. For an instant the word "hallucination" came to him, but her image didn't fade or waver. He said, "Calamity Jane," then lifted his glass to salute her.

"I meant he ruined his health drinking and smoking."

"You're leaving out the effects of tubercular bacilli, I think."

"Then how about a drink?"

"Name your poison."

"I'll have what you're having," she said.

She set her purse on the counter beside her and watched him fill a second glass and add water. She took a step toward him and reached for the glass, and then saw his eyes widen.

"My God, Jane. What happened? Was it a car accident? Have you been seen?" He looked down at her leg, and up to her face, hair, eyes. She could see that his assessment of her appearance was not good.

She took the glass and sipped from it. "A lot happened, not much of it good. And yes, a doctor saw me right away to clean the wound and sew me up. Since then I've taken care of myself."

"You said 'wound.' What sort of wound?"

"Oh, it's a lot to say at once. If you missed me, come give me a kiss."

He stepped to her, set their drinks on the counter, and gently put his arms around her. He did kiss her, but she could tell he was impatient. And he was so gentle it made her impatient, too.

"I won't break," she said. "I'm just a little tender in spots. A lot tender, actually. Fortunately for you, none of them are your favorite spots."

"All of your spots are my favorites."

"After I finish my drink I may be in the mood to let you prove it."

"There's nothing I'd like better."

"Well, I should hope not."

"But you've got to stop trying to change the subject. You're injured, and you look terrible. What happened?"

"I'll tell all."

"How badly are you hurt?"

"I'm actually waiting for your opinion and dreading what it might be. It happened about two weeks ago, so I'm out of danger—not stoically bleeding to death or anything. But I've got some marks on me. There's one that will be at least big and ugly forever, and might even make me limp."

"Okay," he said. "I'm about through waiting in suspense."

"I've been dreading your seeing me, and being disgusted or something."

"Hold on to your drink." He put an arm around her back and the other swung to the back of her knees. He scooped her up and carried her out of the kitchen, across the living room, and then to the stairway. He carried her upstairs to the bedroom and set her on her feet.

"The service around here is slipping," she said. "I almost spilled my drink."

"Disrobe, please."

"You have some nerve."

"This isn't funny. Do it."

She took another sip and set her drink on his dresser, then turned and unbuttoned her blouse, and took it off. She looked into his eyes, and kept looking at them as he bent lower to examine her stomach and ribs.

"Some bad bruises." He turned her around so he could see her back, and gently touched the skin a few times. "And what the hell? Those are burns. How did you get burned?"

"They heated some skewers, the kind you might use for shish kebab. They were trying to make me tell them where Shelby was."

"Somebody tortured you? *Tortured* you? Who did that to you?"

"Enemies of Shelby's, who didn't want him to escape." She felt his arms circle her waist to come around and undo her belt. Her slacks fell to her ankles and she stepped out of them. She reached for her drink and took another sip, then put it back on the dresser.

"This is really something," he said. From the sound of his voice, he had gone to his knees behind her. He unwrapped the bandage on her thigh. "That's an exit wound. Who shot you?" He turned her around again to look closely at the entrance wound in the front of her thigh.

She looked down at him. "I can tell you he was no gentleman," she said.

"Stop, Jane. I told you, this isn't striking me as funny."

"Okay. One of the same men. They were pretending to be cops. When I realized they weren't, I tried to get away, so one of them shot me."

"And who sewed you up and dressed this? Some old mob doctor who doesn't report bullet wounds?"

"He was young. His nurse was his girlfriend. I almost won her over to my side, but she was smitten with him, and a little stupid. The doctor was kind of angry. It was as if he agreed to treat a gunshot, and only after he got there realized it was likely to get him in trouble—that it wasn't an accident, and the victim wasn't going to be grateful for his work and for not reporting it."

"You probably already realized this, but he did a pretty good job. Good closure, no signs of infection, no indication there's anything inside. You were also very lucky. The bullet didn't hit bone or sever the femoral artery. It was a clean through-and-through shot. I'm sure he told you that. It's just a question of the muscle having time to heal now." He rewrapped the bandage. "I want you to tell me who did this."

Jane stared at him. She could see he actually intended to go find the men who had hurt her. "You can't do anything to him, Carey. He's dead." She paused. "The other one is dead, too." She didn't take her eyes off Carey. She could see that she must not let Carey know that the third one, Wylie, was alive. He lowered his eyes and glowered at a spot on the floor.

"You haven't told me what *I* want to know," she said.

"What's that?"

"I guess it's, 'Do you love me?'"

"This is a lousy time to ask that question. I'm damned furious at you for putting yourself in the position to have this happen to you. But that doesn't change the situation between us—either the bad parts or the good. I love you." He paused, as though he dreaded what was coming next. "Anything I'm not seeing? Is this the extent of it?"

"Yes."

He took a deep breath, irritated that he had to be more specific. "Were you sexually assaulted?"

"No. Maybe they would have, but they were very interested in finding Jim Shelby, and everything they did was intended to make me say where he was. Then I got away."

"I guess you didn't tell them where he was."

"No, he's still alive and relatively well." She frowned. "You still didn't really give me my answer."

"About what?"

She put her hands on his shoulders. "Look at me. Do you think I'm ugly now?"

"No. You're beautiful. I'm just upset at what you put yourself through. And I'm really angry. You don't have the right to marry somebody and then, whenever a stranger knocks on your door, run off and act like some kind of amateur police force. You told me that crap was over years ago."

"Yes, I did," she said. "I thought it was. But then one day somebody comes to your door and says, 'My brother, who is innocent, is about to be murdered in prison.' You have only two choices. All you can be is the person who decided to keep him alive, or the person who decided not to. For the rest of your life, that's who you'll be. I decided I would be the one who did."

"No matter what it cost." He looked at her from head to toe. "Well, as I said, you're lucky this time. What you were apparently most worried about didn't happen. Your body is still beautiful and healthy, and with time, you'll be about the same as before."

"Thanks, Doc," she said. Then she waited for a few seconds, looked down at herself and then at him. "Are you even just a little bit turned on?"

He nodded, but grudgingly.

She unhooked her bra, shrugged it off, slipped her panties down and stepped out of them. "Then I'd hate to have all this nakedness and hard liquor go to waste."

He frowned. "I'm sorry, Jane. I don't think this is a good time." He walked to the door, then turned. "Let's get a night's sleep, and then talk in the morning." He walked down the hall.

After a few more seconds she heard him go down the staircase. There were the familiar sounds of Carey checking the locks on the doors and setting the alarm. She showered, brushed her teeth, and got into bed with the light on. She waited an hour for him to come back upstairs, but when she heard his tread coming back up, he went to one of the other bedrooms. She turned off the light and went to sleep.

Later, when the night was at its darkest and the birds in the trees outside the old stone house had not yet begun the predawn chirping, she was aware of him. He was standing in the doorway, silent and motionless. She said, "If you're staring at me, you must have eyes like a cat."

"I'm looking. Can't see you, though. You had sort of an intriguing idea before."

"I thought you said it wasn't the right time."

"It wasn't."

"And now it is?"

"If the offer is still open."

"Always," she said.

14

Jane had been at home for ten days. She spent her evenings and nights with Carey at home in the big old stone McKinnon house in Amherst, New York. To her it was a bit like a honeymoon, a vacation from reality that had turned into a lazy enjoyment of the man she had married. This was not what she had intended in coming home, but she had felt that way the minute she had been in the kitchen with him the first night.

She knew the strength of her reaction to him and this taste of life was partly caused by the fact that she had never expected to be here again. After a few days with Wylie, Maloney, and Gorman, she had relinquished any thought of seeing Carey again. She had become like the old-time warriors, the Grandfathers. All she had hoped for was a chance to fight her enemies at the end—to snatch one of the tools of torture or an unguarded weapon and stab or slash until they overpowered and killed her. After she had become used to that idea and then escaped, even feeling the warmth of sunlight on her face had become a complex and delicious sensation. She had resigned herself to death, and now to be home again with her tall, strong husband was enough to make her feel as though she must be dreaming.

The days, from the time when Carey left at six in the morning for the hospital until late afternoon, she spent trying to speed her recovery. Carey had begun rubbing Neosporin on her burns and scrapes as soon as she had come home. There had been no need by then for any antiseptic effect, but the stuff seemed to help prevent scars. She did her series of tai chi positions, and she could feel herself stretching farther and becoming more flexible. After that she left the house and went for long walks, lengthening her stride a bit each day and raising the rhythm of her steps to go faster. She lifted light weights to strengthen her upper body, but most of the time she concentrated on her right leg. When she was not exercising it she was resting. She took special care to eat well and get lots of protein and take vitamins, and to get plenty of sleep.

On the eleventh morning when Carey left, she took a bus to Rochester, New York, and bought a used car at a big car dealership. It was a gray four-year-old Honda with low mileage. She bought it under the name Emily Westerveldt, an identity she had built with many others, but had seldom used. When she got her car back to Amherst, she had it washed and waxed at the car wash on Niagara Falls Boulevard, and then drove it to her regular mechanic. She asked if he could check it over for a friend of hers. He glanced at it and said, "I'll take a look at it."

"Thanks," she said. She knew he would take care of it, even if it meant he had to drive across the county for parts.

"Pick it up after four."

When she picked it up, she filled it with gas and then stopped to buy the things she carried when she was on the road—a case of bottled water, bags of nuts, trail mix, dried fruit. Then she drove the car to her old house in

Deganawida, put it in the garage, and went inside to make other preparations.

This was the house that her grandfather and his friends had built, the house where her father had been born, and where Jane had lived until she'd gone off to college, then returned to after graduation, and stayed in through the death of her mother. She had lived here until she had married Carey. She had kept it since then, partly because she couldn't sell it to some unsuspecting stranger who might wake up in the middle of the night to hear an unfortunate runner knocking on the door for help—or to hear someone worse coming in a window.

There were still things hidden in the house. For a few years she had stopped thinking of them as the tools of her profession, and had begun to think of them as precautions, like the fire extinguishers in the kitchen and the upstairs hallway in Amherst. She went down the cellar stairs gingerly, trying not to put too much weight on her wounded thigh. She walked to the far end, near her father's old workbench, took the stepladder, and carried it back to the area beside the old coal-burning furnace that had been left here when the oil furnace was installed when she was a child.

She climbed to one of the old, round heating ducts, disconnected two sections, and reached inside. There was a box that contained four pistols, all of them loaded, and boxes of extra ammunition. There was a metal cash box full of money. There was another in the back. When she opened it she found, carefully wrapped in plastic, pieces of identification. Some were for a woman who looked like Jane, and some for a man who looked like Carey, but who had names that weren't McKinnon. There were birth certificates, passports, driver's licenses, and credit cards.

Jane took some stacks of money, and then a Beretta nine-millimeter pistol like the one she had taken from Maloney, and a spare magazine. She set them on the ladder and then fitted the two sections of heating duct back together so they looked as though they hadn't been touched since the 1940s, moved the ladder back beside the workbench, and climbed back up the stairs.

When she came into the kitchen, she partially dismantled the gun, wiped the parts with a soft rag damp with gun oil, reassembled it, and then put it into her purse. She called a taxi to meet her three blocks away and took it home to Amherst; there, she hid the gun and the money in one of the spare rooms on the second floor with a small suitcase she had selected.

On the twelfth day she went to visit the Jo-Ge-Oh, the little people. They were very small, but they looked very much like the Senecas. They had been around for longer than the Senecas, but they had such a peculiar relationship with time that it was difficult to make assertions about it. They preferred to live in places where Seneca villages had been, either because those were simply the best sites in New York state—always near water and close to ground that was fertile and tillable—or because being close to full-size human beings scared off the animals that tended to trouble and annoy anyone their size. Raccoons, possums, skunks, and squirrels were particularly bothersome. For that reason the little people prized fingernail and toenail clippings, which they scattered around their settlements to give off a scent of big people. They were also extremely fond of the sort of tobacco that the Senecas favored, grown in western New York and Ontario, and mixed with a few shavings of sumac.

Jane had often visited them near the site of a large village that had once been along the Genesee River in Rochester. She usually approached the spot from Maplewood Avenue and climbed down the rocky sides of the chasm to the pebbly shore. But today, Jane didn't relish a climb, so she selected another place closer to home. She drove to the Niagara River, and then along River Road to the South Grand Island Bridge. She went over the east river and across the nine-mile-long island to a spot near the northern tip, then drove south along the river road. When she reached the right spot she parked and got out of the car, then walked along the eastern shore of the island to the site of an old, long-vanished hotel called Riverhaven. It was directly across the river from the old ferry landing in the city of Deganawida, and boats had landed here before the bridges were built at either end of the island. But the human occupation was much older than that.

This was a place that had been full of activity since long before the Senecas took the land by conquering the Wenros and Eries in the early seventeenth century. It was the site of one of the very few deposits of flint in the western part of the state, and it had been visited by Native people since the end of the last ice age. Jane walked the shore for a while, and then spoke. "Jo-Ge-Oh!" she called softly. "It's me, Jane Whitefield. I'm Nundawaono, and I've been away. I didn't want to leave again without visiting you."

The Jo-Ge-Oh were known for taking in people who were in terrible trouble and hiding them from their enemies. They would conduct such people to their settlements and let them stay until they were safe. Often the person would think he had been with them for a week or a month, and then come back to the full-size world and discover that many years had passed. His enemies would be long dead and forgotten. Jane had admired the Jo-Ge-Oh and felt close to them since she was a little girl.

"Jo-Ge-Oh! Little people! I've brought you some presents." She opened a foil package that the clerk in the store at the Tuscarora reservation had sold her. "Here's some tobacco. I hope it's good and strong." She made small piles of it on the rocks along the shore. "Here are some clippings from my fingers and toes. I hope it keeps the pests away."

She took out a plastic sandwich bag and scattered the clippings around her.

She spoke to the little people in the Seneca language. "I came to thank you for helping me get home alive and be with my husband." Her speech was in keeping with Seneca practice, which was to thank supernatural beings for whatever they had given, but not to ask for anything. In English she said, "Thanks, little guys." After a few minutes of listening to the silence and watching the flow of the beautiful blue river, she turned and went back to her car. Tomorrow would be the thirteenth day.

That evening Jane had dinner ready early, and made sure she and Carey were in bed at shortly after ten. They began by making love slowly and gently, and then lay still for a time, holding hands. Then Carey moved again and loomed above her, kissing her hard, and she realized that she didn't have to tell him because he had already seen something—the overnight bag she'd packed, maybe—or just sensed the return of the melancholy she always had before she had to leave him. They began again, turning to each other wildly and passionately, as though it would be the last time in their lives and they were saying good-bye to everything that they loved and wanted.

Jane awoke at five a.m. as she had awoken many times, lying with her head on Carey's chest, feeling the rise and fall of his strong respiration, her long black hair spread over him like a blanket. She raised her head slightly and looked at him. His eyes were open, and he was looking at her.

"Good." She put her hands on the sides of his face, and gave him a long, gentle kiss. "One more chance to get that baby started. I'll be gone when you get home tonight."

15

An hour after Carey left for the hospital, Jane locked the door of the big old stone house in Amherst, walked to the driveway, and got into her cab. She took it to Deganawida, walked to her house, opened the garage, and started the used Honda she had bought.

She stopped at a large sporting goods outlet in Niagara Falls and bought a Remington 1200 shotgun and twenty-five double-ought shells. When the man asked her what she wanted that kind for, she said, "Home defense." She bought a gun cleaning kit and a box of rubber gloves; a large, razor-sharp folding knife; a short-handled spade; and a hatchet. She stopped at an electronics store and bought four pay-as-you-go untraceable cell phones with cash.

In another few hours of driving east she was past Syracuse and making the turn onto Interstate 81, heading north to Watertown. From there Route 3 took her east on a winding road into the Adirondacks, and she drove the rest of the day to reach Lake Placid, where she checked into a hotel and slept.

It was mid-afternoon the next day, after she had read the rental listings in the papers and had spent hours combing the area around Lake Placid, when she found the house she wanted. Jane walked the property, climbed on the woodpile outside and looked in the windows, and then walked in the woods nearby. She found the trails: one a game trail that went only as far as a tiny clearing with weeds that had been flattened by deer as a resting place; and the other a man trail, bare of vegetation, that led two hundred feet or so to a small, dark Adirondack lake.

She liked the fact that the building had two stories. The upper story would give her a chance to see what was coming toward her from a greater distance. Because she had driven into the Adirondacks to a place that got cold in the winter, it hadn't been hard to find houses of brick and stone built to hold up to the weather. They would also stop a bullet. This one she judged to date from the 1930s. It had a sloped cellar door that led down steps to a second, vertical door to a basement. The windows were all old-fashioned thick glass, all two-light, opening inward like little doors, secure on the inside and equipped with shutters. She could see through rooms to the inner sides of some of them, and they all had iron fittings so in the winter they could be barred with two-by-fours. The snow in the Adirondacks had been known to pile up to twenty feet, and the windows had been built to hold up against the weight and the winds. The roof had a steep peak to prevent snow and ice from building up and getting heavy.

She took another look around, and then drove up the dirt road to the county highway, and then into Lake Placid to find the landlord. The owner turned out to be a young blond woman whose main business was a store that sold things summer visitors wore—high-end sunglasses; hiking boots; hats for keeping the sun out of the eyes; helmets and bright synthetic shirts and spandex shorts for those who rode the bikes hanging from the rack overhead.

Jane walked in, saw that the blond woman was the only person in the store, and said, "You're Cora Willis, right? I want to rent your house."

"The cottage? Don't you want to see it first?"

"I've seen it," Jane said. "I was just out there. I like it. My name is Janet Keller." She held out her hand and the other woman shook it. "In fact, I was surprised you weren't asking more for it."

Cora Willis shrugged. "I get a lot more earlier in the summer. Usually I close it for the summer at the end of August, and then do whatever upkeep I need to do. There are plenty of years when the nights start to get cold by now. I should warn you about that—you could wake up one morning and find it's fall."

"It's okay," Jane said. "I'm prepared. I saw it was empty, and I'd like to move in later today or tomorrow, if I can."

"No reason not to. I don't need to wait for your check to clear. You seem honest."

"I am. But I assumed you would be careful, so I brought cash." She counted it out onto the counter silently. "Is there a security deposit?"

"Uh . . . no," said Cora Willis. She went to a cabinet behind the counter and produced a rental agreement, a pen, and a key. She walked around her store hanging up clothes that had been left in the dressing room while Jane filled in her false name and address. When Jane was finished, Cora Willis glanced at the agreement as she put it into her computer printer and made a copy for Jane, signed it, and handed it to her. "You should have a nice, quiet time. I always do when I'm out there. My great-grandfather built it."

"It's just right," Jane said. She walked toward the door. "Thanks a lot. I'll be back in two weeks to turn in the key."

"Okay. If you forget, mail it to me. You're the last renter of the season, so there's no rush."

Jane had not intended to move into the cottage right away, but she didn't want anyone around when she got there, and she needed to have the deal be a certainty, so she had started the rental period right away. She drove to Watertown and began to shop for the items she would need. She went to a military surplus store and bought a marine K-Bar fighting knife with a black blade; a blood gutter and a hilt to keep her hand from slipping onto the blade; a whetstone; some basic cooking utensils; a high-intensity flashlight; a camouflage tarp; and a hundred feet of rope.

At a Target store she bought men's jeans, shoes, a shirt, a hooded sweatshirt, a box of rubber gloves, dishwashing detergent, and some sheets and blankets.

She stopped at a copying and mailing store, where she rented a computer and sent Stewart Shattuck an e-mail. Stewart Shattuck was a highly skilled forger and a dealer in false identification with whom she had dealt a number of times over the years. "Stewart, I need a favor. Please make sure that a few of the wrong people find out that I asked you to mail me some new cards—maybe an e-mail acknowledgment that looks as though you accidentally hit 'reply all' would do it, but you know best. Here is the address." She put in the address of the cottage near the lake.

Jane waited nearly an hour before she received the reply: "It's done. If you have any doubts about this, don't ever go there."

Near the mailing store was a party goods store. As she had hoped, the paucity of holidays in the latter part of the summer had forced the staff to lay out the Halloween costumes and decorations early. She went through the displays of masks until she found the one she wanted. It fit over the whole head and had close-cropped brown hair and a smooth complexion. The name on the label said "George Clooney mask." She bought it and a set of rubber hands and rubber feet.

It was nightfall by the time Jane was finished with her shopping. She decided she was not ready to drive several hours to arrive in the dark at a dirt road to an unoccupied house. She drove to the entrance to Route 81, where she remembered there was a large, pleasant-looking hotel, and rented a room for the night. She went back outside to move her car to a spot in the parking lot where it was lighted and she could see it from her room, then went to sleep. She had gone to sleep so early that she awoke at four, then drove the four hours to reach the cottage by eight.

Before she left the highway she refilled her gas tank. She had learned over the years that eluding pursuers was often a matter of tiny precautions, many of them no more esoteric than maintaining a full tank. Afterward she drove the rest of the way to the dirt road and up to the house, where she unloaded her supplies into the kitchen. Then she drove the car back along the dirt road to the highway, and then up the man-made trail she had found in her initial visit. She kept going past the distance where her car would become invisible from the highway, until she found the slab of rock. She parked the car on it, covered the car with leaves and branches, and then followed the trail the rest of the way to the small, calm lake and along the shore to the path that led up to the house.

She locked the doors and began to deal with the supplies and equipment she had brought. She went upstairs and made the bed in the master bedroom, which was at the head of the stairs. Then she went down the hall and selected a second bedroom where she would sleep. There was a lot of work to do, and she had only the hours of daylight to accomplish it. She went downstairs, emptied a half dozen glass iced tea bottles into a pitcher, tied the bottles together with nylon fishing line, and set pairs of them along the upstairs hallway from the stairway to the second bedroom. If anyone came up here in the dark, he would set off a racket with the falling bottles, and very likely tangle himself in the fishing line.

The men's clothing she had bought she filled with leaves, pine needles, and a few sticks, making the most realistic dummy she could. His head was the rubber pullover George Clooney mask filled with crumpled paper bags. His hands were the rubber hands from the party shop. She tried using the rubber feet, but ultimately settled on the shoes with the rubber feet stuffed into them, so the human-looking ankles could be seen. After several experiments with the dummy, she found that the best place for him was seated on the bed in the master bedroom with his back propped up on pillows, the small reading light on the headboard turned on behind his head so his face was in shadow, and a book from the bookshelf propped in his lap. She plumped up some pillows and put them under the covers so it looked as though a woman were asleep on the far side of him.

From time to time Jane stopped her preparations and looked out each of the upper windows, standing still and silent as though frozen, watching the world around the house. She had no reason to imagine anyone could have found her this soon, but the men chasing her now were completely unknown to her. She had no idea what they could do. The thought reminded her that there were many more things she wanted to do before nightfall.

She went to the unoccupied room just beyond hers, tied the rope to the steel frame of the bed, took the screen out of the window, opened the window, and looked down. Directly below the window was clear grass, but on either side there was shrubbery.

In the room she had selected for sleeping, she loaded her shotgun. She dragged the mattress off the bed and put it right at the door, then cycled the shotgun to put a double-ought shell in the chamber, and laid the shotgun on the mattress. She took ten more shotgun shells out of the box, put them in the pockets of her black jacket, and left the jacket there.

She stood still, looked, and thought. The house was stone, impervious to gunfire except through the windows. If people got inside, they would search downstairs, and then they would climb the stairway to the second-floor hall. They might go to investigate the dimly lighted master bedroom where she had left the dummy, or they would come up the hallway and knock over the bottles. Either way, they would warn Jane. If she was stationed in the doorway on her mattress, she could fire eight double-ought blasts into the narrow, dark hallway, reload, and probably fire eight more. She made a few alterations. She adjusted the mattress so she could lie on it and fire, showing only her right eye and right shoulder to the intruders.

She walked to the staircase, descended to the ground floor, and counted windows. There were eight. She went down into the basement and found the eight precut and painted two-by-fours, barred the shutters, and latched the windows.

The front and rear doors each had an assortment of locks and dead bolts. She was a bit uncomfortable with them, because she didn't want it to be impossible to get in. She wanted the shooters to get inside. She wanted them to climb the stairs.

Jane walked the paths through the woods and then among the man-tall reeds at the edge of the lake, memorizing the contours of the land and the marshy places. She stayed out while the sun went low and she could see the water of the lake as a copper-colored mirror shining through the foliage. She knew it was very unlikely that anyone could find her in one day, so she was in no hurry to fortify herself in the house. She walked the deer trails quietly, and heard the deer stir ahead of her, then go crashing through the underbrush and away. She walked out to the highway and stared into the trees to be sure she couldn't detect light emanating from the house. She walked along the grassy shoulder of the dirt road to the house so her footprints wouldn't show.

She picked out landmarks as she walked. The tall pine that rose above the hardwoods stood about halfway to the house. The clearing where the trees had died out was three quarters of the way. As she walked, she heard something big moving through the underbrush, and she suspected it was a bear. She stopped to gauge the wind direction. It was blowing toward her from the lake, so she would probably be safe if she waited for the bear to move on. In a few minutes, she heard it moving off toward the water.

She went inside the house and turned on the downstairs lights. The shutters were all closed, so the light could not be seen from a distance. She made herself some dinner, and washed the dishes. She went to the front door and disengaged the dead bolts. Then she went to the back door and did the same, but left the standard locks on each door locked. If she unlocked a door they would suspect the truth—that she wanted them to come in.

She turned off the downstairs lights, climbed the stairs, and stopped at the top. She turned on her dummy's reading light in the master bedroom, shut the door, and made her way down the hall, stepping over the nylon fishing line tied to the bottles. She showered, brushed her teeth, and dressed for sleep. She wore black jeans, a black T-shirt, and her black jacket. She had a Beretta pistol in her pocket, and the K-Bar knife in its sheath at her back. The shotgun was on the mattress beside her. She lay there in the silence and darkness, and was surprised at how comfortable she felt, with all the physical work done, her hair and body clean, and lying on the firm mattress. It was only a few minutes before she was asleep and dreaming.

16

In her dream, Jane did something she had done a hundred times during the day. She went to her open window and looked outside. This window faced in the direction of the lake. She looked out over the glassy black surface, and saw nothing but the undistorted reflection of the moon and a few stars. Near the shore, where the cold water met the warm earth, there was a layer of fog a few feet thick. She heard a faint sloshing sound and saw the tall reeds forty feet beyond the shore moving a little. A man slowly rose from under the lake and walked with slow determination among the reeds toward the shore, the fog hiding all but his human shape at first. As he approached the shore, the muddy water ran off his head and down his face in streams. He was wearing a coat, and water ran from the sleeves to make ripples on the surface. She knew him, and she felt a deep dread. He was dead because of the worst mistake Jane had ever made—Jane had once been fooled into leading a killer named John Felker practically to his door. And Harry didn't haunt her dreams to bring her good news.

When the man was fully up and out of the water, he stood still for a moment, slowly raising his head to look up at her window as though he had heard her thinking. His eyes focused on hers. There were a few long, mossy strands of water plants on his shoulders. Without moving his eyes from Jane's, he reached up and brushed them off, then began to walk toward the house.

Jane shut the window and barred it, then put her eye to the shutter and watched him walking toward the kitchen door. As he came, water ran down from his clothes, and his shoes made a squish noise with each step. He stopped on the slab of concrete at the back door, and she could see the wet footprints there. He looked up at her again for a moment as though determining whether she would come down to let him in. Then he simply opened the locked door and stepped inside.

Jane slowly moved along the hallway and listened to the watery squish of his shoes as he ascended the stairs. He reached the top and stood on the landing. At his best, Harry Kemple had looked as though he had never cared for himself. He always wore the same sport coat with a very tight herringbone pattern. It must have started out gray, but the fabric had acquired a greenish tint, as though the years of poker table air thick with cigar smoke had reacted with the harsh light to work a chemical change. The elbows were a slightly lighter color because they were worn. He had a bony, unhealthy build, like a too-tall jockey, and his brown pants were too wide for him, gathered above his waist and cinched by a thin belt. His shoes looked as though he had sprayed them with floor wax and given them a varnish-like shine that preserved the scuffs.

"Hello, Harry," Jane said.

"I notice you didn't fall all over yourself to let me in."

"You're a ghost, Harry. Doors don't present the problem to you that stairs present to me. I'm sure you know I've been shot."

Harry nodded. "I know what you know. The nine-millimeter bullet missed the femur and the femoral artery, but it tore the muscle up a bit. In eleven months you'll be as fast as ever. . . ."

Jane's heart beat faster. She couldn't believe the good news.

". . . If your body is still alive."

"You always know how to raise my spirits."

"You raise us yourself," he said. "Me in particular. I get no rest because I'm your mistake. The minute you took John Felker to see Mr. Shaw in Vancouver to get a fake ID, I was a dead man. I could still walk around while he stole Shaw's record of the IDs he'd made and found my new name and address. But I was already on Hanegoategeh's to-do list."

"I wasn't being careless. I believed in John Felker."

"Enough to spend the previous two weeks fucking him, like it was a honeymoon."

"I was an idiot, Harry. I'm sorry. I've been saying it for fifteen years, and I know I'll never stop having these dreams." She reached out and touched his hand, but it was freezing cold from the mountain lake, and bloodless. She withdrew her hand, trying to hide her revulsion.

"What? You can't be surprised I feel like a dead guy."

"No," she said. "I just forget all of that sometimes, Harry."

He looked at her impatiently, then turned his head and looked over his shoulder, taking in everything around him like a man who has suddenly had a blindfold removed. "Oh, shit," he said. "You're the One Who Stops, aren't you? You were running away with the other fighters, and you're the one who stops and fights. That's why you're way up here alone."

"This is the place to do it," she said. "Nobody else can get hurt. The outer walls are stone, and the doors are split timbers. There won't be any innocent bystanders."

"Oh, there won't be," he said. "Not the ones who are after you, and not you."

"Innocent isn't what I want to be."

He looked around again, and she was aware he was seeing through walls and floors. "So this is the spot where you're choosing to block the trail and fight to the death."

"Not 'the' death. Their death."

"Do you know who and how many there are?"

"No. I'll know that when they come."

"What part of the wars is this?"

"What do you mean?"

"Shelby and his sister don't know anything, and neither does Iris. But you know it's about Sky Woman's twin grandsons, the right-handed and the left-handed, Hawenneyu the Creator and Hanegoategeh the Destroyer. So whose work are you doing up here?"

"Hawenneyu's."

"You've made sure that killers will come here for you, and that somebody is never going home. Can you kill for the Creator?"

"I think you can," she said. "If you stop the heart of someone who kills and kills, you can."

"If you're sure, then before they come, do all your thinking. See everything from every direction and tell yourself every story of the fight. Plan what you'll do in every story, so when you see it beginning to happen, you can move. Trade your life for something. Don't throw it at them because you're angry."

"Is that it, Harry? You've finally come to tell me this is my time?"

"Maybe one of the twins knows when you're going to die, and maybe both do. I don't. I exist only in your head. I'm a synapse in your brain that fires when you're anxious."

"Come on, Harry. Am I doing the right thing?"

"You're stopping on the path, turning your face toward the enemy, and preparing to fight alone. The old ones, the warriors and clan mothers from that time, would recognize it, and see you as one of them. I don't know if that makes you right."

"You're hedging, Harry. Are you saying I should do this, or go back to the others and run?"

"You've decided to be Hawenneyu's warrior, fighting death for lives. You'll die this time or another, at this turn in the trail or another." He lifted his head as though he were listening to something only he could hear. Then he said, "Rest tonight. It's too early for them. But tomorrow night, be ready."

Jane slept soundly, then woke at dawn. She rose and walked from one window to the next on the upper floor of the house, looking out. It was cooler this morning, the reminder in the air that it was not going to be summer for much longer. Above the mirror surface of the lake she could see the wispy white fog that she had dreamed of, deep as a man's waist and stretching out past the reedy shore. She saw the first few waterbirds. There was a great blue heron that stepped out from the reeds in the fog, striding in the shallows, then standing still again.

She felt strong. She still had a day, a whole day that would go on until dark. She had realized in the night that time was something she needed, and now she had it. Even if the men were off their flight by now and driving this way, they would not come close enough to be seen until nightfall. They would be searching for the address she had given Stewart, not for a place that could be known and explored. Jane ate breakfast, then took the knife, the hatchet, the spade, and the rolled-up plastic camouflage tarp she'd bought into the weedy fields between the house and the dirt road.

She walked toward the first bend in the road that was also its halfway point, the tall pine. She stayed on the game trail, only a narrow line where the deer had stamped down the weeds on their way to and from the lake. When she found the right spot, she knew it. There was a slight depression in the level field that put it below the surrounding weeds. She moved carefully to the right of the path, and began to dig. The ground here was damp, black with centuries of rotted humus, so it was soft and heavy. She first removed the layer of weeds in clumps, set them away from the hole, and then dug. She used her uninjured left leg to push the spade into the earth, and stood on the right. She dug for four hours, beginning in the cool morning. After a while she discarded her sweatshirt and dug in her T-shirt, feeling the sweat cooling her. The hole was about ten or twelve feet long, and six or seven feet wide. At the end of four hours it was over six feet deep.

She went to work on the long mound of dirt she had shoveled out. She would cause a small avalanche to get a pile of it onto her tarp, and then drag it to a spot at the edge of the woods near the lake. Then she would repeat the process. It took her two more hours to move it all.

Near the pile of dirt she found a stand of hardwood saplings, mostly oak and maple, and used her hatchet to cut ten of them, then cut them into about a hundred inch-thick stakes. With her K-Bar knife she whittled sharp points on both ends of each. She used the foliage to cover the mounds of dirt, then took her stakes to the hole in the field.

She sank each of the stakes into the ground at the bottom of the pit in a pattern that left nowhere for her to stand, then dug her way out. She went back to the stand of saplings and cut two dozen lengths of thin, five-foot saplings, leaving the network of spreading branches on. In the field she laid some of them across the width of the pit, then placed others at angles, weaving some of the smallest branches with others so she had almost a net covering the pit. She placed the camouflage plastic tarp over it.

The clumps of weeds she had removed to dig her pit she placed upright on the tarp. Then she filled in the spaces with new pieces of turf, some fallen leaves, and loose grass, until it was extremely difficult for her to see the difference between her pit and the rest of the field.

By the time she was finished, it was late afternoon. She went back to the house, cooked eggs and bacon for lunch, and ate on the front porch, studying the land in the direction they would come from. In the afternoon she examined all of her preparations in the house again, then walked from the main road along the dirt road to the house, so she would see it exactly as the men would see it. Be ready tonight, Harry had said. And Harry knew what Jane knew.

17

Jane showered, added the bottles from the iced tea she'd had during the hot afternoon to her string of bottles in the hallway, rested, and watched afternoon turn into evening. As darkness came, she reviewed in her mind all of her preparations, and fell asleep. She left the window open in her room. In the night it was easier to separate noises that were natural from sounds like car engines and the jangling of metal, so she was sure she would hear them.

Six hours later, she did. She stood and looked out her window. Her ears had been correct. They were walking in pairs up the dirt road toward the house, and she could hear their boots crunching bits of dirt and stone as they came. There were eight of them, and the number momentarily shocked her. How could there be so many? Maloney and Gorman were dead. It didn't matter—there they were. She hoped one of the men coming toward the house was Daniel Martel.

She closed the window and the shutter so there would be no moonlight behind her, went to lie on the mattress at the doorway, raised her shotgun to her shoulder, and made it snug. She pushed the door closed as far as she could to hide any silhouette she made. Only her shotgun barrel protruded through the open space.

The men were fiddling with the doors downstairs. She heard a faint, battery-operated buzz and knew that one of them had brought a lock-pick gun. A hand turned the doorknob. She half-felt, half-heard the door opening. One by one they entered and stepped away from the door, and she heard the same board creak over and over.

She heard whispering, or maybe it was only the nervous breathing of so many men in a dark, empty house. It occurred to her that they were probably just in from Los Angeles, so their lungs would not be used to the altitude of the mountains yet. There were quiet footsteps on the stairs, climbing up, closer and closer. The men were feeling good now. They had gotten in with little noise and no resistance. They were all together, and taking possession of the house. Jane kept her eyes trained on the hallway.

The first one appeared at the top of the stairs carrying a rifle. She decided to wait. He moved to the side of the master bedroom door, pointed down at the dim light coming from the crack beneath it, then beckoned, and a second man came from the staircase to stand on the other side of the bedroom door. The third man was just visible at the top of the staircase, still half protected by the wall.

She barely moved as she aimed her shotgun at the third man. He stepped up onto the floor of the hallway and raised his foot to kick in the master bedroom door. He kicked, the door swung inward, he fired at the dummy on the bed, and the other two pivoted to fire through the doorway, too. Jane pulled the trigger, and her shotgun blast killed the third man. The other two looked at him and each other, confused, half deafened by the firing in the narrow space, and their confusion gave Jane a second to pump the shotgun and fire a blast into the chest of the second man. The first man, now aware that the fire was coming from behind him, must have heard her pumping the shotgun again. He tried to spin around, but made it in time to see the muzzle flash coming from Jane's shotgun. Her shot caught him in the head, and he fell across the others.

Jane began to reload, but then there was a fourth man running up the hall toward her, firing a semiautomatic rifle. Holes appeared in the wood above her head. She fired at him, but she seemed to miss. She pumped again, but then he had disappeared into the doorway of one of the rooms. If she waited, the other four would be up here in seconds.

She stepped into the hall with her shotgun aimed at the doorway, slipped into the next room, locked the door, jumped onto the bed, and ran on it to the open window. She dropped the shotgun, threw the rope out the window, and crawled out after it. She lowered herself most of the way down, dropped, hit the ground, and ran along the house to crouch at the side of the front porch.

She drew her pistol and rested her arm on the lower part of the railing between the spokes, and took deep breaths while she waited. Two men rushed out the front door heading for the steps. She was so close to them she fired upward into them, not at them. She pulled the trigger five times.

She turned and ran back along the side of the house past her rope, toward the back door of the house. She reached the corner as she heard two more of them coming out. It was too late to ambush them, so she went low, then brought her arm around the corner of the house and fired wildly six times. She knew she hit one, because she heard him yell and fall against the house, and a rifle scraped it, then fell on the ground.

There was no way to be sure of the other, so she ran again, this time away from the house into the brush and weeds. She ran fifty or sixty feet to a thicket, dropped to the ground, replaced the magazine in her pistol, and cycled the slide to put a round in the chamber. She waited for the other man to come around, but he didn't come. He was probably trying to get a better angle to fire the rifle at her.

She had to move before he got a view of her. She would move to where he had been, because that was the one place she could be sure was clear. She would pick up the rifle of the man who had never fired, slip inside, and lie on the floor of the kitchen, where she would be able to hit anyone who came down the stairs or went to the front door. She came around the corner and stopped. There were two men with rifles, both standing up. They quickly swung around to face her, and she dashed back around the corner. She sprinted into the field, trying to dash into the deep darkness. She made it to another thicket, dropped into the weeds beyond it, and aimed at the corner of the house.

It was taking too long. At least one of them was moving to a new firing position. But what was the best firing position? The upstairs window where she had climbed out and rappelled to the ground. From that elevation he would be able to see her perfectly and put a rifle bullet through her.

Jane ran toward the house until she was twenty feet below it. She imagined the man going in the door, through the kitchen, down the long hallway to the foot of the stairs, then up the stairs. He would run along the upstairs hall to the room where she had left the rope. He would kneel on the bed, prop an elbow on the windowsill, and look down the barrel.

Jane stood below the window, her pistol gripped in both hands, and aimed at the center of the small, dark square of the upstairs window. She saw the rifle barrel come out the window, and fired. She fired twice more, but there was no return shot. The rifle rested on the sill, the barrel now pointing out and upward at nothing. She turned and ran.

Behind her she heard more shots. They were rapid, but there was no overlap between them. There was only one man firing. She heard rounds crack as they passed over her faster than the sound barrier, heard thumps as they pounded into the ground. She didn't have the speed that she'd had all her life. It was frustrating and frightening, and she hated it, but she kept sprinting, trying to move as quickly as she could right now, because now was the only time that mattered, that was even real. She couldn't increase her speed, but she could strain to keep moving at the same rate in spite of the fatigue.

She stayed low, running in a particular direction, gauging her position by the tall pine tree jutting upward from the canopy of hardwoods. She crossed the game trail, veered to the right to follow it, and heard a shot hit behind her. She could hear the man now, his loud, heavy footsteps as he ran across the field to get a better shot at her, his heavy breaths coming closer in the silent night air.

Then she was at the pit, much closer than she had imagined it was, and she nearly stepped into it, her right foot dislodging a little dirt from the edge. She straightened her path, then veered to the right again beyond the covered pit. The man fired once more, but the shot went high. He was already trying to cut across her path to make the next shot easier and closer. He was not zigzagging as she was, not slowing at all.

She suddenly realized what he was doing. He had begun to think he could run her down and take her alive. As soon as they had realized she was armed and killing their comrades, the men must have assumed the best they could accomplish was to kill her. But now she was in the open and not running too fast to overtake. She wasn't shooting back, so maybe she was out of ammunition. The man was alone, but if he could catch her, he wouldn't have to split any money with partners. She was worth very little to him dead, but alive, she was priceless. He could sell her to her enemies or torture her, just as Wylie had wanted to do.

She heard it behind her, hardly daring to think it was that, and yet knowing it had to be, and then heard the voice—"Aah! Aah!" again and again, pitched higher than a man's speaking voice but still his voice. She thought she recognized the voice.

Jane slid to put her feet ahead of her, rolled over on her belly, and aimed her pistol in the direction she had come from. There was nothing to shoot at. She could see the whole marshy field all the way back to the house, but there was nothing in it taller than the weeds. She waited, stared down the sights of the pistol, but saw nothing. She stood and cautiously walked back toward the pit. She circled and approached it from the end so she could look the long way into the twelve-foot pit.

The tarp she had used to cover the pit was pushed aside off half the length of it, and the man lay on top of it. She could hear labored, raspy breathing. She could see the man's rifle had fallen about five feet from him. It seemed to be out of his reach, but that could be intentional.

She stepped closer. "I hear you up there," he shouted. "Help me." She had been right. It was Wylie's voice.

"Wylie. How bad are you?"

"Bad. I've got a stake sticking in me."

"Toss your pistol out."

He didn't move. "I can't reach it. I can't hurt you now. Get a stick, something I can hold on to. Maybe I can get up."

She moved to the edge of the pit farthest from him and took the thickest and longest of the branches she had used to hide the pit. She held it out and he grasped it. She pulled.

"Uh," he grunted. "Let me do it."

Jane looked down and she could see that a pool of blood was collecting in the tarp below him. "How many stakes are in you?"

He moved his free hand to explore. “Two. No, three. God, it hurts.” He breathed hard a couple of times, then reached for the stick Jane held.

She said, “Tell me about Daniel Martel.”

“A rich guy. He does what he wants. Sometimes he needs protection from what he does. He wanted Shelby’s wife, he got her, kept her for a while, and then he killed her. He hired us to make sure Shelby got convicted, and then died, so nobody would ever reopen the case or come after Martel. When Shelby got away, Martel hired some more to help us hunt him down.”

“Where is Martel now?”

“I don’t know. Probably LA.”

“Not good enough. I can leave you here just like this, so you can tell the cops who you and all these armed dead men are.”

“I’ll help you get Martel if you’ll help me get through this. I’ll call him and bring him to you.”

“All right. Can you lift yourself? The stakes aren’t in the ground deep. You can probably move them.”

“I’ll have to. I know that.” He pushed up with one arm and dislodged two of the stakes from the ground. “Oh, Jesus,” he muttered. “Oh, Jesus.” Then he moved the third, and lay on his side, regaining his strength.

“Okay,” Jane said. “Here. Hold on to the stick and I’ll pull while you try to stand. Then we can get you up to the surface.”

She saw him grasp the stick with both hands and brace himself. She pulled, and she saw in the moonlight a peculiar look appearing on his face. Then he did what she had expected. He made an incredibly fast tug on the stick, trying to pull her in onto the stakes that remained upright.

She let the stick go, and he fell backward. He was reaching into his jacket pocket when she backed away from the pit. As she turned and ran, she heard him moving. She ran a few more steps and dived into the weeds, just as he raised his hand above the edge and fired in her direction.

A moment later he called, "Come back."

She called, "You're on your own now. Look at your belly. You're bleeding out. I can wait."

"No. Stop. I'll do what I said, and bring Martel."

"Your chances got used up, Wylie."

She crawled a distance away, got up, and went to look at each of the other men to be sure none of them had survived. There were two on the front porch, one in the back. There were three she had caught shooting the dummy in the master bedroom. There was a man lying on the mattress where her rope was tied, his rifle still resting on the windowsill.

She took the rope and began the hard work of moving bodies. She dragged each of the four men lying on the second floor to the edge of the stairs and pushed him so he slid down to the first floor. Each of them stopped at some point, snagged on the railing or jammed against the wall, so she went down and pushed the body with both feet to get it moving. Then she dragged it to join the two who were already splayed on the front porch.

As she stepped off the porch, she heard the report of a pistol come from inside the pit she had dug. She paused for a second, then walked to the side of the house and out to the field, approaching the pit from a new angle so she could look down the long side.

When she was close, she pulled out her gun and stepped close to the pit. She looked inside, then away again. Wylie had put the barrel in his mouth and ended his pain.

Jane walked back into the house, found her cell phone, and called Stewart Shattuck's number. When he answered, she said, "I knew you'd be awake. Do you recognize my voice?"

"Yes."

"I just killed eight of them. If there are others who might know you helped me, be ready."

"I'm pretty sure there aren't. I got the impression they were one little expedition after a reward. They wouldn't have passed on a tip to anybody. But thanks for the warning. You all right?"

"I'm the only happy person for a few miles in any direction."

"Good enough. See you."

"See you."

Jane went upstairs and took the blanket off the bed where she had slept. She rolled one of the bodies off the porch onto the blanket and used it to drag him to the pit. She carried the blanket back and rolled the next one onto it. She worked hard and tirelessly. She had decided to do as much of this work as she could tonight, while it was cool and the bodies were fresh, and it was dark and she didn't have to look at their eyes. By the fourth body the blanket was soaked with blood. It didn't matter, she thought. The men were just bleeding into the grass. The ground of the state of New York, the country her people called their longhouse, had been soaking up human blood nicely for about fourteen thousand years.

When she had all seven bodies at the pit, she went through each man's pockets, dumped the contents onto a growing pile on the grass, then rolled him into the pit. When she had rolled the last one in, she lay back in the weeds and stared up at the dark sky. Clouds were coming in, and she knew that later on, there would be enough to snuff out the stars. After a long time, she got up, put the men's belongings into one man's ammo bag, and carried them to the house. She turned on the porch light and read the names on the licenses and credit cards. Wylie had not been lying—none of them was Daniel Martel.

She found the spade, then began to fill the pit. It was hard work. She took her jacket off and shoveled, letting the sweat pour off her, and soak the spine and armpits of her

T-shirt. Her hair was a long, wet rope down her back. The volume of eight men and their weapons was considerable, but after the mass grave looked even with the rest of the field, Jane still kept bringing dirt until it was a bit higher. She had saved the layer of turf and weeds she had used to hide the pit, so she replanted them now in the topsoil. When she was finished, she took the tarp and spade to the house.

She turned on the hose at the side of the house, hosed off the grass, then went to the front porch and washed off all the blood she could from the high-gloss enamel paint.

She knew the men had come in some kind of vehicle, and she didn't want to leave it where they must have parked it, halfway up the dirt road. She went inside, searched the men's belongings, found three sets of car keys, took them all, walked up the road, and found the van. She tried a set of keys, got in, and drove the van to the house, then around the side to the back, where it would be hard to see from any angle.

Her night of killing was nearly used up. She began to pile things in the big brick barbecue behind the house—the tarp, the blanket, the leather wallets and other perishable items the men had in their pockets. She kept the money, identification, credit cards, and loose slips of paper. In the kitchen she found a glass jar and a rubber tube that attached to the faucet for spraying dishes. She went to the van, siphoned off a quart of gasoline from its tank, and soaked the things in the barbecue. She rinsed the jar and tube with the hose.

The last thing she did was stand on the grass in the moonlight and strip off her clothes. When she was naked except for her hiking boots, she took a windproof lighter that had belonged to one of the men, lit it, and tossed it onto the pile.

The air gave a "huff" sound and the fire came into being above the pile of human things like a little explosion that puffed against her hair. It was a big flame, at least ten feet tall at first, bright orange with an aura of blue around it. Jane watched it for a minute, until it had begun to calm down and settle into devouring what it had been given. Then she walked out of the firelight and went about two hundred feet to the edge of the lake.

She kept walking, and her boots sank into mud at first, making a sucking sound as she lifted them for the next step. The water was icy, but to her it felt clean and fierce and scouring. She kept going until the water reached her chest, and then bent her legs and ducked under. She came up gasping, feeling as though her skin were burning instead of cold. She took two more deep breaths and then went under again, scrubbing herself all over with her hands. She took off her boots and cleaned them of the lingering bits of mud, then walked up through the reeds to the shore. She put her boots back on and walked up toward the fire.

She was shivering when she got there, but she stood in the heat for a few minutes, feeling the fire evaporating the moisture almost instantly. Already there seemed to be nothing recognizable in the fire, only ashes and black residue. She walked to the house, and left her boots on the back porch to dry. She locked every door, barred every window, and went upstairs. She stepped into the shower and washed herself carefully and thoroughly, beginning with her hair and ending with her feet, then dressed in a clean sweatshirt, jeans, and sneakers.

She reloaded her pistol and her shotgun. Then she went to a room that had not been touched, lay on the bed, and went to sleep.

Over the next few days she would search the van, remove its license plates and VIN tag, and abandon it deep in the woods. She would perform many hours of scrubbing in the house, fill holes in walls, and paint over them. She would do some more planting over the grave. But most of the time, she would rest and recover.

It was not until the fourth day, while she was indoors during a heavy rain organizing the information she had gleaned from the men's belongings and the contents of the van, that she admitted to herself what she was going to do next.

18

Jane drove west on the Southern Tier Expressway over a hundred miles before she stopped at Oil Springs. This was a tiny bit of land that had been left as a Seneca reservation to preserve Seneca ownership of the spring. The water flowed into a pond and was clear and cold, but had a coating on top that was oil. In the old times, the Senecas used to collect it by dragging a blanket along the calm surface and then wring it out into containers. She had heard that the prophet Handsome Lake, who had lived not far from here in the 1790s, used to come to make medicine.

The spring was at the end of Cuba Lake on County Route 50. She parked her car, put some equipment in a bag, and began to walk west from the pond. It didn't take her long to get far enough inland on the swampy ground to begin spotting the flower she was looking for here and there. She looked for healthy plants over seven feet tall with complicated branchings that each ended in the flat white groups of tiny flowers that looked like circles of lace.

Harvesting was dangerous. She had retained a few pairs of surgical gloves from the housecleaning, and she put on a pair now. She used the long, razor-sharp blade of the K-Bar knife to dig up the muck around the bottoms of the plants so the roots would come up easily. She collected the roots of about fifty of the tall water plants.

She loaded the roots into one-gallon ziplock bags, then went to a spot in the shade where there were a few large flat limestone slabs. She set the bags on the flat stone surface and used the blunt side of her hatchet to pound the roots into a mash. She repeated the process with each of the bags. Finally, she stretched the leg of a pair of panty hose over a glass jar, put a pinhole in the first of the plastic bags, and squeezed the pale yellow juice from the pulverized roots out the hole and through the homemade filter into the jar.

Jane was always extremely cautious with water hemlock. Just handling the stems with bare hands could make a person lose consciousness, but the strongest poison was concentrated in the roots. It was a powerful nerve toxin, and eating a couple of bites of a single root would kill a person in minutes. She kept working with her bags of root mash, moving the panty hose occasionally to present a fresh filter. She filled four quart jars with the filtered root juice before she ran out. The juice she obtained was strong and clear, free of root particles. She capped the jars, reloaded her equipment into her backpack, walked to her car, and put everything in her trunk.

She drove on, bought a ten-foot coil of copper tubing and a camp stove in a hardware store in the next town, then stopped in the cooking section of a small department store and bought a teapot and a cooking thermometer. She drove another thirty miles and followed signs to a picnic area by a campsite. Cicutoxin, the poison in water hemlock, was a complex alcohol. Alcohol boiled at a lower temperature than water, so purifying and concentrating the juice was done by distilling it. She set the covered pot on the stove, attached the copper tubing to the spout, sealed the openings with duct tape, and let the tubing extend in a downward spiral into an empty jar. When the juice in the teapot boiled, the cicutoxin would vaporize at around seventy degrees Celsius, then condense in the long copper tube, and drip into the jar. The water wouldn't boil off until it reached one hundred degrees Celsius. She boiled the juice until about a quarter of the liquid remained, then refilled the pot and repeated the process. When she had finished, she had about a quart of highly concentrated poison. The clear liquid had lost almost all of its yellowish tinge.

She sealed everything she had contaminated in a big plastic bag, put that into a second plastic bag, stopped after dark at a Dumpster behind a large store, and put the bag in the Dumpster, a few feet down where no human being might touch it. The Dumpster would be lifted by the mechanical arms of the garbage truck and dumped in a landfill. All she had kept was one quart jar of concentrated poison. She wasn't sure that it was as strong as the best batch she had ever made, but she was sure it wouldn't take more than a tablespoon of it to kill a person.

In Erie, Pennsylvania, she turned in the rental car and went to a car lot and bought a used Camry for a down payment of five hundred dollars and a promise that Heather Gollensz would begin paying two hundred dollars a month after a three-month grace period. She drove on into Ohio. As she traveled, she fell back into the old discipline. She never let her gas tank go below half full, and the nearer she could keep it to full, the better. She traveled at night by preference, moving along the highway at a steady, unchanging speed with feigned patience.

She was so familiar with the east-west interstate highways that she noticed if a new sign for a restaurant or a hotel appeared where it hadn't been last trip. She had driven these night roads with exhausted, sleeping fugitives, staring at the mirrors every few seconds because any set of headlights that lingered in her wake too long might be death waiting for its best chance. She'd driven the same routes alone, pushing the road time and the speed, because an extra day of travel could mean a helpless victim would disappear forever. This time her eyes were usually fixed on the road ahead, and her mind was occupied with trying to move forward to the day when she would find Daniel Martel.

As Jane drove, she thought about Martel. He would be getting a bit anxious by now. He had sent out eight hired shooters to the place where he'd known Jane, and probably Shelby, would be, and the eight had simply vanished into silence. There were no news reports, no police investigations, no complaints of a disturbance. Jane was satisfied with that. She hoped the disappearance of his men kept Martel awake at night, and made him compulsively turn to look over his shoulder in daylight.

Driving back to Los Angeles meant putting herself in the one place where her breakout of Jim Shelby wasn't a distant event rapidly fading into memory. She was going to a city where any police officer might be actively watching for her. It was also Daniel Martel's country, not hers. The Adirondack Mountains where she had ambushed Martel's men were part of her ancestral world. She had been there many times since she was a child, and it was a place where she felt comfortable. Southern California was not part of that world. It was a hot, inhospitable place for her at this time of year, when the sky would turn clear like a gigantic, unchanging blue bowl, and the temperature might rise to 110. Los Angeles was a single suburb eighty miles north to south, and a hundred east to west, and Martel probably knew it better than she ever could.

Hunting him would mean stalking him from a distance. She stopped at a hotel in Phoenix. She began by going out to buy a computer in an Apple store and then going back to her room to begin her search. She began with Google and moved quickly to the tools she had developed to help place her runners. She signed out and then signed back in as a corporation she had invented about ten years earlier to provide work histories for her clients. She performed searches on Lexis and Nexis. In Lexis she found deeds and mortgages, motor vehicle registrations, and personal legal histories. He had never been convicted of a crime, never even been arrested. But he did have property.

He had a house in Los Angeles. That struck her as revealing. When he had lived with Susan Shelby in Los Angeles, it wasn't at his house. He had made her rent an apartment and moved in with her. He must have been expecting to do something that would get him into trouble. He had probably never told her his real name.

He also had a condominium in Las Vegas, which was his official residence. That made sense to her. He had some kind of business as a cover for selling prescription drugs diverted from legal distribution channels, and he seemed to have quite a bit of money. Nevada had no state income tax. There was a Porsche Carrera registered in Nevada, and a Mercedes 735 registered in California.

She found the mortgage he had taken out to buy the house in Los Angeles, and she almost cried out in frustration. He'd had to give his Social Security number, but it had been blacked out. That number would have given her access to his credit reports and his financial records and eventually would have told her where he was.

She still didn't have him. She had used the computer to get specific bits about him, like stakes to drive in a circle around him, the beginning of a definition. But she had not found a picture of him, had no certainty about where he was. Each time he could have made a mistake and been caught, he had avoided it and escaped. He had been supernaturally careful and thorough about removing all traces of himself from the apartment in Los Angeles he had shared with Jim Shelby's wife. In the apartment the police had found no fingerprints, no DNA traces. He had been nowhere near the building where Jane had been held and tortured, and nowhere near the house where his men had held Sarah Shelby. The underlings Jane might have used to connect him with crimes were dead.

Jane spent some time organizing and studying the information she had found about him, then teased it to make it more useful. She used aerial maps and surface photographs to get pictures of his house and his condo and the streets on all sides of them. She got more aerial photos for each hour of the day or night, and signed into traffic cameras that were permanently trained on the major thoroughfares nearby.

She used the driver's license numbers to bring up replicas of his actual licenses so she could see his photographs. He had thick, dark hair; a smooth, unlined face; and large, light blue eyes. She wasn't surprised that he was handsome. He had gone to Austin with confidence that he would have no trouble meeting and manipulating a woman he only expected must exist—a pharmaceutical saleswoman who worked at the nearby company headquarters. According to the licenses, he was tall—six feet two inches—and he weighed 180 pounds. She could see from the photos that he was trim, with big shoulders and chest. It was a body acquired not by playing some game, but by consciously shaping with weights and repetitive exercises. His skin was evenly tanned. It had been done not by being outdoors in some active way, but more likely by using a tanning bed. He controlled his appearance like an actor.

She studied the pictures of his face until she was sure she could recognize it even if he added something to change his appearance—a beard, glasses, mustache, hair dye. Then she packed her clothes, computer, and guns into the car, and drove toward Los Angeles. All of the men he had sent after her had been carrying California driver's licenses.

Jane was heading for a city where she had committed the crime of the year. Before she left Phoenix, she stopped in a wig shop and bought three wigs. One was light brown with natural-looking highlights, one was darker brown with a hint of red, and one was short and blond. She knew from experience that she could get away with even light blond hair with her blue eyes, but the wig made her look very different. In another shop she bought two pairs of sunglasses, one that wrapped around her face, and one with big saucer-shaped dark lenses that made her face look small.

As she drove the last hundred miles to Los Angeles on Route 10, she thought about the ways of getting to Daniel Martel. When she reached Santa Monica she took her Camry to a Toyota dealer and told the service manager to do all of the checks, replacements, and maintenance it would take to make the car into one he would buy his daughter. When she picked it up a day later, she filled the tank and had the car washed and waxed. She knew that a dirty car caught people's attention in Los Angeles, and made it look as though the driver had just blown in from elsewhere.

She drove to the neighborhood in west Los Angeles where Daniel Martel's house was. She spent over an hour driving around the area before she swung past his address for the first time. His house was a two-story Spanish-style building with a red tile roof and a balcony with an ornate wrought-iron railing. She could see signs on the lawn for a security company, and a few decals on the lower windows and front door.

Jane returned to her hotel and laid out a set of dark clothes, a baseball cap, more of the surgical gloves she had used for cleaning, about fifty feet of the rope she had brought to the house in the Adirondacks, her folding knife, and her two identical Beretta M92 pistols.

At two a.m. Jane drove past Daniel Martel's house, parked a block away, and walked back to the house. She stepped around the outside, peering in windows. There was an alarm keypad that she could see beside the front door, but she could also see that the display said, "RDY": ready. It was not turned on. Did that mean he was at home, that he was in there waiting for her? There were no lights on, and there was no car in the garage. She wondered if it meant that he had no fear of a break-in, or that he had known she would be coming but didn't want the security system to summon anyone. She decided it probably meant he wanted her to find her way in.

She continued around the house, looking inside. She knew she could break a window, reach a latch, and slip inside without worrying about the alarm going off. If he was gone, that would be safe, but she sensed something was wrong. She picked up a fallen branch from beneath a tree in the yard, cleaned it of twigs, tied her rope around it, stood to the side of the balcony, and threw it over both railings so it dangled free on the other side without hitting anything and making noise. She reached up and removed the stick, tied the two parts of the rope into a slipknot, tugged it to tighten it, and began to climb. As she did, she used her arms more than usual to save her right leg. When she was just below the balcony she reached up, clutched the edge, and pulled herself up to grasp the railing. She braced her left foot against the wall of the house, used the railing to climb up, and stepped over it onto the concrete surface of the balcony. Then she pulled the rope to bring the knot up to her, untied it, drew up the rest of the rope, and left it coiled on the balcony where it wouldn't be seen from below.

She leaned close to the double doors on the balcony and stared in at the master suite. There was a king bed with gauzy covers and two long pillows. She moved to look from the left side of the left door along the wall to the closed bedroom door, then beyond it toward the right, when she saw the spring gun aimed at the inner side of the bedroom door on the far side of the room from her.

It was a pump shotgun set up on a table using a bench rest designed for zeroing in a rifle at a range. There was a thin wire running across the closed bedroom door, through an eyebolt screwed into the woodwork on the wall beside the door, through another one in the wall behind the shotgun, then attached to a piece of wood set inside the trigger guard just in front of the trigger. When the door opened, the shotgun would blast the intruder at the height of the table, about thirty inches above the floor. For someone standing upright, the blast would hit the lower abdomen. It was a prolonged, painful death.

Jane stayed at the double door on the balcony studying the room to spot signs of more traps. She saw nothing, so she slid the blade of her knife between the two doors, lifted the latch, then stepped aside and placed her back to the wall before she tugged the right door open.

She remained still and listened. There was no gunshot, no sound of an alarm system, no low growl of a dog that he'd locked in. She leaned in far enough to see all sides, but kept her feet planted until she was sure there was no threat in this room but the spring gun. She stepped carefully to the shotgun, clicked the safety in so the red stripe disappeared, removed the piece of wood from the trigger guard, and let the wire go slack.

The spring gun had been aimed at the closed door that led out of the bedroom to the hallway. She stepped to the door and listened. She stepped back a pace. Something was wrong. There was no sound out there. Nobody was on the other side waiting for her, but she sensed that the spring gun she had disarmed couldn't be all. That wasn't the way this man thought. He was a murderer who had framed his victim's husband for the murder and then tried to get him killed in prison. One strike, one murder, one trap would not be enough for him.

As she thought, she knew what it must be. There would be a second spring gun in the hallway, aimed at the outside of the bedroom door. If she entered the bedroom through the balcony doors, as she had, she would see the spring gun in the bedroom and disarm it, and then confidently open the door. The second spring gun, the one in the hallway that she had never imagined, would go off and kill her. If instead she had entered the house another way and come along the hallway toward the bedroom door, she would disarm the spring gun in the hallway and then be killed by the one trained on the door from inside the bedroom. It was a simple, elegant way to build a booby trap: disarming the first gun didn't make you safe; it made you only a confident victim of the second.

She used her knife to unscrew the doorknob and remove it from the inside, then pushed the outer knob out of its hole and let it fall to the floor in the hall.

Through the circular hole where the doorknob had been mounted, she could see the dimly lit hallway. Exactly as she had predicted, there was a second table with a shotgun mounted on a bench rest, aimed at her. She followed the trip wire with her eyes. It ran from the piece of wood in the trigger guard to an eyebolt screwed into the surface of the table behind the shotgun, and then straight to the bedroom door. Since the door opened inward, any attempt to open it would pull the trigger and kill the person coming out of the bedroom.

Jane studied the spot where the wire led to the door, then worked with her knife to carve away the wood from that part of the door. It was taking time, but Jane had already determined that Daniel Martel wasn't here. If he showed up now, she would hear his car through the open balcony doors. She kept working until her blade scraped the screw end of the eyebolt. When she freed the bolt from the door, she heard a clink. She put her eye to the hole and saw the bolt and the slack trip wire on the floor.

She pulled the door open and walked to the shotgun. She pushed the safety on and continued down the hall. There were four more bedrooms up here, but none of them had any furniture. There were just polished hardwood floors and spotless white walls.

Because stairways were easy places to plant booby traps, Jane used great care in descending to the first floor. She kept her feet on the outer edges of the stairs, where she could see what she was stepping on. When she reached the bottom, she found an insulated wire and followed it to a pressure pad Martel had installed under the runner on one of the steps.

She could feel the man's mind at work. He had a problem. He had murdered a woman and framed the woman's husband. The husband was always the easiest one to get the police to accept, because most female murder victims were killed by male family members or friends. Probably Martel had always planned to have the husband murdered in prison, because as long as the framed man was alive, someone might take a second look at the crime. When Jane had taken Jim Shelby away from him, he had sent eight men after her, and this must have struck him as no more than prudent. She had buried the eight, and disappeared again. Clearly he was now aware that she was coming for him, and he was retreating and leaving booby traps in his wake, not staying to wait for her.

She searched, moving methodically through Daniel Martel's house from room to room, opening all the spaces where things might be hidden. She searched for photographs of Daniel Martel. She searched for medicines in the cabinets that might indicate a chronic illness or an addiction. She examined the figurative paintings to see whether any of the landscapes might be pleasant places he had visited once and might return to if he felt he had to lie low for a period of time.

When she had been everywhere on the ground floor, she climbed the stairs again to look in the master suite. She opened the walk-in closet and the lights went on automatically. The poles where clothes were hung had been disarranged, with some clothes taken and the other hangers pushed to the sides. She studied the clothes that remained to see whether he had been searching through the cold-weather clothes, taken hiking boots or beach sandals, taken expensive suits and shoes or left them. To her it appeared that he had left out the extremes. Judging from the locations of the empty hangers, he had apparently taken something from the jeans section, several shirts, a couple of sport coats, and a windbreaker or light jacket. The shoes were in rows of small cubbyholes. There seemed to be a pair of sneakers or running shoes gone, and a pair of dress shoes, probably brown, since that was the color of the others in that row.

She pushed some hangers aside. There was a compartment built into the back wall. It wasn't a safe, just a doorless cabinet that must have been hidden by a set of shelves on rollers that he had pushed aside. She looked inside to see if she could determine what he had chosen to take. There was an empty envelope with the return address of the West Valley Bank printed on it, the kind a teller would offer if you withdrew too much cash to carry in a pocket. There was a second envelope, this one with the return address of the county clerk in Dayton, Ohio. The name of the addressee had apparently been typed on a sticker, and it had been torn off. The receipt inside said that it was for a duplicate of a birth certificate, but not the name of the baby. There was another envelope that was from Sioux Falls, South Dakota, and said, "Do Not Forward." It had to be a credit card he'd ordered in a false name.

He was running, and that put him in a world she knew better than he did.

She took her rope from the balcony, closed the doors, went down the stairs, and stepped across the never-occupied living room and out the front door. When she reached her car, she started it and drove to the first freeway entrance and turned north. At this hour, it would only take a few minutes to reach the 101 freeway, and then the junction with the 134. In an hour she'd be nearly to the edge of the desert at Victorville, and she would be in Las Vegas by morning.

19

Daniel Martel seemed to Jane to be someone who went to some trouble to be unreadable. His house in Los Angeles wasn't a home; it was an investment. It had expensive paintings but no books, no old clothes, no magazines, no computer, and no personal effects. It was a place for him to stay while he was in Los Angeles without having to be visible or sign a hotel register. It was also a place to store some of his wealth. And real estate was the easiest commodity to manipulate—to give equal credibility to either a big profit or a big loss, whichever he wanted. Martel had apparently never before been close enough to danger to need to run. But Martel was cagey, cunning.

He'd had enough imagination to foresee the possibility that if he kept making money through criminal acts, he might someday have to run. Maybe when he was with Susan Shelby, he had seen in her whatever quality it was that ultimately had made him kill her, and prepared. Maybe she was a talker, who might reveal his business. It might have been as simple as Susan getting irritating, and Martel beginning to think about what beginning a future without her might require. Jane was aware that Martel was psychologically sophisticated. His simple booby trap had been dangerous because it displayed acute attention to how the human mind worked.

But he was still a novice at running. He had not had time to think through the predicament of a runner and invent strategies for each obstacle. He would drive to Las Vegas—almost certainly, he had done so as soon as he'd realized his hired men must be dead—and collect whatever he thought he needed. The Las Vegas condominium would be another place for Jane to learn more about him.

She rechecked the two Beretta pistols she was carrying, put one in her jacket, and put the other under the seat. She drove as fast as she could without attracting the police. The drive to Las Vegas was a long roller coaster—an incline that rose five thousand feet to the Cajon Pass, then a descent into the edge of Death Valley at sea level again, then a couple of smaller ups and downs, ending at two thousand feet on the Las Vegas Strip. She was driving outside the fence past the taxiway at McCarron Airport when the sun rose. The look of everything—blinding and sun-bleached with a promise of cruel heat just outside the car window—reminded her of the morning only a few weeks ago when she'd been wounded, alone on foot with no money, no food, no water, no name. Things were so different now that as the two impressions merged, she felt stronger and more determined.

She knew approximately where Daniel Martel's condominium was. The address included the name Silverstrike Club, and she remembered seeing a building with that name on it just east of the Strip. She looked it up on her laptop and saw that it was between a midsize hotel and a nightclub. There were a couple of pools and a nine-hole golf course behind it.

The problem was going to be getting inside to the upper floors where the condominiums were. Las Vegas was an island in a river of cash, so it was full of people who had come to steal. It was, consequently, also heavily populated with security technicians, guards, rent-a-cops, and others whose job it was to prevent incursions by the thieves. It would be best to assume she was always under surveillance.

There was little time for the things she would have to accomplish here, so she started immediately. She drove to the hotel beside the Silverstrike Club, checked in wearing her short blond wig, and then went out shopping for a dress. The Forum at Caesar's was close, and at its heart was a collection of high-end stores for women. She spent an hour finding the right dress, purse, and shoes, and returned to her hotel with enough time to take extraordinary pains with her hair, makeup, and accessories.

She was a bit thinner than she had been when she'd gone to get Jim Shelby out of the courthouse, so she supposed she looked more appealing by Las Vegas standards than she had before she'd been shot and starved. Before she left the room, she made sure the marks that Wylie and his friends had made on her were hidden by her long sleeves and high neckline.

As she walked the two hundred feet to the front entrance of the Silverstrike Club, she could feel the drying and tightening as the surface moisture of her skin was seared away by the sun. The white building was about twenty stories high with a broad, roofed-over drive in front like the gigantic hotels on the Strip. Jane stepped inside, heard the automatic door swing closed behind her, and felt the refrigerated air embrace her. The lobby was an empty marble cavern except for a wide concierge desk with a woman in a man's sport coat standing behind it. Jane approached and said, "Hello."

"Good afternoon." The girl was as well trained and disciplined as an acrobat. Her smile was an artful blend of dental bleaching techniques and willpower. "How can I help you this afternoon?"

"I'm supposed to meet Mr. Martel for lunch at one. Can you please call him for me?"

"Of course." The voice was lilting. There was nothing in the range of human activities that she would rather do. She punched numbers with a fingernail manicured by a nameless artist. Next came the moment when the eagerness was replaced by uncertainty. She hung up. "He's not answering." She had already filed this incident in the archives of thoughtless errors men commit. Her left eyebrow gave a twitch of commiseration. "Would you like to wait for him in the bar?"

Jane looked only mildly surprised by his absence, but certainly not ready to disregard the slight. She glanced at her watch with the eye of a prosecutor silently building a case: the time was now entered into the official record. "Well, all right," she said, as though the outcome had been anything but sure.

"I'll take you there." The girl was around the counter and gliding across the marble floor, so Jane had to move quickly to keep up. The girl reached the door a half step ahead so she could push it open before Jane's progress could be impeded. They entered a space with a large dining room on the left, and a long bar on the right with a liveried bartender wielding a cocktail shaker before a couple of men in polo shirts and shorts.

Just inside the door was another perfected young woman at a lectern. The concierge whispered something about "Mr. Martel" and "bar." The hostess was launched a few steps toward the bar, turned her head only, and held her hand out to Jane. "I'll watch for him and let him know where you are."

"Thank you," Jane said. She sat at a small metal table in the bar and took her phone out. She pretended to look down into the display at e-mails or text messages, but she had pressed the button for "camera" and was using the viewer to study the men in the vicinity. There were only about a dozen in the bar, but all of them had taken a moment to watch the concierge, the hostess, and Jane. That was fairly promising.

As she studied the room through her phone, she thought about what she should do if it all went wrong—if Daniel Martel suddenly walked in. There was no chance he could get across the lobby without being reminded by the concierge that he had a date waiting. The ladies' room was at the end of the space, to the right of the bar. She would probably be able to head into that hallway and follow it all the way to the other side, where the restrooms would be accessible to the dining room. The door to the kitchen was in the same direction, a little farther on. She could slip in, go down the long aisle that was always in the center for waiters to pick up orders, and be out the back door before he had any idea what to do.

The waiter appeared at her table, and Jane looked up and said, "May I have an iced tea, please?"

He had barely had time to step away before a new man replaced him, standing above her. "Hi," he said. "Are you waiting for somebody?"

He didn't appear to have been out golfing or swimming. His summer-weight sport coat and jeans could have been work attire in an informal office, but his T-shirt and sandals could not, and his Patek Philippe watch raised the question of whether work was necessary. He was handsome, but in a way that was too old for the way he dressed. She decided to take a chance rather than wait for another one. "Well, I have been waiting, but I'm beginning to wonder whether I should. Being late is manipulative. If I put in the time and effort to wait much longer, I'll have to persuade myself that he was worth it. Then I'll have to be willing to devote more time and effort to him."

"He sounds very sophisticated."

"It's not working. I'm just getting irritated."

He shrugged. "Anger is a passion, and it makes your blood circulate and starts you thinking about him. That's much better than indifference."

"Not if you want to get laid this year instead of next."

He threw his head back and laughed. "Good point." He took a fake step away, then stopped, as they both had known he would. He looked back. "If you'd prefer some company while you wait, you might make him jealous."

"I may as well inflict whatever pain I can. Have a seat."

He sat at the small table with her, gave a half wave to the waiter, and, while the waiter approached, said, "Is that iced tea?"

She nodded.

"Two Long Island iced teas." To Jane he said, "You like to trade up, don't you?"

Jane said, "Thanks, but four kinds of liquor and sweet and sour mix?"

"It's just your iced tea's more fun-loving sister."

"No alcohol."

He nodded, and the waiter disappeared. "So what's your name?"

"Tina Guilford. And you?"

"Rick Chambers." He held his hand out, and when she shook it, he held on a half second too long.

She freed her hand. "Pleased to meet you. Do you golf here?"

"Not often," he said. "And never in the summer. It's a hundred and six out there. By three it'll be a hundred and ten. I mostly just live here."

"Do you like it?"

"Sure. It's a block from the Strip. It's got all the amenities, and the view in every direction is fantastic. It's safe from random people wandering in and out whenever they please. Not like the big hotels."

"I never got the idea they were unsafe."

"They're not, actually. But do you want all the people you see walk in their doors to walk into yours?"

"I suppose not." She looked at her watch.

"Are you hungry?"

"Well, to be honest with you, he did ask me here for lunch."

"It's getting to be mid-afternoon. Come on. Let's get a table." He leaned forward, his hands on the table as though he were about to push off.

"No, I don't want to impose. I'll just finish my tea and order lunch for myself."

"You're out of luck, Tina, honey. This is a private club. You can't pay for your iced tea, let alone lunch. We're too snobby to use money. It goes on a tab. Please. I'm hungry, too. I'll sit here and suffer with you if you want, just because you're beautiful. But it would be much nicer to watch you eat lunch."

She looked at the hostess, visibly uncomfortable. Then she smiled at him. "I'll take you up on your kind offer. You're a true gentleman."

"It's just my upbringing, and when I find a beautiful woman at my mercy I overcome that pretty quickly." He waved at the waiter and said, "We'd like a table in the dining room, please."

They went into the dining room, which was still well populated, and ordered. They ate and had a pleasant, unhurried conversation. Jane kept steering the conversation away from the way she looked, and moved her arm twice because he had the habit of laying his hand on it for emphasis. When they'd been there for nearly an hour, she said, "Well, I guess he's not going to show up at all, and he lives here."

"What's his name?"

"Today, it's Fool. But he'll still be calling himself David Cavendish."

"If he comes in now, please don't make a scene. I'm too much of a coward for a fistfight."

"Do you know him?"

"I don't think so. But he sounds Scottish. Probably throws the caber and drinks his single malt neat, and all that."

"Pretty close. I'm picturing him in a kilt now. This would be a better climate for a kilt than Scotland."

"Too much wind off the desert. It's the only show in town nobody would pay to see."

A few minutes later, she determined it was time to force him to decide whether to commit himself. "This was a lot of fun, Rick. I really enjoyed our lunch. You turned what started as a horrible day into a nice one."

"Oh, we can't just end it here. You were curious about the club. Let me show you around."

"I don't want to waste your afternoon."

"Afternoon is nothing. Half the people in town are asleep waiting for night. Come on." He came around behind her to pull out her chair, then led her out the far door that led to the residential part of the building. There was another door, and he used a key card to open it. Jane felt a blast of heat, but stepped into it after him.

"Out here is the pool I like best. Over here, by the jungle." There was a thick barrier of sago palms, elephant ears, and flowering plants. The pool was a complicated shape with waterfalls and grottoes that opened onto some other part of the pool she didn't see. The impression was of a place apart, somewhere other than the desert. "Very pretty."

"The golf course is up that way, and the tennis courts are over there. You can follow the ambulances picking up the sunstroke cases."

He opened the door again with his key card, and stepped to the elevator. He pressed the "up" button.

"Where to now?"

"You've got to see the view from the upper floors." When the doors slid aside he stepped in, pushed "18," and swiped his card on the reader beside the panel. The elevator rose. Jane followed him out on the eighteenth floor to a door marked 1829. "Here," he said. "Look the other way, and prepare for a sight."

Jane covered her face with her hands and looked up and down the corridor to spot the security cameras. She didn't see any. He pushed the door open, then said, "Now look."

She stepped across a symbolic expanse of marble into the large living room. In the floor-to-ceiling windows were the backs and sides of the hotels on the east side of the Strip—MGM and Venetian, Paris—and on the west side she saw the facades of Mandalay Bay Luxor, Caesar's Palace, Bellagio, Mirage. "This is absolutely breathtaking," she said.

"I love it. I'm glad I got to show it to you."

"I am, too."

"Now take a look on this side." He opened a door and they walked into a room that was a sort of den, but had a desk with papers on it. The big window in this one was on the other side, and looked out onto the dry hardpan and distant mountains.

"That's incredible, too," she said. "But it doesn't look any more real than the other side."

"Let's have a drink," he said. "You have to keep hydrated around here, or you fall over and get stepped on."

"What do you have?"

"Nonalcoholic?"

"Not necessarily."

"How about a nice, icy vodka martini?"

"Well, okay."

"Great. I'll make them."

She followed him through the living room to a counter that was near the entrance to the kitchen. He took two martini glasses and walked off to put them in the freezer.

He took the shaker and ice and poured in the touch of vermouth. She saw him shake and pour off the vermouth, pour in the vodka, then begin to shake it. As he shook it, he went back to the kitchen with the shaker, took out the two iced glasses, and walked across her line of vision to an angle she couldn't see. He returned with the two martinis, smiling. He handed her one, clinked his glass against hers, and said, "To serendipity."

He tipped his glass back, and Jane raised hers. She saw that the stems of the two glasses had small metal rings around them. His was a silvery color, like platinum, and hers was gold with a little ruby on it. She touched the glass to her lips and turned her head to survey the windows again. The rings were obviously part of a set that people attached to guests' glasses at parties so they could identify their own drinks and not take someone else's. "That's a nice martini," she said.

"I'm glad you like it," he said. "Anybody can make a good second martini. It's the first one that's hard, while people can still taste them."

She looked at the far hallway. "I think I noticed your bathroom on the tour. Can you excuse me, please?"

"Sure. Right down there."

She wanted to take her glass with her and pour it out, but that wasn't normal. He would suspect she knew. She set the martini down on the counter, went into the bathroom, and locked the door. The rings had not been on the glass stems when he'd taken them to the freezer. Why would he put those rings on the glasses this time? There were only two of them. And did it really matter? It wasn't as though the drinks were different but looked the same. They were the same, exactly. Only they weren't. They couldn't be.

Jane looked around her for a solution. She spotted a dispenser on the wall of the bathroom that held paper cups. She flushed the toilet, and then ran the water while she pulled two cups out, put them into her purse, and left the bathroom.

He wasn't visible. His drink was on the counter with hers, but he was gone. There must be a second bathroom. She poured her drink into the two little paper cups, poured his drink into her glass, and poured the paper cups into his glass. As she lifted her glass and took a sip from it, her eyes rose and saw him coming from the kitchen. Without thinking about it, she realized he had used the moment to get rid of the concoction—the chloral hydrate, Rohypnol, GHB, whatever he used—just in case she went in there. Or maybe one of the times he'd done this before, he had forgotten to hide it before he carried the girl into the bedroom, and forever after he was worried about his own competence. He smiled, snatched up his drink, and took a large gulp. "You're right. That's good."

He walked into the living room and sat on the couch. She came and sat near him. He looked closely at her as he said, "So, Tina. What do you do?"

"I'm a loan officer for a bank." She smiled. "That's why I've got time for an extra little unpaid vacation this summer. We're hardly making any loans, so they're happy to let anybody who wants to take time."

"Sounds good. And bad, of course."

"How about you?"

"I'm good, too, and bad."

"I meant your job."

"I'm semiretired. I was one of the people who put up money for this place, and we made quite a profit, so I don't really need to punch a clock."

"That must be nice."

"I thought it would be," he said. "I thought that I'd have a good life. I had a wife, and some kids. The kids were already out of college, and my wife and I had planned to travel and have a great time after I quit the contracting business. But I never seemed to be able to get there. Finally, this place got finished, and I came home one day and said, 'I've retired.' She said, 'That's odd.' I said, 'What do you mean, odd?' She said, 'I've just filed for divorce.'"

"Really? I'm so sorry."

"She was right, though. It was odd." He was getting tired, having a hard time keeping his eyes open. "We lived in California, which is a community property state. She took half the money and left. But I still have enough." He stared at her for a moment. "You did something to my drink, didn't you?"

"Did I?"

He lowered his head. "I'm sorry."

"That's a really creepy thing to do," she said. "You could go to jail for the rest of your life." She took the Beretta pistol out of her purse, then pressed it against his temple. "Or you could run into somebody who woke up mad enough to kill you for it."

His eyes widened, but then a moment later the chloral hydrate overcame even his alarm. His head tilted back on the top of the couch and his body seemed to melt into it. He began to snore.

Jane listened to him for a few seconds, and decided his breathing was strong enough to keep him alive, and wasn't getting any weaker. She hadn't originally planned to do anything to Rick; she just intended to have him use his key card on the elevator. She would pretend to go toward the lobby, then stop the elevator on the fifteenth floor and get out. She rolled him slightly to the side and reached into his pocket, then pulled out his key card.

She went into the kitchen and searched the cabinets and drawers until she found a small brown unlabeled plastic bottle with pills inside. She poured the pills out into the garbage disposal, ground them up, and ran the water for a minute to be sure they got out into the drain.

Jane took a last look around. She wiped off the two glasses, the doorknob and faucets in the bathroom, and the plastic pill bottle, and took the two paper cups with her. She checked on Rick again. He was breathing steadily, if noisily.

She remembered that he had told her he'd been one of the developers of the building. Would this man give up all that control? Wouldn't he hold on to just a remnant of it, even if it was only a symbol? She rolled him onto his side and took his wallet from his back pocket. She looked among the credit cards and found the second key card she'd been looking for. The first one bore a photograph of the building. This one was plain gold with the silver letters *Silverstrike Construction*. She looked out the peephole in the door, then opened it and left.

She walked to the elevator, stepped in, used Rick's key card to activate it, and rode it down to the fifteenth floor. When she got out, she used the card again and sent the elevator back up to the eighteenth floor. She didn't want it to arrive on the ground floor, open, and reveal itself to be empty.

She looked both ways and saw that the hallway was deserted. She kept her head down, because she assumed she was being taped. She stopped at Martel's door; tried Rick's key card in the lock; saw, as she'd expected, that it wouldn't work; and put it away. Then she took out the second key card, the one she had found in his wallet, and inserted it into the lock, then pulled it out. The little light shone green and she heard a click. She was right: Rick had retained a master key. She pushed the door open and stepped inside.

After all of her effort, she was inside Daniel Martel's condominium. She stood still and looked in every direction. She didn't want to come all this way and get killed by another one of his booby traps. She studied the big living room. It was the same layout as Rick's, and she saw no alterations that would hide a booby trap. The door sign indicated that he had a maid service come in to clean, and he could hardly have warned the service about any booby trap. He must have been counting on the regular security system of the club to keep everyone out of this place.

She could see he had the same built-in cabinetry Rick had, the same furniture facing the same tall windows. But the paintings on the walls were peculiar. They were stylized nearly naked showgirls that seemed to be taller than a man and menacing, with emaciated white-painted faces accented by collagen-puffed, bloodred lips and bared teeth. Their cheeks had round smears of rouge that were almost clownish. The eyes were luminous and cruel, like the eyes of the big cats in animal trainers' acts. They had the quality of unmasked falsehood, yet still grinned with triumph over the viewer like vampires caught with their fangs showing. She could feel the hatred of women that had inspired every feature.

Jane put on her gloves and began to open drawers and cabinets, searching for all of the things that would give her more information about Martel. She moved into his bedroom. That was where burglars looked first, because it was the place most likely to contain valuables. The bedroom was painted dark gray, and it had two sets of curtains that could shut out all light from outside. The bed was a California king with a fake fur bedspread and silk sheets. Six pillows were piled on it at the head.

She opened the drawers of the nightstands. The one farthest from the door held a box of .45 ammunition, but no gun. The other held two pairs of handcuffs and a blindfold. She closed it, and the sense of foreboding she'd felt since she'd arrived intensified. It might be nothing. There were plenty of people who played games with those things, and it meant nothing about their lives. But Daniel Martel was a murderer, someone she knew had already killed a woman. How could it not mean anything? She found herself staring at the bed. It had a steel head piece and foot piece with vertical bars. Some of the bars looked as though the paint had been marred by something scraping on them.

The closet door was on the other side of the bedroom. It was a walk-in the size of a second bedroom. There was a chest-high island in the middle, and the walls were covered with drawers, cabinets, and poles with hangers. Of course Daniel Martel would be unusually interested in his appearance; he made money seducing foolish women. She closed the closet door, but there was a full-length mirror on the back of the door, and she kept catching her own reflection in it, so she opened it again.

The clothes on hangers had been pushed to one side so there was a section that was bare in the middle. She opened the drawers on the wall to her right, and saw that some of them had been emptied.

The island in the center of the room kept drawing her eye. It was a chest-high rectangle about seven feet long and four feet wide, with drawers on all sides. She opened a few drawers. A couple near the top contained accessories—cuff links, watches, sunglasses, rings, an ID bracelet. Others had socks and underwear still in packages. But she soon lost interest in what was in the drawers. The most intriguing thing about them was their size. They were wide, but they weren't deep enough from front to back. Behind them, inside the center of the island, there had to be a long empty space. She tugged on one of the drawers to pull it free, but it wouldn't come out. She studied the island, ran her fingers under the overhanging top surface, and then knelt and looked up at it. There was a pair of hinges on one side. She walked to the opposite side, found the catch, and pushed it. The top opened like a chest.

In the center of the island, between the drawers, was a rectangular box like a tray. Stored in it were four pistols with extra magazines, two boot knives, a couple of knives that could be opened with a flick of the thumb, two electronic stun guns, and a short Japanese sword designed for fighting in close quarters. She lifted the tray out and set it on the floor, then looked in the tray below it.

There were bundles of letters and three photograph albums. She picked up the first stack of letters and leafed quickly through it, looking at the envelopes. Then she did the same with each of the others. The letters were in different handwriting, from several different people, sent to him at a succession of addresses. But all had been mailed in Indianapolis, Indiana.

She took up the first of the photograph albums. There was a shot of a man about thirty-five to forty years old, with a handsome face. It was Martel. He had longer hair than seemed stylish at the moment, but the picture might be old. On the next page, there he was again in a tuxedo, with an attractive woman with long, shiny blond hair wearing a strapless gown and holding a matching clutch. She was a stereotype, a trophy girlfriend at some big event.

Jane turned the page and saw them both again. The woman had her wrists and ankles tied to a bed, and she was bent over a pile of pillows. There was a gag in her mouth. She seemed to be in genuine distress, not posing or pretending. Sitting at the head of the bed near her was Daniel Martel again, as naked as she was, but smiling. He held a leather belt in one hand. Jane turned the next page, and then the next, and the next. Daniel Martel was a sadist. All the photos were of him and a succession of women, and all of them involved some kind of bondage. In a few of the photographs they were in the midst of intercourse, but even then, the woman would be restrained somehow, while Martel was merely naked, always smiling for the camera. The smiling pose reminded her of a snapshot of a fisherman on a dock standing beside the hoist where his prize tarpon hung.

She took the two photograph albums and the letters from Indianapolis. She lifted out the tray and found the other thing she had been waiting for—financial papers. She found a tax return and copied his Social Security number. Then she returned the three trays to the island, closed the top, and went back through the bedroom and living room to the door.

In the hallway she used Rick's key card to operate the elevator, and rode it to the lobby. She walked out of the club, returned to her hotel room, and quickly began to pack. She wanted to be far from Las Vegas before Rick woke up. As she prepared to put Martel's letters into her suitcase with the albums, she opened the top one and looked at the signature. "Love, Mom," it said. "P.S. We can't wait to see you on the 25th. Let us know if we should get your old room ready." Jane looked at the postmark. The letter was only six days old.

20

As Jane drove toward the east, the sun behind her illuminated everything so brightly that it seemed to glow against the blue of the sky. Within a few hours the sun sank, and she was propelling herself into empty night. She had spent only one day in Las Vegas and had left without sleeping there. Probably Daniel Martel had not dared to spend a night there, either. He had simply stopped to pick up a few things, and then had driven on toward Indianapolis.

She spent four days and nights driving and thinking about what she was doing. For most of her adult life, she had tried to guide her runners away from spots that had become dangerous to new, safe places. She had never encouraged her runners to stand and fight. She had taught them to be rabbits, and shown them how to run from the hounds that were hunting them. Each time she succeeded, the hounds failed, and the rabbits got to live another day. This time would be different. This time, when the hound plunged into the next hole expecting to sink his teeth into the rabbit, he was going to find out that a hole didn't always harbor a rabbit. Once in a while what was down there was something that bit back.

When she reached Indianapolis she drove around the city a bit, trying to get a feel for the area. It was like a lot of other cities in the Midwest, a small central area of tall buildings all jutting upward like a set of teeth, surrounded by a wide circle of one- and two-story buildings stretching outward like ripples in all directions, fading into suburbs.

Daniel Martel's mother had written to him on an occasional but consistent basis. She mentioned his father regularly, and a few people who seemed to be friends and neighbors, but there didn't seem to be any siblings. Jane searched for the address on the envelopes as she explored. It was on Meridien Street.

The houses on both sides of Meridien were large, set back on big pieces of land that had been planted and cultivated into lush gardens and vast lawns that looked as though they had been laid down by golf course greenkeepers. The architecture was mainly copied from the British gentry, much as it was in rich neighborhoods in other cities. There was the usual riot of Tudor and Georgian and a few neoclassical mansions, but the American federalist period and the modern didn't seem to offer anything grand enough.

When she found the correct house number she drove past, scanning it hastily. It seemed to be much like the others. It was three stories high, a Tudor with a steep roof and chimneys on either end. There were thick-trunked old hardwood trees on the lawns and somewhere in the back, serving as witnesses and guarantors of the antiquity of the building. There was a stone fence that separated the house from the next on each side, with exactly the right number and kinds of climbing plants on it—some rambling roses, a few climbers with white or yellow flowers.

She tried to get a look at the cars, in the hope of spotting Daniel Martel's Porsche or his Mercedes, but the driveway was like the one at the McKinnon house in Amherst, New York, where she lived with her husband, Carey. It ran straight back until it was past the house and then turned and went out of sight. She thought she could pick out the corner of an old carriage house converted to a garage like hers and Carey's, but it could have been something else.

Meridien continued through some small, elegant enclaves and out into suburbs where the big houses tended to sprawl at ground level on lots that could have accommodated cornfields, and probably once had.

Jane needed to find a way to keep watch on the Martel house without being caught at it. The problem was that wealthy neighborhoods were generally watched by many unseen eyes, some of them natural and others electronic. Strangers were not especially welcome unless they had specific, useful business there. It was possible to be arrested going for a walk in some cities if you couldn't prove you were there to offer some service to a specific resident.

She drove to her hotel and turned on her computer. She got an aerial view of Martel's parents' neighborhood, and then a ground-level view from the streets on all sides, and studied them to find a good way to get close. Under her business name, she ran another credit check on Daniel Martel using his Las Vegas address and the Social Security number she'd found on his tax return.

There was nothing in the credit record yet to indicate he had arrived in Indianapolis. She guessed this meant that he was traveling the way she did and was using cash and credit cards in a false name. It was possible that since he'd arrived in Indianapolis his parents had been paying for everything, so there was no record that he'd spent any money.

She arrived in the back yard of the house on Meridien at four in the morning, while the world was still dark. She climbed a neighbor's wall and walked along a dry ditch that had apparently been constructed to channel rain runoff from the yards to the next street. She had seen it on the aerial imagery on her computer. She used it to get to the rear of the Martel yard. She wanted to be comfortably settled and able to watch before the first person in the household awoke.

The first one was a woman servant, who turned on the light in a third-floor window at five, and then turned it off a few minutes later and appeared in the kitchen as cook. She was wearing a dress that wasn't quite a uniform, but was designed for work. It was light blue with a white collar and cuffs and buttoned up the front. Jane watched her in the kitchen making coffee, laying out food on serving platters, and doing other chores that Jane couldn't see well. She went into the dining room and set the table.

At six thirty the father came down the stairs and into the dining room. He wore khaki pants, a belt of military webbing with a gold buckle, brown leather shoes, and a blue shirt. The wife was down a minute or two later, wearing a dress that appeared to be light silk with a pattern of blue and white like Delft china. These were people of the last generation, but they had the air of an earlier generation.

She felt a small tug of sympathy for them. She wondered if there was a hidden feeling of doom because they had raised a murderer and were trying to keep from knowing it. Either way, they betrayed no evidence that they weren't delighted with their lives.

The mother had apparently been a beauty when she was young. She was still straight and slim, and her summer dress had a flow and a dignity that showed she was used to being looked at. Her letters to her son that Jane had read were what old-fashioned mothers wrote—little newsy paragraphs about how "Dad" was doing, and what had been said when they'd had the Stevenses or the Putnams for dinner and bridge. It was like reading a message from the 1940s.

Jane waited for the son to come down. At nine thirty, she was losing patience. There were probably eight or ten bedrooms in this house. In her experience, what fugitives were doing when they went home was resetting the calendar. They were trying unconsciously to go back to a time before their lives had become chaotic and dangerous. It was a time when they had been safe. She supposed that when he was growing up, this big, imposing house must have provided a sense of security for Daniel Martel.

She waited until noon, but there was no sign of him. At twelve thirty, the cook came out and supervised a younger woman wearing the same light blue dress in setting a large round table on the patio with utensils and china for something that looked a bit like afternoon tea. At one fifteen, two couples came outside on the patio. The women both wore broad-brimmed hats and thin summer dresses. One of the men wore a seersucker sport coat; the other wore a loose white shirt with no collar. After a few minutes the host and hostess reappeared.

There was a pleasant, unhurried lunch followed by a period of sitting at the table in the shade under the old trees drinking lemonade and sparkling water freshened by the younger maid every fifteen minutes. At a little after three the sun, which had hung high overhead so the big trees provided shade, sank lower, to an angle that threw bright, harsh rays into the diners' faces. Jane watched the two visiting couples go through the ceremonial steps. The wife would throw a glance at her husband, who had received very little of her attention until then. He would look at his wristwatch in surprise, as though the device had suddenly jumped up from the ground and wrapped itself around his arm. Jane was too far away to hear words, but she could see all the mimed expressions of surprise at how quickly the time had passed, and then a brief recitation of responsibilities that had to be met—Billy's baseball practice, Madison's piano lesson. The women all hugged each other and then hugged each of the men. The men shook hands, with one quick, tight grip and release. Then the host and hostess walked their guests through the house to the front door.

Jane waited while the maid and the cook cleared the table and disappeared into the kitchen. The afternoon had been dreamlike, a turn-of-the-century painting of life among the bourgeoisie. But her attention had never flagged. She'd watched to see whether each phase would be the one that signaled the arrival of Daniel Martel. Would he come to see these visitors? Wait for them to leave?

She was patient. She had succeeded in preventing him from murdering Jim Shelby, and for now, Shelby was safe. Martel would stay in Indianapolis for a time, probably until he realized how vulnerable it made him to hide in his hometown, or until he began to see the futility of trying to return to a world that had a place for him as a child, but didn't have a place for somebody like the man he had become. It could take months, and it was almost sure to take weeks. She could wait.

In the old days, during the wars of the forests, there were always warriors out in groups of three or two, or even alone, simply staying in the countries of enemies, living unseen in the woods, and observing. Sometimes they would stay there for a few weeks, sometimes for as long as a year.

Jane left the yard during the late afternoon, and returned to her hotel. She showered, ate, and changed into clothes for night, then drove to a Sears store and bought a green-and-brown plaid stadium blanket. When she was back in the car, she put a gun and a knife in her jacket. She returned to the house at dark, parked her car on the street around the corner with its front wheels aimed in the direction of the Martel garage, and walked back into the yard. She stationed herself in a row of ornamental shrubs, wrapped herself in the blanket, and became one of them.

The night was warm, and the windows and sliding doors were all open, with only the screens to cut the sound. She could see into the living room, the kitchen, and the dining room. Upstairs there were lights on, and she could see a couple of ceiling fans spinning to keep the air moving.

The cook and maid came through briefly to finish the last of the kitchen cleaning, and then disappeared into the upper levels, probably for the night. At eleven, Jane stretched out full length with her feet down the incline of the ditch and her blanket wrapped around her. She slept peacefully for a time in the silence of the residential neighborhood. When the noises came, they were not loud. It was just the sound of the mother closing the first-floor windows and sliding doors.

Jane opened her eyes, rested her chin on the blanket, and watched the mother appear at one window, then the next. Then she disappeared for a moment. The back door of the house opened, and then Mr. and Mrs. Martel went down the back steps carefully, and walked, arm in arm, toward their garage. Jane looked at her watch. It was after one thirty.

It was too late for them to be going anywhere for a social engagement. They had to be doing something extraordinary. Jane rolled up her blanket, went low, and trotted quietly along the ditch to the street where her car was parked. She got in behind the wheel, rolled down her windows, and waited. She heard a car door slam, and a moment later she heard a second one slam. The electric whirring of the garage door opener as it raised the door was surprisingly clear in the night air. She heard their car start, counted to thirty, then started her engine and moved ahead to the intersection. She sped up and turned the corner in time to see the Martel car at the end of the block, just disappearing into a right turn.

Jane had spent many hours thinking about the ways of following a car, because she had needed to be sure she wasn't making herself easy to tail. There were plenty of tricks—using two followers in cars and taking turns staying in sight, changing the driver's appearance every few miles, passing on a long, straight stretch and then watching through the mirror instead of the windshield. Police departments sometimes installed two different sets of headlights so they could change the way their cars looked from the front. Others planted electronic transmitters or GPS units and followed without ever coming in sight. Tonight Jane could only drop back as far as possible and stay aware.

It was unlikely that the Martels were very good at spotting a tail, but even in a city the size of Indianapolis, there was much less traffic to hide her Honda as the clock moved toward two a.m. She tried to stay behind a car that was going in the same direction, but it soon turned and disappeared. She knew that the moment of greatest danger for her would be when the Martel car stopped for a red light. That would give the driver—probably the father—nothing to do for a couple of minutes but keep his foot on the brake. He would spend some part of it looking into his rearview mirror at whoever was coming up behind him.

A light ahead of the Martels turned red. Jane continued to the next intersection ahead of her, turned right, went about thirty feet, turned around, nosed out at the corner where she had just turned, and looked up the main road toward the Martels.

The Martel car didn't wait for the red light. The driver paused at the edge of the intersection for a second, saw there was no car coming to his left or right, and accelerated through and kept going.

Jane hesitated. If she came after them, the Martels would see her car and think she was a cop who had witnessed the infraction. The driver wouldn't be able to take his eyes off her. She stayed where she was, waiting and watching their car move farther and farther ahead. She waited until it had moved far enough along the slight curve of the road so a glance in the rearview mirror would not include her pulling back onto the road and following.

There was something she had not anticipated. She had hoped they had simply been told to wait until the middle of the night to visit their son. But they seemed to be doing things that would force a follower to reveal himself. Had Daniel told them to do that? Were they so wised-up on their own? They didn't look like criminals, and they didn't live like criminals, but neither did their son.

Jane sped up. Her turn and pause had reduced the likelihood that they would recognize her car as the one behind them earlier. She was virtually starting over again as just another car that happened to be out late. Another stoplight was coming up. It was already red. Probably now that Jane was visible again, they would be afraid to run it.

No. The driver tapped the brakes at the intersection, then accelerated through it. Jane kept coming. She was far enough behind them so that she arrived at the intersection just as the signal turned green.

The Martels were speeding. Jane hadn't thought much about it at first, but now that she was closer, she could tell that they weren't just a bit over the limit. They were going at least fifty in a thirty-five-mile-per-hour zone. She concentrated on keeping her distance steady by timing lights without going too fast. No matter how eager she was to find out where they were going tonight, she couldn't afford to be pulled over by a police officer.

At the next big intersection the Martel car turned to the left. Jane followed it into the left-turn lane, but she was too late to catch the green light. She watched, and saw the car far away, making a right turn into a driveway at the side of a large building.

When the light changed, she followed; then she saw a big red sign that read, "Emergency," and a blue sign that read,

"St. Vincent Hospital." She made the turn and followed the driveway up the side of the building in time to see the Martel car stopped under the roof at the emergency room entrance. The wife was out of the driver's seat, and she and an orderly were helping her husband get into a wheelchair.

Jane drifted past and turned to enter a parking lot about fifty yards away. She swung into a parking space and switched off her engine and lights. The orderly wheeled Mr. Martel into the doorway where the doors automatically slid apart to admit them. The wife seemed torn, doing a little dance toward the doors, then looking back at her car sitting there blocking the entrance circle with both doors open and its engine running. She ran to it, slammed the passenger door, continued around the front end, got into the driver's seat, and drove the rest of the way around the circle.

Jane realized that there was only one place for Mrs. Martel to go. Jane rolled over into the back seat of her car, then pulled the blanket over her. Seconds later she heard the car pull into the space beside hers. The engine stopped, the door slammed, and she heard the sound of high heels clicking away toward the emergency room entrance. She waited for a few minutes, then sat up. The lot was empty of people again for the moment.

What this looked like was a heart attack. The wife's erratic driving had nothing to do with being followed. She had not noticed other cars and had not cared. She had just been rushing her husband to the hospital.

Jane stayed where she was and watched for cars coming up the driveway to the emergency room. There was an ambulance. Two big male EMTs pulled a gurney out the back. There was a small, slim girl EMT with long black hair tied tight behind her head perched on the gurney above the patient, doing chest compressions to restore his heartbeat as the gurney clattered through the doors into the emergency room.

A few minutes later, a car pulled up and six teenagers—three boys and three girls—got out. In front, one of the boys was holding his left arm as though it was giving him pain.

It was nearly an hour before a black Porsche wheeled into the lot and parked. Jane listened while the door slammed, then waited for the sound of male footsteps, trying but failing to determine where the man was. Finally she raised her head a bit and looked. It was Daniel Martel. He walked in long, quick strides to the emergency room door and disappeared.

Jane got out of her car and walked to his. She saw that the Nevada license plates had been replaced by Indiana plates. She wrote the license number on a receipt, then the VIN number from the top of the dashboard, on the chance that having it would help her find the address he was using here. She checked to see if he had forgotten to lock the car, then to see if he had left a window open a crack, but it was a halfhearted effort because she knew Martel wasn't the type. She also felt fairly sure that Martel would have bought whatever optional high-end alarm system Porsche offered, so she left the car alone.

She sat for another hour and then made a call with her cell phone.

"Hello?" The voice was sleepy, and Jane felt guilty.

"Hi, Sarah. I'm sorry, but I need some information right away. Are you anyplace where Jim can't hear you?"

"He's asleep, and I'm in my room with the door closed. He can't hear."

"Can you describe his wife, Susan, to me?"

"Well, let's see. She was about my height, five six. She had long blond hair. It was natural honey-blond, and it was thick, as blond hair usually isn't. And shiny, always, like a shampoo commercial. She had the kind of green eyes that sort of change color—bright if she wore bright colors, gray in low light, even a little blue if she wore blue. She was thin, but with a terrific body, with curvy hips and big boobs. She did zero to deserve that body. Her exercise was going to the bar to pick up her drink herself."

"What would be the most distinctive characteristic? Any marks, moles, scars?"

"Not on her. She was perfect-looking, like a nasty little doll. If there was anything unusual, it was probably her lips. They were cupid's-bow lips, you know? They were big, kind of turned up at the corners with a little dip in the center of the upper lip."

"I know the kind you mean, exactly," Jane said.

"Can you tell me what—"

"Not today. I hope another day, soon. Thanks." Jane hung up.

She spent the rest of the night in the lot, thinking about what she had to do. At five thirty, Martel and his mother came out of the main entrance of the hospital and headed for the lot. Jane studied their posture, the way they spoke and walked. They seemed exhausted, but they didn't look like a pair who had just lost a close relative. There were no tears from the mother, no gestures of comfort or condolence from the son.

The son walked the mother to her car, and she got in and drove off. The son got into his car, started it, and pulled out of the lot. But when he reached the street, he turned in the opposite direction from the mother.

Jane followed him at a distance. There were the cars of early commuters and delivery trucks for her to hide behind now, so following a car seemed easier. He drove out of the city to a clean, quiet suburb just off a major highway. As his car approached the entrance to a big hotel, she expected him to turn, but he didn't. When he approached a large, modern apartment complex she prepared to turn in at a different entrance from the one he chose, but he didn't stop.

He went on, and pulled the Porsche into the driveway of a house. He stopped in front of the garage, and the garage door opened. He eased the car in.

Jane accelerated so she would be far down the street and around the first corner before he got out and walked to the house. It was best to let everything be a surprise.

21

When Daniel Martel woke, it was already late afternoon. He remembered immediately what had happened. His father had been lucky. If Mom hadn't thought quickly and gotten him to the hospital, his little warning heart attack probably would have killed him.

Daniel didn't relish the fact that he would have to spend much of his time during the next few days going to visit the old man in the hospital. They hadn't had much to say to each other while he was young, and now he could hardly bear to listen to the old man's voice. The irrelevance of his words to Daniel's life made all conversation an ordeal. The old man's thoughts never reached the world he lived in. He didn't know it existed.

He'd had some hope of sampling the nightlife around here, and trying to meet a few interesting women. He hadn't spent much time in Indianapolis in the past fifteen years or so. There had been just a few one-day or two-day stops on the way to somewhere else, so he didn't know what the stock of women was. When he had been young they'd been plentiful enough. For the past few days he had not gone to any bars or clubs, because he'd been trying to get settled first.

After dinner he would stop by the hospital. Visiting hours ended at nine, so he would go out after that. It occurred to him that he should get the house in order just in case he brought a woman home with him. He remade his bed, fluffed up the pillows, picked the dirty clothes off the floor and put them into the hamper, then went into his closet. He unfolded his tripod and extended the legs, then mounted the video camera on it, aimed the shot, and looked through the viewfinder to be sure. He turned it off. He selected some clothes, tossed them onto the bed, and went into the shower. He dressed, took another look at the bedroom, and stepped into the living room.

The black-haired woman was sitting in his living room in his new wing chair. There was a short cocktail glass in front of her on his coffee table with a little paper napkin under it as though she were protecting the finish of the table, and beside it his previously unopened bottle of tequila taken from the bar across the room. He could see that the clear liquid in the glass had the same crystal clarity, with a slight oily quality, as the liquid in the bottle. Drinking his liquor was a deliberate affront. "Who—what the fuck do you think you're doing here?"

"You started with who. Did you stop because you already know?"

"What do you want?"

"So you *do* know," she said. "I gave you lots of reasons to leave Jim Shelby alone. Now I'm here to give you a chance to end it."

He was near the sideboard that was against the wall. "What are you talking about?" He leaned his right elbow on the top of it.

"You killed Shelby's wife, Susan. I want you to go to the police and tell them you were the one who did it, and that Shelby's innocent."

He laughed. "Are you crazy, or just stupid? He's convicted. Cooked. No matter what I say or anybody else says, he's finished. He escaped. That's a crime, too. And why would I even—" He opened the top drawer, snatched the gun he kept there, and aimed it at her.

"Try?" she supplied the word.

"You made a mistake coming here."

"Maybe." She picked up the cocktail glass from the coffee table, holding it with the little paper napkin.

"Get up," he said. "This way."

"Which way?" she said.

"Through this door. Into the bedroom."

"Not an attractive offer." She shook her head.

"Get in there!" he shouted. "Now!"

"I'm not here to give you another victim."

The mention of it titillated him. Her knowing it was coming made it even better. She would be fearing his power, knowing the uselessness of resisting, long before he did anything. The gun in his hand meant that anything he wanted was his. He said, "Put down that drink." He watched her hand, hoping it would be shaking when she held out the drink to set it down.

She leaned forward and set it on the table, but when she stood, he saw there was already a gun in her other hand. She'd had it hidden behind the arm of the chair. "Yes. I've got one, too."

"If you were going to use it, you would have," he said. "Put it down."

"Here's how it is," she said. "I found your photograph albums. I'm pretty sure there are other things—I'm guessing the still pictures were image grabs taken from video—but it doesn't matter. I'm also pretty sure a few of those women are dead. And I think one of them—the first one in the second album—is Susan Shelby."

"So here we are," Martel said. "What do you think the trade ought to be?"

"I'll teach you something about yourself. Then you'll clear Shelby."

Jane had already begun to walk. She sidestepped slowly, steadily, around the back of the big chair. She stepped close to the heavy wooden furniture along the wall, her gun on him, aimed always at the center of his chest.

Martel could not allow her to use his sideboard and the heavy cabinets to shield herself from his fire. He moved away from her along the wall, circling. He detested the weakness of appearing to retreat from her. He had to find a way to reassert his dominance, to expose the fear she must be feeling, and deflate her empty bravado.

He was near the wing chair now. He noticed the glass of tequila she had poured herself on his coffee table beside the bottle. Keeping his eyes on hers, he bent his knees, took up the glass, sniffed it, smelled the tequila, and took a drink. He winced. It tasted much rougher than he'd expected—almost corrosive. He smacked his lips. "A little strong for you?"

Jane shrugged. "It's almost pure."

He lifted the bottle and poured a little more over the ice, then took another drink. A few seconds passed, and then his eyes widened, and he gripped his belly. His face assumed a grimace and for the first time he seemed to forget to keep his eyes on Jane. He bent over, facing the floor. Both hands were on his knees. "I get it," he said. "What am I supposed to do? How do I stop this?"

"You're not supposed to do anything," she said. "You don't stop it."

His head jerked upward, and then he raised his gun. He pulled the trigger, but there was only a click. He held on to the empty gun. "Give me the antidote!" He seemed to become more determined. When he bent over in pain, he dropped the gun, jammed his trigger finger down his throat, and began to retch, but nothing came out.

Jane stood where she was. "Throw up, cut your head off—whatever you like. What I came to teach you wasn't that you were scared. It was that you were stupid."

He kept trying a few more times, but he couldn't get his vomit reflex to work now because the neurotoxin was taking over. He lost his balance and fell to the floor. He rocked back and forth, holding his belly for a few minutes, and went into convulsions. Then he lay still.

Jane put on her surgical gloves as she watched. She picked up his gun from the floor, using only the pen from her purse in the barrel, and set it on the coffee table beside the glass of hemlock distillate and tequila. She set the full magazine she had removed from the pistol beside it, then carefully pressed the magazine release with the pen so she could remove the empty one she had inserted.

She walked into his office and brought out his laptop computer. She plugged it in and read over the confession and suicide note she had written on the laptop. It was filled with the remorse and self-loathing he never had felt. The crime that the note claimed he regretted most was the murder of Susan Shelby and the framing of her husband for it. But there had been many other crimes. Jane saved the note, then knelt beside the body and pressed the fingers on the proper keys—the right hand on J, K, L, and all the right-side keys, and the left on A, S, D, F and all the left-side keys. Then she brought back the final note and left it on the screen. There was no printer in the house, so she was relieved of the chore of forging his signature.

The fact that his prints were on the gun, the glass of poison, the bottle, and the computer keyboard would be sufficient. She went back into the kitchen and left the bottle of *Cicuta maculata* poison she had brought, so there would be no question of why cicutoxin was found only in the drink and the tequila. She went to the den again and brought out the two photograph albums. She opened the second one to the pictures of what must have been the last hour of Susan Shelby's life, and propped the other album to keep it open.

Jane went through the house making sure everything else was the way she had found it, and there was nothing left that she had touched bare-handed. She went into the bedroom and found the video camera. She saw it was turned off, but turned it on, pressed the rewind button, then pressed "play," and watched the viewfinder just to be sure nothing had been taped. She rewound it and turned it off. It struck her that if Martel had gotten his way, he would have been taping himself killing her just about now. She went back through the living room to the entry.

It was dark out when she opened the door. She set the lock button and closed the door before she took off her surgical gloves. She used one to hold Martel's spare key to lock the bolt from outside. As she walked away, she felt as though she had just lit a very long fuse.

The gray Honda moved onto the interstate and out of the vicinity of Indianapolis, and then out of Indiana entirely. It was as though over a period of less than two days, a small shadow had passed over the town, and if people had seen it they had not separated it in their minds from all of the other variations in light and dark that had come and gone.

As Jane drove, thoughts of death had already receded and become distant to her—once again, just one of the things that she knew. What she was thinking was that right now it was time for Jane McKinnon to go home while there was still enough left of her marriage to coax back to life. She was almost certain that, even with the new scars to remind him of her imperfection, she would be able to make Carey glad she was back.

Read on for an excerpt of *The Boyfriend*, the latest masterwork of suspense from Thomas Perry.

"Perry is a marvelous plotter, and he builds suspense with all the subtlety of a master chef nursing a risotto to a buttery perfection. It's nothing new to call Perry a master of the genre, but it's no less true for being widely acknowledged."
—*Booklist* (starred review)

Available March 2013 wherever books are sold!

1

James Shelby sat in the white prison van looking out the tinted window. The tint was so dark it was hard to see out, and the grate on the inside that kept inmates from touching the glass made it worse. He was shackled to a ring welded to the side of the van, so he couldn't move around much.

Five prisoners were going to court this morning. Everyone in the California Institution for Men at Chino had already been tried and convicted, so they all knew the routines—how they should stand, how their facial muscles should be set, where their eyes should be aimed. Three of the five men were going to be tried for crimes they had committed before they'd gone to jail—one man whose DNA had been taken at his prison intake physical and later matched to the sample swabbed from a rape victim, another man who had turned up on three bank security tapes committing robberies, and a liquor store bandit whose gun had been matched to a killing.

The fourth man was shackled a few feet from the others on the opposite side of the van with Shelby. His name was

McCorkin and he was the former cellmate of an embezzler. McCorkin was going to testify that the embezzler had been bragging about using the money to buy drugs for resale. This was McCorkin's fourth trip to court to testify against cellmates, all of whom seemed to tell him things they hadn't told anyone else.

He and Shelby were shackled away from the others because they were both considered informers. Shelby had not concealed the name of the man who had stabbed him in the back two months ago. Being seated with McCorkin had its advantages. None of the others wanted to say anything in his presence that he could use to get more privileges or a shorter sentence. They didn't want him to be aware of them, because his mere notice brought with it a risk of future prosecutions.

Shelby looked out at the road, and not at his companions. From the start he hadn't let his eyes rest on any of them, because they were volatile. And today they were more dangerous to him than ever, because all any of them had to do was notice that something was odd about him and say so. If they even joked with him about being different today, the guards would hear it. He knew the malice and perversity that had tangled the prisoners' minds. If they knew he was planning to escape, they'd be resentful that he wasn't freeing them, too. They would be envious that he had a plan, because they didn't. And the ones who considered him an informer would find it simple justice to snitch on him.

On the way into Los Angeles there were mountains, then dry-looking pastureland and a succession of telephone poles, and then a big highway with cars driven by bored civilians who saw the marshal's logo on the side of the van and the reinforcement of the side and back windows, and tried to see through the tinted glass. They wanted to see a sideshow, a few ferocious beasts whose ugly faces would give them chills, and maybe even more, the poor, sad bastards who didn't look mean or crazy. Shelby was one of those. If they could have seen him through the glass, they would have said he looked just like their brother or nephew or cousin—a man in his late twenties with light hair and a reasonably handsome face. There was some unholy fake sympathy in people that made them think, "There, but for the grace of God . . ." and not mean it. The idea that they were the favored ones seemed to titillate them. They were not the ones inside the bars with the monsters and the freaks, and never would be.

The ride took another hour, and then the van pulled off the freeway at Grand Avenue, and went south to First Street and then up Broadway toward the Clara Shortridge Foltz Criminal Courts Building. It was still early morning. Through the tinted glass Shelby could make out lots of people on the sidewalks of the court district. The lawyers all wore suits, mostly in shades between light gray and charcoal, with white shirts and neckties. The female city bureaucrats all wore pantsuits, and the males had dress pants and light-colored shirts and ties, and all of them wore plastic badges dangling on lanyards from their necks like jewelry. The jurors dressed more casually. Each of them had a red-and-white paper badge for jury duty stuck in a plastic holder with an alligator clip to hold it.

In the period of his life long before his troubles started, Shelby had lived for a year in Los Angeles. He'd served on a jury here, so he knew. They always started the day by herding a couple of hundred men and women into that small assembly room on the fifth floor. Then they waited, and at irregular intervals one of the clerks would come out of their office and read some juror numbers.

Benches lined the hallways of the court building, and they were always occupied by lawyers, their clients, witnesses, and the defendants' families. The first time he had seen the hallways, they had reminded him of the marketplaces in the Middle East, with people haggling and gossiping and scheming, their private conversations all out in the open, but unheard because there were too many people talking at once. Everyone had something pressing of his own to worry about at that moment—legal papers to look at and stories to repeat and get straight before going into the courtroom, or plea deals to evaluate before they were withdrawn.

The building was modern, with floors marked by rows of identical windows a person couldn't see into. The main entrance consisted of steps descending into a sunken patio. At the edge of the patio were glass doors leading into the building. The court building seemed worn. Everything had been walked on, rubbed, touched by human hands so many times that it was old while it was still new. Inside the tall glass doors was a security area that could have been transported from an airport. Long lines of people waited to put their belongings on conveyer belts that took them through X-ray machines, and then waited to walk through the arch of one of the three metal detectors.

Big, hard-eyed male cops and a few women cops operated the machines and funneled the mass of people into single-file lines and off into the rows of elevators on both sides of the lobby, first the ones for floors twelve through nineteen, and then the ones for floors two through eleven. During the past weeks Shelby had spent hours remembering every detail he could bring back.

Shelby prepared himself while the van pulled up behind the building and then into an underground garage. The van stopped. The guard yelled, "Listen up," and paused to hear the silence. "When you're unlocked, get out on the right side through the open door. Follow the man in front of you and line up in that order with your toes on the yellow line. Do not walk, do not move, until I tell you."

Shelby and the others got out and remained in line. They were all experts by now at hearing the order and following it without allowing it to linger in their minds to chafe. Following orders had become the only way forward in their lives.

The second guard got out with them and stood a few feet back, so they couldn't rush him without getting shot. The driver pulled the van ahead and around to an extra-long parking space reserved for the vehicles from the lockups. He came back and stood near his companion. "All right. We're going in through that door over there. When we're inside, you'll be given instructions and taken to a holding room. Walk."

The group of shackled prisoners walked ahead in single file to the door and then continued inside. The second guard handed a police officer a piece of paper, and he read it and handed it to another police officer at a desk, who used a pen to check something off against a list and wrote something down. All of the cops' faces were set in a wary distrust, making sure they were seeing the same things they'd seen ten thousand times before, and not something new.

The men were shackled to a railing that was attached to the wall in a holding room, in the same two groups. Shelby wondered where the black-haired woman was right now. He had listened closely to what she had told him during her visits to the California Institution for Men at Chino. She had told him where things were going to be and how he should reach them, but she'd never said where she was going to be or what she would do. Now he couldn't help wondering whether she hadn't told him because what she intended to do was insane, and she had been afraid he would lose his nerve. Maybe she had already set everything up before dawn, and had taken off, to be as far away as possible before things began to happen. She'd said only that she would give him a chance to free himself, and he had to be ready.

There was a television set on a metal stand high up in a corner, but it wasn't turned on. On the center of the wall was an electric clock. He and the others sat in silence for a long time watching it and waiting for something to happen, but nothing did. He began to worry again that he was not exuding the same air of bored emptiness that he had on other days, in prison. If he seemed nervous or unusually alert, one of the other inmates would know that he was hiding something. He half-closed his eyes and pretended to be dozing, but he tried to figure out where the guards were. About once an hour one of the sheriff's deputies in tan khaki shirts and green pants would come through the room as though he were taking a shortcut to somewhere else. Twice Shelby heard prisoners' names called over an intercom, but they must have been in other holding rooms.

At eleven thirty Shelby began to get nervous and agitated. The time was coming. Either it would happen soon, or it would not happen. There were a hundred reasons why it couldn't happen, and only one reason why it might—the woman's sheer mad certainty—but as long as that one reason wasn't dead, the tension in his chest kept growing. In a half hour he would be free or he'd be dead. Less than a half hour, now.

His eyes began to lose their ability to stay focused on one spot, because they weren't able to rest anywhere long enough. A cop came to the door and called out, "Shelby!"

"Yes, sir," Shelby said.

"There's an attorney waiting to speak with you. Stand up."

He stood and the cop unlocked his shackles from the rail on the wall and guided him out the door. Shelby took deep, even breaths. This was the start, and he was going to need to be sharp. The cop led him along the back hallway to the first open door, a room with a small window that started head-high with steel mesh over it. The cop ushered him in and closed the door behind them.

Seated at the table was the woman with black hair. Today she was dressed in a black suit, and she had draped a black raincoat over the table. The cop led Shelby to a chair across the table from her and began to shackle Shelby to the ring welded to the table.

The black-haired woman dropped something that sounded like a pen, and crouched to pick it up. For a moment Shelby and the guard lost sight of her under the table. The guard suddenly released Shelby's chain and stepped back. "Hey! What are you doing?" He reached for something on his belt and took a first step to go around the table toward her. Before he could make the turn, his legs bent at the knees and he pitched forward. He fell to the floor, and rolled over to get his radio off his belt, but she batted it out of his grasp with her hand, and it clattered across the floor.

She held up her other hand to show him a hypodermic needle she had used on his leg. "It's a low dose of anesthetic. It won't hurt you, and the effect will be gone in a little while. I'm sorry."

The cop stared at her with wide eyes, but he didn't seem to be able to move. In a few seconds his eyes closed. She said, "He'll be out for a half hour." She knelt; unbuckled the cop's utility belt with his gun, mace, and handcuffs and set it across the room in a corner; reached into his breast pocket to get his cell phone; and took the battery and put it with his other equipment.

Shelby saw that the cop hadn't managed to close the hasp to lock his chain to the ring, so he pulled it through and freed himself.

She took the key from the cop's limp hand and removed the chains from around Shelby's waist and between his ankles. "Take off the jumpsuit."

Shelby unzipped it and stepped out of it, then stood in his underwear feeling cold and vulnerable. The woman looked out the screened window and took off her suit pants, which had been rolled at the waist to conceal their length, and cinched with a belt at her hips. She took off her black stretch turtleneck and handed it to him. This left her in a pair of tight black pants and a fitted vest over her white blouse. The suit coat she had left inside her raincoat when she'd taken it off, she now extricated and handed to Shelby. He put it on, and it fit reasonably well. She put on her raincoat.

She turned to him again, and he felt the blue eyes sweeping down from his face to his feet.

"How do I look?" he asked.

"Not like a prisoner." She knelt again beside the cop, took off his black shoes, and handed them to Shelby so he could put them on. He kicked off his plastic sandals, stepped into the oversize shoes, and tied them as tightly as possible. The last thing she handed him was her briefcase. "Ready?"

He nodded. She unlocked the door with one of the keys from the cop's belt, and went out to the narrow, empty corridor. There were doors all along the left side that led to rooms like the one they'd just left, and one windowless steel door at the end with a clipboard hanging on it. The sheet on the clipboard listed Kristen Alvarez, but she took out a pen and added the name Gregory Campbell to the list with the same entry time as Kristen Alvarez. She looked at her watch and signed them both out. They stepped out into the main hallway of the building. As they walked, she and Shelby looked straight ahead and never met the eyes of passersby. Shelby noticed that any eyes passed over him and lingered on her. She was beautiful, tall and erect, and took long, purposeful strides. They made a turn and stepped through the exit door into the staircase.

They hurried down four floors without meeting anyone on the stairs, and then she stopped at a small glass door with a fire extinguisher inside. She opened the door, reached behind the extinguisher, and produced a red-and-white juror badge in a plastic holder and clipped it to Shelby's breast pocket. She looked at her watch. "We're on the fifth floor.

Just go out into the hall near the jury room and sit on one of the benches. In three minutes it will be noon."

"How can I ever thank you?"

"You're not even out yet. Make sure you get one of the first elevators."

He nodded and went out into the fifth-floor hallway. In two and a half minutes the staff in the jury assembly room would let the two hundred or so bored prospective jurors go to lunch, and they'd all stream out to jam the hallway and the elevators and stairs. He walked toward the jury assembly room, but stopped outside the door and sat down on the bench by the wall closest to the elevator to wait.

JANE WHITEFIELD RAN DOWN THE stairwell the rest of the way toward the first floor, but just as she was reaching for the door handle to go out to the lobby, she heard a door a few floors up flung open, and she could hear the measured sound of leather-soled shoes on the metal stairs, and the murmur of voices—jurors. She almost smiled, but instead kept her face blank and serene as she stepped out into a narrow corridor to the back of the lobby near the elevators.

Then Jane saw the three men. Shelby's sister had given her photographs of them when she had come to Jane in Deganawida, New York, to ask for her help. "I took these during Jim's trial," she said. "These are the three who helped frame him. They bribed some witnesses to say that Jim had done violent things when he got mad at people, some to say they saw him sitting in the parking lot waiting for Susan to come home that night, and scared at least two other witnesses away so they couldn't be found in time for the trial."

The pictures had been taken from different angles: one photo of them taken as they were coming out of some public building together, one taken when they were getting into a car, and one taken through the open side window as they pulled away. The men were all about thirty to forty, with short, well-barbered hair, all wearing suits. They looked like lawyers or business clients arriving for a case.

Jane watched them. They had already passed through the metal detectors to get in, so they couldn't be carrying guns. But they were moving against the crowd of jurors and lawyers departing for lunch, standing in front of the bank of elevators, and as each door opened to let jurors out, the three men moved a little closer to get in. There were six elevators on each side of the lobby. There was still a good chance that when James Shelby's elevator arrived they would be entering another one, or at least not looking in his direction.

Jane moved closer to them. This was developing into a situation where she might have to pay a high price for James Shelby. She had prepared herself for this possibility a long time ago, something that was implicit in the promise she made to her clients. If she was going to save innocent people from the enemies who wanted them dead, there would be times when she must fight.

She was close to the three men now, almost to their backs. The door of the elevator to their left opened and she saw James Shelby. He was in the middle of the crowded elevator, and as the door opened he spilled out with a dozen jurors, all pushing forward, weaving to get past the surge of people wanting to get in. A hand shot out as one of the men in front of her grabbed Shelby's arm, and Jane pushed off with her back foot to throw her body into the arm, wrenching the hand off Shelby. The man grunted in pain and surprise and half-turned to get a look at her over his shoulder, but she pivoted, her back to him and his companions as she moved toward the main exit. Ahead of her she saw Shelby heading across the lobby with the torrent of people.

"That's him!" the man yelled.

"What are you talking about?" That seemed to be one of his companions.

"It's Shelby! He's leaving!"

The voices were behind her as she caught up with Shelby and pushed him out with the crowd into the narrower space at the glass doors.

"Stop him!" the man said. "It's him!"

Jane got Shelby out onto the sunken patio outside the entrance where the steps went up onto Broadway. "Go!" she said to him. "Just as we planned."

He looked at her in panic, but his legs took him up onto Broadway, and he kept going.

Jane planted herself at the foot of the steps. She reached into a pocket of her purse, took out a black elastic band, gathered her hair in a ponytail and slid the elastic over it, then tucked it under so the hair was tight to her head. She stood straight and held on to her purse.

The man who had grabbed Shelby had wasted fifteen seconds keeping his companions out of the elevator and another fifteen getting them to plow through the crowd and across the lobby. The people in the crowd were unwilling to let anyone push them aside to get out of the building ahead of them, so getting out took time and the three men weren't much faster than anyone else.

Jane felt the seconds passing. Shelby should spot the parked car soon. Within another minute or two he should get in, find the keys, start the engine. Next he would head for the freeway entrance. Maybe the crowd would delay the men long enough.

But the three men burst out the double doors. They had been craning their necks to see what went on through the glass while they fought their way to the exit, so they all dashed toward the steps where Shelby had escaped to the street. Jane knew Shelby was still not completely recovered from the stabbing two months ago, so he would be slow. Not enough time had passed since she'd freed him from the man's grasp. They could still run him down if she didn't stop them.

Jane took two steps and turned on the bottom step to face them. She could see that they still hadn't grasped what she was. To them she was a lady lawyer, and they planned to push past her and endure her look of irritated disdain.

The first one was easy, probably because he was bigger and faster than the other two. He didn't seem to be aware that she could possibly be a lethal opponent. He charged ahead, barely seeing her as he dashed to the steps. All Jane had to do was sidestep, trip him, place one hand on his spine and the other on the back of his head to direct his face downward into the steps. Her push increased his momentum enough so he hit hard and lay still.

The second man was the one who had grasped Shelby's arm in front of the elevator, so he was ready. He didn't try to get around her, but went straight for her with both his hands up, preparing to throw a punch. Jane knew she couldn't fight toe-to-toe against a male opponent who outweighed her by a hundred pounds, so she never did. She retreated up two more steps to place herself beyond the man's fallen companion. He took a wild swing at her with his right fist, and when he missed, he had to put one foot on his unconscious comrade to keep from falling over him.

Jane swung her purse into his face. He grabbed it, and she wrapped the strap around his wrist, tugged him toward her over his unconscious companion, and delivered a quick jab to the bridge of his nose. When both of his hands went to his face, she stomp-kicked his kneecap from the side. He went down, landed on his friend, and rolled down the last step clutching his knee while his nose bled down the front of his clothes.

Spectators were beginning to gather, jamming the crowd that was still trying to leave the building. In the corner of her eye Jane caught the third man moving up the steps toward her back, but he threw his arms around her from behind in a bear hug before she could evade him. In a single motion she threw her head back into his nose and upper teeth, heel-stomped his right instep, made a fist with her right hand, and swung it behind her into his groin. She felt a puff of his hot breath on the back of her neck as he released her and rocked back.

His momentary distress seemed to give bystanders courage. A dozen men swarmed in at once, getting between Jane and the three attackers, holding them back and pinioning their arms. It was surprisingly quiet, just a bit of grunting and "You don't want to hit a woman, pal." "Calm down." "Just don't struggle." "Fight's over."

Suddenly there was a loud, authoritative voice. "Stand aside. Police officers." Five big cops in black LAPD uniforms moved in, parting the crowd as they made their way toward the three men.

Jane turned instantly and walked off, away from the center of the crowd, adjusting her steps to put as many people as possible between her and the policemen. She hurried along the sidewalk in front of the building and into the other, separate crowd of curious people who had retreated half a block before stopping to watch. As she burrowed deeper into the group, she took off the black raincoat, pulled the elastic band off her hair, and shook her long hair out. She set her face in a slightly amused expression, an implication that whatever had been going on down there had nothing to do with her and was, in any event, incomprehensible.

She got past the spectators and moved on with the stream of people going to lunch. She walked downhill on Broadway to First Street, and turned right to head for the Metro station at Hill and First. She walked quickly, taking long strides that carried her past most of the other pedestrians. The sidewalks were full of people wearing juror badges clipped to them or security ID on lanyards for the city and county offices in the civic center. There were male lawyers with thick briefcases and female lawyers pulling cases on wheels with long handles like suitcases. She spotted the tall red sign with an "M" on it, glanced behind her to look for anyone running, and kept going.

She reached the sign and turned into the walkway toward the escalators. A plain, dark blue Ford Crown Victoria sped up Hill Street toward her, veered to the curb, and stopped. Two men in suits got out quickly. One of them yelled, "Stop right there, miss. Police." He opened his coat and she could see a gold badge clipped to his belt. His companion stayed by the driver's door, but he had pulled out his gun and was steadying it on the roof of his car, not quite aiming at her, but showing it.

Jane's mind raced ahead. If she managed to get down the escalator without being shot by one police officer or wrestled to the pavement by the other, she might reach the platform and have to wait ten minutes for the next train. She couldn't outrun their car on these streets. She stood still and held her hands out from her sides. "What's the matter, officer?"

"Just stay where you are, with your hands in sight." He ran up to her, grasped her right wrist and brought it behind her, snapped a handcuff on it, then took the left behind her and closed the other handcuff on that wrist. He clutched her arm and tugged her toward the car. "Now come with me. We're going to get into the back seat of the car. Keep your head down."

He opened the door and put his hand on her head to keep it from bumping as she slid onto the seat. He moved in after her, and the lock buttons clicked down. The driver put away his gun, put the car into gear, and drove.

The car went up Hill to Temple, turned left away from the court building, past the cathedral and the concert halls, and swung onto the Hollywood Freeway moving north. Obviously, they were taking her, not back to the courthouse, but to their precinct station. She decided to introduce doubt.

"You've got the wrong person," she said. "I haven't done anything wrong."

"I didn't ask you," said the cop beside her. "There will be plenty of time to talk later." He had small, close-set eyes and the sort of thick, dark hair that went down too far on his forehead so it looked like a cap.

"I was just getting on the subway and you came along and arrested me, so you must think I did something." She had begun the urgent business of keeping them from holding her long enough to connect her with Shelby's escape.

"I didn't say that."

"But whoever you're looking for is back there somewhere laughing at us. She's getting away." She didn't have much hope of persuading them it was a case of mistaken identity, but she had to keep probing to see if she could derail the inexorable process of getting her into a jail cell, where she'd be when the escape was discovered.

The cop beside her sighed wearily. "You had a little scuffle on the courthouse steps, didn't you? You hurt some people. Does that ring a bell?"

She knew cops lost their sympathy when somebody lied to them, so she'd have to try something that didn't contradict what they'd seen. "I was in front of the building when these three men rushed out of the building and attacked me. There are at least a hundred witnesses who saw what happened."

"These men just attacked you for no reason."

"If they had a reason they didn't tell me what it was."

The cop shrugged. "Could it be because you had just helped James Shelby to escape?"

"Escape? All I was there for was to get excused from jury duty."

"Consider yourself excused," the driver said.

"Those three men were trying to hurt me."

The cop beside her said, "I'm not arguing with you. I believe that's what happened."

"So why are you arresting me?"

The cop beside her said, "When you see three men who mean you harm, how do you know that there aren't more?"

The driver laughed. "There could be a couple more waiting in a car nearby."

Jane turned to face the man on the seat beside her. "What are you?" Her hands were cuffed behind her, but she used them to grasp the door handle.

"We're the guys who caught you pulling a jailbreak."

She kept her eyes focused on his, but she was watching the speed of the fixed objects passing the window behind him—trees, buildings. The freeway was crowded, but the car was still moving about forty miles an hour. Even if she managed to survive a fall to the pavement at that speed, she would be hit by at least the car behind, and probably the next two after it. She had to wait and hope there was a bottleneck somewhere ahead that would slow the traffic to the stop-and-go crawl that was typical of Los Angeles freeways.

She said, "Since you're not cops, this is kidnapping, false imprisonment, and about eight other things. If you drop me off at any police station and say you saw me get James Shelby out, they'll arrest me and you'll be heroes."

"Sorry. We've got orders, and that isn't what they are."

"Whoever told you this was a good idea isn't doing you any favors. Will he be with you while you're serving a life sentence in a federal prison?"

"Nobody's going to prison," said the driver. "Just sit back and relax for a little while, and everything will be fine."

"There's nothing fine about this," she said.

She watched for her chance impatiently, but the car never slowed below forty. It was still only a few minutes after noon, so the traffic was moving smoothly. She watched for police or highway patrol or sheriff's cars, but the only one